SHADOWS OF DISCOVERY

THE SHADOW REALMS
BOOK 2

BRENDA K DAVIES

BRENDA K. DAVIES

CHAPTER ONE

C OLE LEFT bloody footprints behind as he stalked up the palace steps toward the open doorway. He stopped walking when an approaching shadow grew larger and spread out from the doorway a second before Brokk skidded to a stop in the entrance. His aqua blue eyes widened when he spotted Cole.

"Cole? Holy shit! What *happened* to you?"

Then his gaze went past Cole; his eyes roamed over the pathway leading to the gates and fence surrounding the dark fae palace. Cole knew his brother was searching for their father, but he wouldn't find him.

When Brokk's eyes returned to him, sadness filled them as they ran over the blood covering Cole's naked body. The stench of blood filled Cole's nostrils, and though it was the normal, coppery scent, it smelled putrid to him.

He wore the blood of their *father* mixed with that of a dragon's.

"What happened?" Brokk croaked out the words. "Where's... where's Father?"

Then his gaze went past Cole again, and his jaw dropped. Cole didn't have to look to know his brother had finally spotted the body of their ex-helot, Sindri, and the dragon head Cole staked to the fence.

"Is that a *dragon* head? And Sindri?" Brokk's eyes shot back to Cole. "What the *fuck* happened?"

"The Lord ordered a dragon to kill Father."

Brokk blinked at him, and his attention returned to the bloody remains on the fence. "Why?"

"Because he didn't think he would do enough to hunt Orin and Varo. He thinks *I* will do more. He intends for me to rule after I survive the trials."

Cole did not say *if* he survived the trials. He didn't care that numerous dark fae had tried and failed to make it through the trials. He. Would. Not. Fail. He would become the king of the dark fae and destroy the Lord of the Shadow Realms if it was the last thing he did.

Brokk didn't speak as he stared unblinkingly at the fence. Tears brimmed in his eyes, but he didn't shed them.

Cole knew Brokk's tears would come with time; so would his, but right now, the horror of what happened to their father was still too fresh in his mind. And though there was grief, there was also a white-hot fury that burned away the sorrow and left ashes in its wake.

"Where did the dragon head come from?" Brokk asked.

"I destroyed the dragon that killed Father. I took its head to warn away all those who will try to stand in my way of claiming the throne."

If his brother's eyes got any bigger, they would pop out of his head. "You killed a dragon by *yourself*?"

"Yes."

"*How* did you manage that?"

Cole could only think of one answer for how he succeeded in destroying the powerful creature. "Rage."

"And you killed Sindri because...?"

"He was happy to see me wearing Father's blood."

"Killing him makes sense then."

As Cole finished climbing the stairs, Brokk stepped back to let him enter the palace.

"Where are you going?" Brokk demanded when Cole brushed past him.

"To see Lexi."

"Who?" And then Brokk's mind started working again as he blurted, "*Del's* daughter?"

"Yes."

"You're going to see her *now*?"

"Yes."

"There are a thousand things we will have to take care of and do; why would you go see her now?"

"Because I have to."

The door shut behind him, and then the padding sound of Brokk's soft boots sounded against the stone as he hurried after him. Cole didn't look back at his brother while he navigated the palace halls toward his rooms.

He'd spent his entire life within these walls, and during that time, he'd passed these doors thousands of times. He'd learned which doors would never open to him, and he'd accepted that he would never satisfy his curiosity about those rooms. They belonged to someone else and would not open to anyone but their owners, even if those owners were dead.

Will the palace seal off my father's rooms now too? Is that how it works?

A pang of sadness broke through his rage; it pierced his heart, but he swiftly buried it. This was not the time or place for it; he had far too much to do. First things first, he would see Lexi, then meet with the dark fae council and arrange to start the trials.

When he finished the trials, they would plan his father's memorial. He would prefer to do it before the trials, but the longer the Gloaming went without a king, the more likely turmoil and uprisings would begin to unfold. And the authority of the throne would help him crush any rebellions before they took root.

Once he claimed the throne, he would use his power to help him sink his claws into the Lord and rip him to pieces. He would celebrate when that fucker's blood covered him.

CHAPTER TWO

"Cole."

Brokk reached for his arm but hesitated when he saw the bite mark from the dragon and the blood coating him so thickly. His brother lowered his hand without touching him.

"The fae council is going to descend on this palace as soon as they learn of Father's death," Brokk said.

"I know."

"They won't want either of us to rule. We're only half-breeds."

"They're not going to have a choice."

"Great. Fantastic. Glad to hear you say that because I'd really like to kill the Lord, but if you're not here when the council arrives, then what? I don't plan to throw myself in the ring as a contender for the throne as I want *nothing* to do with ruling the Gloaming."

"I know."

"You never wanted to rule it either."

"I still don't."

"Then—"

"I don't have a choice. I *am* going to rule, because if I don't, the Lord is going to destroy us all," Cole interrupted. "I will rule because I'm going to kill that prick if it's the last thing I do. But I *have* to see Lexi first."

"Cole—"

When Cole spun on him, Brokk stopped speaking and took a startled step back. "She's my mate, Brokk, and I'm going to see her. I *have* to make sure she's safe. If the council arrives before I return, then you'll have to stall them. I don't care how you do it. Just *do* it."

Brokk gawked at him, and this time when Cole walked away from him, it was a few seconds before his brother scrambled to catch up again.

"Your mate as in your *lycan* mate?" Brokk demanded when he arrived at Cole's side once more.

"Yes."

"Why didn't you say something? I could have checked on her."

"I wasn't expecting to be gone for so long." Or to come back soaked in his father's blood. "I didn't expect any of this."

He'd also never expected to watch his father die, to endure the trials, rule the Gloaming, or have the Lord breathing down his neck about his rebellious brothers. He certainly never thought he'd be leaving Lexi for nearly two weeks when he walked away from her manor.

Because of his dark fae nature, she probably believed he'd abandoned her; she had every right to think that, but he would make sure she learned the truth soon. And he had to see her before he started the trials.

He had no idea how much time the trials would take, and he would never get through them if he were concerned about her. There was also *no* way he would let her keep thinking he'd used and abandoned her.

"Why didn't you tell me she was your mate?" Brokk demanded.

"I wasn't ready."

Brokk didn't speak again as Cole continued toward his rooms.

He hated the silence that descended because it allowed the memories to bubble forth. His father had taken great pride in walking these halls and ruling over this land.

With every corner Cole turned, he expected to find his father gliding toward him. A smile would brighten his face the second he saw Cole; then his arms would open for a quick embrace.

Tove, king of the dark fae, was a ruler who did not tolerate disobedience. To his sons, he was a man who loved them deeply, and they loved him in return.

Cole fingered the wedding rings his father gave him before everything went to shit. The rings once belonged to his father and mother, and he hoped one day, Lexi would wear his mother's.

But that was an obstacle for a later time. Now, Cole had to make sure she was safe before returning here to endure the trials and take control of the Gloaming.

He sneered at the reminder.

He'd never believed anything could happen to his father. His dad ruled these lands for over seven hundred years. He was the longest-reigning dark fae king, and in a moment... one lightning-fast moment, he was dead.

Cole shuddered as some of his grief crept back in, but he shoved it aside. He had no time to mourn.

He had trials to survive, a throne to ascend, and hell to unleash.

CHAPTER THREE

LEXI FINISHED HANGING the last feed tub over the horse's door and turned. When she saw the man standing behind her, she gasped and stumbled back until she crashed into the stall door. She never heard him enter the barn or realized he was standing a foot away from her.

How long had he been watching her?

She opened her mouth to demand answers, but he wouldn't give them. Instead, she clamped it shut and lifted her chin. Her eyes narrowed when he leaned against the wall far too close to her.

Anger and revulsion warred inside her as she glowered at him. There were few people in this world she disliked, and this arrogant prick was one of them.

When he smiled at her, his smug attitude set her teeth on edge. How *dare* he waltz in here as if he belonged in her life and on *her* property?

Normally the familiar, much-loved scents of hay and horse made her worst days better. The soothing sounds of the horses eating their breakfast was typically a balm to her soul, but nothing could calm her now.

To make matters worse, with as quiet as he'd been, he could

have caught her entering or leaving the tunnels below. And if he learned of the refugees, they would all die.

Then she realized she'd never heard him enter the barn because he'd teleported in. She could never enter the tunnels from the barn again.

Entering them through the house meant Sahira had a better chance of catching her, but she'd take her chances with her aunt over Malakai. She would *not* risk the lives of the refugees.

"Hello, Elexiandra," he practically purred.

Though outwardly she remained unmoving, everything inside her recoiled when his brown eyes leisurely perused her. He'd never seen her naked, and he *never* would, but she felt like those eyes stripped her bare.

She resisted the impulse to cover herself with her hands, but she would *not* give him the satisfaction of knowing he unnerved her. Instead, she stared disdainfully back at him as his eyes met hers again.

"Malakai," she said.

Her crisp tone didn't faze him as his smile revealed his straight, white teeth and fangs. As a half vampire, she had a set of fangs too. However, his were elongated like he was about to feed.

And she would *never* be the thing he fed on.

"How are you doing?" he asked. "I feel like we haven't seen each other in a while."

Not long enough.

It had been almost two weeks since they last saw each other. At the time, Cole chased him off, but Cole was gone, and she was all alone with *him*.

But she didn't need anyone to chase him off again. Her father was gone, Cole was gone, and *she* would somehow get him to leave her alone.

How? She didn't know, but she would find a way to get him out of her life.

Her shoulders went back. "I've been good, and you?"

"Unfortunately, I haven't been so good. Would you like to know why?"

"No."

Her surprise over the unexpected, blunt response was only exceeded by his. The smile slid from his face as his eyes glinted with malice.

"I'm sorry, Malakai, but I don't have the time for this. If you'll excuse me."

She'd prefer not to go anywhere near him, but the way she always exited the barn was behind him. She could walk out through the paddock and climb the fence to get out, but she refused to back down from this man, or anyone else, anymore.

Keeping her shoulders back, she started toward the open door behind him. The sunlight streaming through it caught the specks of dust dancing through the air.

It was such a familiar sight that most of the time, she never noticed it. She focused on those particles now as they drew her toward freedom.

Her mind shouted at her to run, and her senses remained focused on the man behind her, but she kept her step steady as she approached the door. *I will not run from this man. I will not run.*

She was almost to the door when Malakai transported directly into her path. She almost walked into him, and his six-two frame blocked out the welcoming rays of the sun as he towered seven inches over her.

"Where's your boyfriend?" he growled.

His smile was gone, and the malevolence shining in his eyes caused ice crystals to form in her blood. Those crystals crept across her skin until they encased her in a frozen tomb.

She would not back down from him, but she wasn't sure she'd survive what he planned to do to her.

CHAPTER FOUR

"Please, get out of my way," she replied in a steady voice that didn't reveal her increasing alarm.

Malakai tilted his head to the side as red gleamed in his eyes. "Did you fuck him, Elexiandra?"

She barely stopped herself from gaping at the crude, unexpected question.

"Did he part those pretty thighs?" He prowled closer as he asked the question. "Did you let that half-breed rut between your legs like the dog he is?"

Despite her determination not to back down from him, she edged away from the hatred he emanated. As much as he wanted her, he also despised her and planned to make her pay for the years she spent refusing him. And he especially intended to make her suffer for choosing Cole over him.

What he would do to her should be done to *no* living creature.

"And like the dark fae he is, he grew tired of you and took his cock to his next whore," Malakai continued.

The truth of those words stung like a slap to the face, but she hoped she kept that hidden from him.

"You're disgusting," Lexi said and planted her feet as she refused to take another step back. "Get off my property."

"And how do you plan to make me?" he asked.

When he stopped before her, the toes of his boots touched the front of her sneakers. The five o'clock shadow lining his jaw matched the dark brown of his hair.

She contemplated knocking that shadow right off his face, but the look in his eyes froze her. She'd punched Cole's brother, Orin, and he was one of the deadliest creatures in all the realms, but Malakai wasn't Orin.

Orin was lethal, but he was also sane and had a bit of a moral compass, even if it was broken most of the time. Malakai was a monster who would tear her apart if she gave him a reason.

He was a twisted freak who was a lot stronger than her, and if she punched him, he would attack. But then, he might attack without any provocation too.

Lexi prepared herself for that possibility as he loomed over her. He could stomp her, but she wasn't going down without a fight.

"Did you like fucking him?" Malakai inquired.

Tired of him, Cole, Orin, and every other "man" in her life since her dad died, Lexi had no idea what came over her, but she smiled as she replied. "I *loved* it."

She had only a second to gloat over the rage clouding his face before his hand clamped on her throat. He moved so fast she didn't see him before his fingers bit into her flesh.

As he choked her, he cut off her ability to breathe. Lifting her, he propelled her backward and into the wall. The air in her lungs managed to escape on a gurgled *ah*.

"You whore!" he spat the words into her face with such vehemence that spittle sprayed her.

Her disbelief over being attacked in such a way faded, and her survival instincts kicked in. Determined to get away from him, Lexi lashed out. When her fist connected with his cheek, the blow knocked his head to the side.

Malakai's grip relaxed, and fresh air briefly filled her lungs before his head swiveled back toward her. She didn't see the punch coming at her until a crushing blow battered her temple.

Her head shot to the side, and blood filled her mouth as dizziness assailed her. When her legs gave out, his grip on her throat kept her standing. She was still trying to recover her senses when he shoved his leg between her thighs.

Realizing exactly what he would do to her, Lexi swung and kicked and squirmed as she battered him. The blows sent shock waves through her hands and arms. The adrenaline coursing through her gave her a strength she'd never shown before, but it still wasn't enough to get him off her.

She couldn't breathe. She was going to pass out. And once she did, he would do whatever he wanted to her.

That reality dragged her back from the brink of unconsciousness. She continued to punch at him, but he caught one of her wrists with his free hand and bashed it into the wall. Something cracked, and she was sure bones shattered in her hand, but she continued to swing at him.

And then, blessedly, he released her throat. She greedily sucked in oxygen as she coughed and sputtered. She was just getting enough air in to scream when he seized her other wrist and pinned them together with one of his hands.

Her scream choked off when he recaptured her throat and squeezed until her windpipe threatened to give way. Then the bastard kissed her.

The force of his kiss was nearly as punishing as his grip on her throat. He split her lips until she tasted blood. Then the asshole licked her blood away before shoving his tongue into her mouth.

~

COLE KNOCKED on the manor door one more time before stepping back to examine Lexi's home. No lights were on within, but that could be because no one was home or the electricity was out again.

It had taken him more time than he would have liked to wash all the blood off him and arrive here. By the time he finally finished scrubbing himself, his arm had nearly healed and now was nothing more than a dull throb.

He ran a hand through his hair and tugged at it as he studied the ruined remains of the marketplace in the distance. No one resurrected it after the Lord unleashed his dragons on it.

So, she hadn't gone to the market. However, she could have traveled to another marketplace or *anywhere* else. He'd been gone for almost two weeks; any number of things could have happened since then.

He tried not to think about that as he started around the manor. He stopped when the barn caught his attention. If she wasn't in the library, then her second favorite place was the barn.

And it was around the time when she usually went out to take care of the animals. He didn't know where Sahira was or why she hadn't answered the door, and he didn't care.

Eager to see Lexi again, he started toward the barn at a brisk stride. He stepped into the open doorway and peered into the shadows cloaking the barn.

It took only a second for his eyes to adjust to the darkness, and when they did, his blood rushed into his ears until he was certain his eardrums would rupture. A thick, red haze descended over his eyes to block out the embracing couple.

He was glad for that because he'd seen enough to make him spiral into a pit of madness as encompassing as what consumed him after his father's murder.

The urge to kill and shred overtook him as he imagined digging his hands into Malakai's bowels and ripping them out. He would make all the vampire's insides visible to the world as he spilled his blood across the ground.

Cole's fangs burst into his mouth; his claws sliced through his palms and scoured his bones. The blood dripping from his hands sounded like cannon fire to his lycan ears as it plopped onto the dirt floor.

He was on the verge of shifting, changing, becoming a beast who would decapitate her new lover and eat his head.

How could she?

When he left her, he promised to return in a day or two, but those days had come and gone. *He* never would have remained faithful to someone who did the same to him, but he hadn't expected the same from her. He'd believed her to be different than himself and the other women he'd been with; she was *his*, and she'd already moved on to a man she despised.

Wait. That made no sense. She *hated* Malakai. A lot could change in two weeks, but he didn't see her going from hating to screwing this man in such a short period. Although, he'd fucked more than a few women he despised.

Still, Lexi wasn't like him, and he couldn't shake the feeling something wasn't right here. With a control he hadn't believed he still retained, he pushed aside some of the red haze clouding his vision. He didn't want to see them locked in their passionate embrace again, but he did.

And as his breath thundered like a bull about to charge, he took in more details of their embrace. When he did, things beyond the knife twisting in his heart sank in.

Lexi's body bowed toward Malakai in a way that indicated she craved more. Cole's teeth ground together as he recalled how wonderful it felt to have her lithe body melding against his, but...

This *wasn't* melding.

She was as rigid as a board against Malakai. Her wrists, bound by Malakai's hand, were pressed against the wall, and her fingers were hooked into claws.

Blood spilled from the corners of Malakai's mouth a second before he reeled back from her. Blood flowed from both their mouths, and Cole realized she'd bitten him when she spit a gob of blood into his face.

"You bitch!" Malakai spat.

Lexi jerked and somehow lifted a knee to slam it into the vamp's stomach. Air exploded from Malakai as she tried to twist away.

"Let go of me!" she screamed.

Cole was shifting as he ran toward them, but he wasn't fast enough to stop Malakai from pulling his head back and smashing his forehead off her face. Lexi cried out as blood poured from her nose.

A roar built within Cole, but he didn't release it. He couldn't alert Malakai he was coming. That roar built to a crescendo as Malakai released her wrists and hit her. Lexi's head bounced off the wall as more of her blood spilled free.

CHAPTER FIVE

It took everything Lexi had to keep herself from passing out. If she did... well, she couldn't think about what would happen if she did.

Still, she felt like she was trying to claw her way out of quicksand as her knees gave out. Malakai's thigh between her legs was the only thing keeping her up. She blinked away the stars erupting before her eyes, and her head fell back.

No!

Her hands moved like someone had tied concrete blocks to them, but she somehow got her palms up between them. With a strength she hadn't known she still possessed, she drove her palm up and under Malakai's chin. His head snapped back as his fist flew.

Lexi braced herself for another blow as the whistle of his hand cutting through the air came at her. She didn't think she'd remain standing after this punch as her head still rang from the last blow and blood dripped off her chin.

She clawed at his neck and twisted her head away as Malakai was ripped off her. Lexi staggered forward and nearly went down.

She threw herself back against the wall as a flash of black soared past her.

Without Malakai to keep her propped up, Lexi hit the ground. But she refused to stay down; it could mean death, or worse, if she did.

She rested her hand against the wall and rose. Dizziness assailed her, and she almost fell again, but she refused to give in to the weakness consuming her.

Instead, she slumped against the wall as a massive wolf landed a few feet away from her. With its jaws locked around Malakai's abdomen, the vampire dangled from the wolf's mouth. Its head and body were the size of a lion's—an extremely large, extremely powerful lion. Its paws were the size of her head, and its claws could eviscerate a T. rex.

Malakai beat against the wolf's head as it opened its mouth and bit down again. Malakai's shrieks were like toothpicks to her eardrums. Blood spurted from his mouth as the wolf shook its head back and forth, turning Malakai into nothing more than a rag doll.

Normally, such a thing would have appalled her, but though she didn't enjoy Malakai's pain, it didn't upset her either. He would have raped her and maybe killed her; he deserved to be eaten.

When the wolf opened its mouth to chomp down again, Malakai vanished as he transported out of the wolf's hold. Lexi's eyes darted around the barn in search of him, but he didn't materialize anywhere nearby.

She squeezed her eyes shut when her vision blurred but almost immediately opened them again. *Is he going to return?*

But as the seconds stretched on, and he still didn't reemerge, she slid down the wall. Once on the ground, the thundering in her head became louder as her attention shifted to the wolf.

Its head moved around as it searched the barn. The blood dripping from its muzzle reminded her that it hadn't gotten the chance to eat, and she might be next.

When she scrambled to rise again, the abrupt movement caused nausea to twist in her belly, but she got to her feet. She rested her hand against the wall as she panted for air.

Turning its attention away from the barn, the wolf focused on her. When its silver eyes met hers, a certainty hit her as hard as Malakai's fist.

"Cole," she whispered before her knees gave out.

She didn't know how he moved so fast, but he transformed and his arms enveloped her. Blood stained his face, and his black hair was disheveled as he cradled her against his bare chest.

Joy soared at the sight of him, and though blood coated him, she relished being in his arms again. As she drank him in, she saw that he'd shaved his beard.

That was her last coherent thought before blackness descended.

～

"Lexi?" Cole whispered and rested his hand against her cheek. "Lexi?"

She didn't respond as her head lolled against his chest. Blood still seeped from her nose and caked her split, swollen lips. Her nose was three times its normal size and already turning the color of an eggplant. More bruises seeped out from her nose to shadow her closed eyes.

The imprint of fingers was evident in the black bruises marring her elegant throat. Her neck was swollen and red. More blood streaked her dark auburn hair with its various, brilliant strands of red.

He cursed the fact Malakai had gotten away. When this was over, he would finish tearing that vamp in half, but he wasn't going to part from her any time soon.

He stalked past his shredded clothes, into the day, and toward the manor. He was almost to the house when Sahira emerged from behind the house. She had gloves in hand, dirt streaked her cheeks, and a basket of vegetables hung over her arm.

She froze when she spotted him, and then her gaze landed on Lexi. When the basket fell from her grasp, tomatoes rolled across the ground, and she stomped them as she ran toward them. She was only a few feet away when she skidded to a stop.

When her amber eyes flew from Lexi to him, they darkened, and a breeze stirred the air. Some of her mahogany hair had fallen free of her bun; the loose strands started to blow around her face as she drew on the air currents surrounding them.

"Don't," he cautioned when the wind stirred around him.

Despite only being half witch, she had control over the elements. The breeze intensified as her nostrils flared.

"Put her down," she hissed.

"No. I didn't do this."

Sahira's eyes practically crackled with fire.

"I would *never* do this to her," he said.

"Like you've never laid a hand on her before."

Then her gaze ran over his naked body, and like Medusa's snakes, her hair whipped around her head. Her words were more of a blow to him than the increasing wind.

He hadn't injured Lexi on purpose, but she was right; he had left bruises on her throat when she tried to wake him from a nightmare. But this…

"I would *never* do this to her," he repeated as the wind buffeted him.

It was a good thing Sahira wasn't near any flames. Otherwise, she would have tried to torch his ass. If she wasn't Lexi's aunt, he would put a stop to her continued use of power against him, but she had Lexi's best interests at heart, she was the only family Lexi had left, and Lexi loved her. Stopping her would turn physical, and he couldn't let that happen.

"Malakai did this," he said and turned away from her.

He started toward the manor again. No matter how pissed Sahira was at him, she wouldn't do anything harmful while Lexi remained in his arms.

CHAPTER SIX

COLE DIDN'T LOOK BACK at Sahira as he climbed the steps to the manor. Shifting his hold on Lexi, he opened the door. Sahira arrived at his side as he stepped into the cool, dark interior of the home.

"Malakai did this?" she demanded.

"Yes."

"Are you telling me the truth?"

He glanced at her before striding down the hall toward the stairs. "Yes."

"I swear if you're lying to me, if you did this—"

"I didn't do this, and I'm not a liar," he interrupted. "When I get my hands on Malakai, he *will* pay for it."

"I have to gather some of my supplies."

She didn't leave his side as she hovered nearby and peered at Lexi's face. When she tried to touch her, Cole moved Lexi away without realizing that's what he intended to do.

Sahira glared at him; he glared back.

"What are you doing back here?" she asked.

"I came back for her."

"Why would you do that? She's not a play toy or a game. I will *not* let you hurt her."

"I'm not going to hurt her."

"You already have. Where have you been?" she demanded as they started to climb the stairs.

He didn't reply. He owed Lexi answers, not her.

"Conveniently, you showed up again today, and this is what she looks like," she said.

"More like lucky. Where were you when Malakai was attacking her in the barn?"

"Where was *I?* Where have *you* been?" she retorted as he opened the door to Lexi's room.

The familiarity of her scent and the memories of their time here almost mollified him. However, nothing was going to calm the lycan while Lexi remained like this. He hit the light switch to chase away the shadows and get a better look at her, but they remained off. The power was out again.

Carefully, he set Lexi on the bed and sat beside her. Sahira tried to push past him, but he caught her wrist to hold her back.

"Don't get between us," he warned.

She started to say something, but then her mouth parted. He didn't know what she saw on his face as she took a small step back.

"I'll get my supplies," she said.

"Go."

She glanced from Lexi to him and back again.

"She's safe with me," he said.

Clasping Lexi's hand against his chest, he ran his hand up and down her silken skin as he sought to pierce through her unconscious haze.

Sahira hesitated before bowing her head. "I'll be right back."

Cole didn't look up as she left the room. Leaning forward, he brushed the hair back from Lexi's face and ran his fingers along her temple. Despite the damage Malakai inflicted on her, she was still strikingly beautiful and *his*.

Setting her hand down, he carefully touched the bruises marring her throat and face. Her other hand was turning black and blue, and when he carefully lifted it, the broken bones in it shifted as they ground together.

Hair sprouted from the backs of his hands, and his claws lengthened as he continued his exam.

CHAPTER SEVEN

LEXI'S HEAD pounded like the drummer from the Foo Fighters was using it as his drum set. Afraid that opening her eyes would only result in more pain, she kept them closed as she struggled to recall why she ached so badly.

Through the drum solo in her head, the bits and pieces of what happened fell into place. Malakai's stranglehold on her throat explained why it felt like she'd swallowed fire. The rest of his assault explained why her nose and hand throbbed.

Every part of her was sore and battered. She couldn't think about moving without wanting to groan, never mind actually attempting to do so.

And then she recalled the wolf.

Cole!

Her eyes flew open, and she whimpered when the influx of light burned them. She closed them again and squinted before she realized it hurt to do so.

"Shh," someone soothed, and a hand rested on her shoulder. "Here, drink this."

She turned toward the voice, but for some reason, she couldn't place who spoke. Was it Cole? Was he here with her? Had she imagined him?

Or was it Malakai?

The possibility caused her to bolt up in the bed. She cried out as her head exploded like fireworks were going off in there, and her stomach revolted. She wanted out of bed, but she couldn't resist the gentle hands on her shoulder, pushing her back.

"It's okay," someone whispered. "You're safe."

Malakai wouldn't say those things to her, and even if he did, she didn't have the strength to fight him. She tried to open her eyes again but couldn't crack them without her head spinning.

When cool glass touched her lips, she opened her mouth and allowed the liquid to fill it. It tasted of peppermint, apple, and the sand of the demon realms. She was certain a lot more ingredients comprised the drink, but she couldn't name them all.

It had to be something Sahira had created as only her aunt could mix such eclectic ingredients and make them delicious. As the liquid slid down her throat, it eased the burning and some of the pounding in her head. This time, when she opened her eyes, the light didn't burn them.

Sahira's face loomed before her. Concern etched her forehead as she tenderly brushed the hair back from Lexi's forehead.

"Do you feel better?" she asked anxiously.

"Yes," Lexi croaked and winced at the sound of her raw voice.

"Did Malakai do this to you?"

"I told you he did," Cole stated from behind her.

Lexi's heart leapt at the sound of his voice. Trying to see beyond her aunt, she searched for him, but Sahira blocked out everything else.

"I'm going to hear it from *her*," Sahira retorted.

Her eyes never left Lexi's face as she leaned closer and clasped her hands. "Did Malakai do this?"

"Yes," Lexi whispered. "He tele...."

When she broke off and winced, Sahira brought the bottle to

her lips again. Her aunt tenderly cupped her head as Lexi drank the rest of the contents. After she finished, Sahira capped the bottle and set it on the stand. When she moved, Lexi glimpsed Cole standing by the window.

His silver eyes met hers, and excitement flooded her, but she tamped it down.

No matter how happy she was to see him, she wouldn't allow him to roam in and out of her life whenever he chose. He was here and had saved her from Malakai, but no matter how much she cared for him, she would *not* be the piece of ass he kept on the side and visited when he was bored.

Sahira sat on the bed beside her and clasped her uninjured hand. "What happened?"

"Malakai teleported into the barn." It was still raw, but her voice sounded a lot better, and her throat already didn't hurt as much. Her aunt truly was a miracle worker with the potions. "He attacked me."

Sahira's eyes darkened, and from behind her, Cole released a sound that would have made a dragon tuck tail and fly. The noise caused a flash of unease to cross Sahira's face, but her attention remained riveted on Lexi.

"I let you give her the potion, but I'd like to talk to her alone now," Cole said.

"I'm not going anywhere," Sahira replied.

Lexi squeezed Sahira's hand as Cole stepped forward, but he didn't come any closer. He emanated an air of brutality she'd never seen before. Without the beard shadowing his face, the tips of his ciphers licked the bottom of his chin.

An ominous look clouded his face, but there was something more to the glint of rage in his eyes. There was also concern as he smiled hesitatingly at her. Despite her every intention not to let her heart melt toward him, it softened.

"It's okay," Lexi said to her aunt. "I want to talk to him."

Sahira's hands tightened on Lexi's good one. She'd never

approved of them together; she approved even less since he'd taken off.

"I'm sure that whatever he has to say can wait," Sahira said in a clipped tone. "You're wounded and—"

"It's fine," Lexi assured her.

She'd prefer to get this over and done with. It would be easier on her heart if he left again sooner rather than later.

Sahira didn't look like it was fine, but she released Lexi's hand and rose. "I'll make some more healing potion for you. I won't be gone long."

She gave Cole a pointed look before leaving the room. Lexi stared at the empty doorway after Sahira vanished, but she couldn't put off dealing with him forever.

Taking a deep breath, she finally tore her attention away from the open door to focus on the man standing near her window. Her heart raced, sweat coated her palms, and her stomach contracted like someone had punched it.

He was as gorgeous as she remembered with his chiseled cheekbones and square jaw. It was strange seeing him without his beard, but he was impossibly more handsome and ominous without it.

The tips of his pointed ears poked up through his short, black hair. When she used to run her fingers over the tips of those ears, he would turn into her touch.

Now that she could smell him and see him again, she was acutely aware of everything she missed while he was gone. Heat flooded her body as the memories of *all* the things he enjoyed her doing to him returned.

She spent the first few days after he left trying to recall every detail of their time together. She was determined not to forget a second of it.

Once she realized he wasn't coming back, she spent a lot of time working to bury *all* of those memories. They were far too distressing to recall during the day, though they tormented her dreams. As those memories rushed back, they refused to be stifled again.

It didn't help that he was back in her father's ill-fitting clothes like the last time she saw him. She assumed he hadn't arrived here naked and his clothes had torn from him when he transformed.

Even in the too-small outfit, he was still striking and commanding and so tempting it took all she had not to beckon him closer to kiss him. The shirt's short sleeves revealed the black ciphers around his lower biceps, forearms, wrists, and the tips of his fingers.

She knew from experience those flame-like marks also ran across his shoulders, neck, and down his back to his waist. Those ciphers hinted at the plethora of power he possessed, but it was only a small hint. She'd probably never know the full depth of it, but then, *he* might not know.

Like her, he was also a half-breed. Unlike her, he possessed a *ton* of power.

As he stared at her, the silver bled from his eyes until they were once again their beautiful Persian blue color. Her heart warmed further before she slammed a wall around it.

She would *not* let him hurt her again.

CHAPTER EIGHT

"You shaved your beard," she said.

It was a stupid thing to comment on, but she had so many things running through her mind that she had no idea what to say to him first.

Why did you leave me for so long? You promised you would be back sooner. Your brother and a bunch of refugees are hiding beneath my manor as we speak.

This reminder was a knife of fear to her chest. He couldn't know about them. He'd turn them in faster than he transformed into a wolf, and she couldn't let that happen.

He rubbed his chin as he approached the bed. "I did."

She almost asked why but held back the question. He was honest enough that he would tell her if it was for another woman. Maybe he'd met someone who didn't like his beard while she loved the feel of it against her skin and between her thighs.

She tried not to blush at the reminder but couldn't stop it. Damn her fair complexion and tendency to embarrass far too easily. After all this time and all the intimate moments they shared, she should be beyond embarrassment.

It was something she had to work on.

"How do you feel?" he asked as he stopped beside her bed.

With him beside her, she was reminded of how large he was. He possessed the black hair and ciphers of the dark fae but the impressive size of a lycan. It was an alluring combination that grated on every one of her bruised nerves.

"Fine, thank you," she replied stiffly.

When he frowned at her, she focused on the window behind him. She couldn't see anything out of it, but it was better than looking at him.

"Lexi."

The way he said her name was like a caress against her. She *hated* it.

"Lexi, look at me."

She couldn't sit here, stubbornly refusing to do so. It was childish, and she refused to back down from him or Malakai or anyone else ever again. She lifted her chin as she stared defiantly up at him.

Those blue eyes warmed, but when they slid to her throat, they hardened again. When he reached out to touch her, she recoiled from his fingers. His hand froze between them before falling to his side.

She hated the hurt look in his eyes but having him here again was worse than not having him here. The sooner he left, the better off she'd be.

~

COLE SAT on the edge of her bed. He'd expected her to be upset with him; he hadn't expected to walk in on her brutal attack. He wasn't sure if it was the attack or the fact he'd been gone so long bringing such sadness to her eyes, but he hated seeing it there.

And those eyes. It took everything he had not to smash the walls as he took in her battered face and throat. The whites of her eyes were completely red, probably from being strangled. Sahira's potion had made her voice better, but the welts and bruises on her throat were worse.

The swelling in her slender nose caused it to be twice its normal size, but a few of the freckles dotting its bridge were still visible beneath the bruises. In her hunter green eyes, the emerald flecks were more vivid against the red that had filled the whites surrounding them.

He longed to pull her into his arms. He needed her warmth and comfort as badly as he wanted to shelter her from the world, but she wasn't going to allow it until he explained what happened.

"What are you doing here, Cole?" she asked. When she spoke, the tips of her fangs glinted in the fading daylight.

"I came back for you," he said.

"Why would you do that now?"

"I never meant to be gone so long," he said. "The Lord called my father and me to him, and when I say called, I mean he *ordered* us to attend him. I wanted to send you a crow and considered sending Brokk, but the Lord's man was there, and the Lord can't know about you."

Her mouth pursed. "And why is that?"

"Because you're a weakness to me, one that he *would* exploit."

"You think I'm a weakness?"

"I know you are, and I'm going to do everything I can to protect you from him."

"I don't need your protection, and I'm *not* a weakness."

He took a deep breath. "I'm not explaining this well. You're *my* weakness, Lexi. If something happened to you, it would destroy me."

She looked like he'd told her dogs could fly and sing the alphabet by burping it while in flight.

"If the Lord learns that, he will use you against me every chance he gets. It's only a matter of time before he learns about you, there's no stopping that, but I'm going to keep you from him for as long as possible."

After what happened with his father....

Cole shut his eyes as he tried to block out the memory of his father's demise. He could still feel the hot wash of blood spraying him as the dragon consumed Tove. As fresh sorrow swelled in him, his jaw clenched until his teeth ached from it.

Taking a deep breath, he pushed aside the memory and opened his eyes to focus on Lexi. The sight of her helped keep the memories at bay, but they wouldn't remain buried. The dead had a way of returning; he'd learned that after the war... when they started haunting his dreams.

Concern radiated from Lexi as she rested her hand on his. "What happened?"

"My father is dead," he said.

Her mouth dropped, and the fingers of her good hand clamped around his. Sahira entered the room with a tray of tea and another bottle of healing potion. She froze when she saw Lexi's expression.

"What is it?" Sahira asked. "What happened?" Then her eyes narrowed on him. "What did *you* do?"

Cole turned his hand beneath Lexi's and tenderly squeezed it. "My father is dead," he said to Sahira.

Sahira lowered the tray but didn't set it down. "That's not possible."

"But it is."

"King Tove is dead?"

"Yes."

"I never thought I'd see the day," she murmured.

"Neither did I."

"Sahira, I need to talk to Cole alone," Lexi said.

Her aunt walked over to set the tray on the nightstand beside her bed. "There's another bottle of healing potion, and I added a soothing mix to your tea, so make sure you drink it."

"I will," Lexi promised.

This time, when Sahira left, she closed the door behind her.

CHAPTER NINE

"TELL ME EVERYTHING," Lexi said.

So, he did. And as he did, she watched the emotions playing across his face. Fury tinged his voice as he told of his imprisonment in the tower with his father. She heard his uncertainty when he stood in the Lord's hall and finally his distress as he spoke of his father's murder.

Her heart broke for him. Then her concern for him grew as he revealed what he did to the dragon and the helot who once worked in his palace. A chill crept down her spine when he told her what the Lord commanded him to do.

The Lord expected Cole to be the next king of the dark fae. That meant Cole would have to survive the trials. She had no idea what those trials were, but before she could ask, he rubbed his face and lifted his beautiful blue eyes to her.

"I couldn't get my father's blood or the smell of it out of my beard," he said. "That's why I shaved it."

Those words and his sorrow-filled voice broke something inside her. Tears spilled down her cheeks as she leaned across the distance separating them and wrapped her arms around him.

With tender care, he pulled her onto his lap and cradled her against him with such desperation it made her tears come faster. This big, powerful, magnificent man was looking to her to help ease his suffering, and she would not let him down.

They cleaved to each other while she tried to ease his grief. She knew what he was going through, knew what it was like to lose a father who was loved and cherished. She could never take that loss away, but she would do her best to help get him through this.

As she nestled the back of his head in the hollow of her shoulder, she recalled the time he told her that his father would tease him because he always got lost in the palace. At the time, she was stunned to learn the dark fae king teased anyone, but he'd loved his children. And Cole loved him.

"I'm sorry," she whispered.

Her anger with him was gone. He hadn't abandoned her for other women or decided to return for a booty call. He'd been imprisoned with his father before watching him die.

And she'd been here, mad at him and trying to bury her heartbreak. Because of that, she'd taken in his fugitive brother and a bunch of refugees, who now resided in the tunnels beneath *her* manor.

No, *not* because of that.

Lexi hadn't aided Orin because of her anger at Cole; she did it because she couldn't turn away those suffering people and immortals and because she was taking a stance in this war. One that put her in direct opposition of Cole.

But there was no *way* Cole could still be on the Lord's side after the homicidal maniac slaughtered his father. She should talk to him about it and maybe tell him about Orin, but now wasn't exactly the time.

～

COLE HELD Lexi in his arms as he stared out the window. Outside, the birds were singing the last of their songs for the day.

He'd spent the past hour regaling her with stories of his father. With her head against his chest and her hand absently stroking his stomach, she listened and laughed with him. She also cried some more.

He hated her tears as he wiped them away, but those tears were because she understood his loss and cared for him. It was that caring that touched him most.

He'd come back for her because she was his mate and he cared for her, but as she cried and laughed, he realized how much she cared for him too. That knowledge warmed his heart at a time when he never would have believed such a thing possible.

When he finished speaking, they fell into a companionable silence as the setting sun's rays bounced off the walls and lit the room with a rainbow of colors. If they were in one of the realms, pixies might be dancing through those rays, but the pixies didn't often come to the human realm.

"I'm sorry about your father," she said after a while.

"Thank you. He was a good man."

"He raised an amazing son."

Cole smoothed back her hair and kissed the top of her head. Little had gone right since the war between the immortals started and the Lord unleashed his dragons on Earth, but she was one thing that had gone *so* right.

And he wasn't letting her go again.

"I'm sorry I didn't get word to you sooner," he said.

She lifted her head and frowned at him. Some of the swelling had come out of her nose, but the bruising was worse. "Don't apologize; I understand why you didn't."

"But I bet you were cursing me," he said with a small, teasing smile.

"Never," she teased back.

He laughed and kissed her forehead. "I wish I could say that I'm going to stay, but I can't. I have to get back to the Gloaming and state my intentions to endure the trials."

Her beautiful eyes darkened. "How bad are the trials?"

"Not much is known about them, but few have survived, and all who did were named king of the dark fae afterward."

"I don't want to lose you."

"You don't have to worry about that."

She tried to suppress it, but he felt her shudder.

"I *will* survive the trials," he said.

"What are they?"

"I don't know. There could be two of them or hundreds. What each of them entails is a mystery; my father never revealed what he endured. They're probably designed to test my dark fae powers."

"But you're only half dark fae."

"And stronger than the rest of them."

"Yes, but even if you survive the trials, will the dark fae accept you as king?"

"They'll have no choice. Whoever survives the trials claims the throne."

"What if someone is already on the throne when someone else decides to go through the trials? Or what if another dark fae decides to do the trials too?"

"As far as I know, the first has never happened, but there can only be one king. If two fae survive the trials, a fight to the death will ensue, and the survivor would wear the crown."

"That sounds horrible and brutal."

It most certainly would be, but he kept that to himself. Lexi stifled a yawn, and her lashes fluttered against his chest as her eyes closed before opening again.

"You should rest," he said as he ran her hair through his fingers.

"I will, but I'm not ready yet."

"I'm not going back yet. I'll be here when you wake."

"I'm still not ready," she said around another yawn.

He decided not to push her on it. Soon exhaustion would win out over her stubbornness.

"How many times has Malakai been here since I left?" he asked.

"Today was the first time. You both returned on the same day."

"If I have my way, it will also be the last time."

"Good," she murmured before her eyes drifted closed and didn't open again.

CHAPTER TEN

WHEN LEXI WOKE, Cole stood by her window while Sahira sat in a chair next to her bed. Cole crumpled a piece of paper in his hand as a crow flew away. The last crow that arrived here took him from her, and judging by the look on his face, this one hadn't brought good news.

"You're awake," Sahira said as she leaned over and rested her hand on Lexi's.

Lexi couldn't look at her aunt as her attention remained riveted on Cole. "What did the note say?" she asked.

"Don't worry about that." Sahira rose and lifted a teacup from the table; she handed it to Lexi. "You just focus on getting well."

Lexi held out her hand to stop her aunt when Sahira offered her the cup. "I'm okay."

"You're still healing."

"I'm fine."

With a sigh, Sahira pulled the cup away.

"What did it say?" Lexi asked Cole again.

"The dark fae council has learned of my father's death; they have descended on the palace. I have to return," he said.

Lexi's heart sank. She'd just gotten him back, and he was already leaving.

To start the trials that few survived.

Shit.

She bit her lip against begging him to stay and shot a panicked look at Sahira, who watched her with worry.

"Come with me," Cole said to her.

"I can't," Lexi said a little too fast.

She pushed herself up on the bed and propped her back against the headboard.

"We've had this discussion before," she continued. "I have too much to take care of here. I can't leave."

"I'm not leaving you here after what Malakai did," Cole said. "He could come back."

"I can't go."

"Yes, you can," Sahira said, and Lexi shot her an irritated look.

"You *hate* the stables. Who will take care of the horses if I leave?"

"I'll have George come to help with the horses. But he's right, you can't be here when Malakai returns, and he *will* return."

Lexi's teeth ground together. The two of them were like oil and water, but they were ganging up on her. Malakai would have won the fight between them, but she'd gotten in her fair share of hits against him too.

"I can defend myself, and next time, I'll be more prepared. I never expected him to teleport into the barn," she said.

"And he can do that again," Sahira said. "It's not safe for you here."

"Cole was gone for almost two weeks last time. I *can't* stay away that long."

"No, but if it means keeping you safe, then you have to go."

"And you're going to stay here? You think Malakai won't do something to you or George if he returns? I can't leave you here alone and unprotected."

"I am not unprotected; I'll set his ass on fire or put a curse on him if he tries anything."

"And if he attacks you? You're not a fighter."

"I'll make up a couple of potions that will burn off his skin if he tries anything. Believe me, Lexi, I'll be fine."

"You could give me some of those potions."

"When you come back and when you're stronger. You're far too easy to take down right now, and you know it."

Sahira was right, and she also didn't like the idea of sending Cole back to the Gloaming alone, not when he wanted her there with him. But Orin was in her tunnels with a bunch of refugees.

She couldn't leave them alone down there. Orin supplied most of what they required, but she was part of their food chain and had taken on the responsibility of protecting them.

And what would happen if the Lord's men somehow discovered them while she wasn't here? They would blame Sahira, and she could *not* let that happen. But how much could she protest without drawing suspicion or hurting Cole?

"I'll have you back by tonight or tomorrow at the latest," Cole said. "Even if I have to send you back with Brokk. However, I'm not leaving you here while you're injured, but I have to speak with the council and make it clear that I *will* be their new king and they *will* follow me."

Lexi gulped as his eyes burned with silver fire.

"You should go," Sahira said.

There was no way she could tell her aunt she couldn't leave because she would be putting *her* at risk.

"You can't be here if Malakai comes back," Sahira continued.

"Neither can you."

"He's not going to mess with a witch."

"Half witch," Lexi reminded her.

Sahira wiggled her fingers as she grinned. "But full-on bitch."

Cole snorted with laughter, and Lexi rolled her eyes. "Bitchiness isn't going to stop him," she said.

"You can come with us," Cole offered.

"No," Sahira said as Lexi said, "Yes!"

"We can't leave George here completely unprotected if Malakai does return. But you *can* go," Sahira said when Lexi started to protest. She clasped Lexi's good hand in hers and squeezed. "Go, Lexi. I'll be fine, but most importantly, you'll be safe."

She couldn't believe her aunt was arguing for her to go *with* Cole. Apparently, her concern for Lexi's safety outweighed her dislike and distrust of the dark fae. It figured such a thing would happen now.

"I can't be gone long," she said to Cole.

"You won't be," Cole promised.

~

WHEN THEY STEPPED through the portal Cole created, Lexi stopped dead in her tracks as she gazed at the fence spikes. The first time she came here, it was night and the moons hanging over the palace cast a silver radiance over the land.

Now, the night sky was overcast and none of those moons were visible. The peaks and turrets of the palace stretched so high it was almost impossible to discern where they ended and the sky began.

Wings stretched out to the side of the building, and the structure went so far back the end of it vanished into the night. The golden light shining out of the towering palace's numerous windows spilled across the grounds to illuminate the fence.

They also illuminated the remains stuck to the spikes on that fence. Remains Cole created.

He'd told her about the dragon, but hearing it and *seeing* it were two completely different things. The head was monstrous and enormous. It had to be at least eight feet long, and the thick sinew hanging from its severed neck revealed how heavily muscled the beast was.

It was a gruesome spectacle, and this thing had killed Cole's father, but she couldn't help feeling a little bad for it. It had only followed orders and died because of it.

Had it wanted to follow those orders?

Everyone saw dragons as merciless monsters now. But though they were known as dangerous and protective of those who ruled them, they'd never destroyed lands until the Lord commanded them to.

A part of her really hoped they were cruel creatures who enjoyed killing and not beasts enslaved by a vindictive master who made them do things they wouldn't normally do.

That possibility caused her chest to tighten. No matter what they wanted to do, this dragon was huge and lethal, and Cole had destroyed it.

"How?" she whispered.

He didn't pretend not to know what she was talking about. "It killed my father."

That didn't entirely explain the how, but she understood. Grief and wrath could compel someone to feats they never dreamed possible.

Beside the dragon head were the remains of the helot Cole killed. She hadn't known his name then, but she briefly met Sindri when he introduced her to the king and his sons at the party the king threw to celebrate the end of the war. And now he and the king were dead.

It was a turn of events she never could have seen coming then. *It's all so short and fast,* she realized as she gazed at the remains.

She'd always known that, but standing there, with a small breeze tickling her hair and the song of the night creatures filling her ears, it had never been more precarious or precious.

"Cole...."

He turned to look at her, but she had no idea what to say to him. Instead, she held out her hand to him. It was the hand Malakai broke, but it was fully healed.

When Cole took it, his fingers fit perfectly as they entwined with hers. As she gazed at his hand, she wondered how many more times she would get the chance to hold it.

She shook off her melancholy musings as Cole opened one of the gates and stepped back to let her enter the palace's outer courtyard. The stables to her left were quiet, but a single lantern burned in one of the windows. She suspected it was the room of the stable boy who most likely resided there.

A couple of greenhouses and some gardens were to the right of the stone pathway they trod toward the stairs leading to the looming palace doors. Beyond those gardens were more buildings. Plates of armor hung on fences and posts outside some of those buildings.

"What are those?" Lexi asked and pointed to the structures.

"The homes of the king's soldiers," Cole said.

"How many are there?"

"Homes or soldiers?"

"Both."

"There's a little over a hundred soldiers now. We lost many to the war. And there are a few hundred homes with an option to house more in homes behind the palace."

Lexi studied the buildings as they ascended the steps. It helped to distract her from her nervousness, but not much.

Things had changed so much in such a short amount of time. The last time she was here, she didn't know the man walking at her side, and now she knew him in the most intimate of ways.

She was also falling in love with him.

"Since the council is already here, I'll have to see them immediately, but I'll show you to my rooms first," Cole said as they climbed the steps to the doors.

"*Your* rooms?"

"Unless you prefer to stay somewhere else."

"No," she blurted and then started to blush. "I, uh... I didn't know what to, ah... what to expect."

"From now on, Lexi, you can expect to be by my side in all things."

Her heart melted a little as she inwardly groaned. Yes, she was definitely going to have to figure out what to do about Orin and Cole soon. She couldn't keep this big of a secret from Cole when he was saying things like *that*.

But could she trust him? And how was he going to react when he learned she'd kept this from him?

He wouldn't do anything to harm her. She was certain of that.

She was also certain he was going to be pissed.

CHAPTER ELEVEN

COLE RELEASED Lexi's hand to clasp her elbow as they ascended the stairs. The door opened before they arrived at the top, and Brokk stepped into the light spilling out of the palace. He smiled when he saw Lexi, but it didn't reach his eyes, and it faded when he saw her bruises.

"What happened?" he demanded.

"Malakai doesn't like the word no," she replied.

"Is he alive?"

"Not by choice and not for much longer if I have my way, but he teleported away before I could finish him," Cole said.

"Of course that coward did. Are you okay?" Brokk asked Lexi.

"I'm fine," she assured him.

Brokk stepped back to let them enter. "The council is waiting for you in the great hall."

"I'm going to show Lexi to my rooms before I meet with them," Cole replied.

"They're getting impatient, Cole."

"I'm going to be their king; they'll *wait*."

"I'll go with you," Lexi offered.

"It's a meeting for the dark fae," Brokk said.

"Then I'll wait outside the hall."

"The meeting could take a while. I'd prefer to see you settled first," Cole said.

She shifted her hold on the small bag of supplies she brought with her and rested her hand on his arm. "Don't leave them waiting. I'll be fine. Go on," she urged.

Cole took a deep breath before releasing it. "I won't have you standing in the hall. I'll take you somewhere quiet."

Brokk followed as Cole led Lexi past the main entryway to the great hall and through another doorway. They slipped into another corridor and climbed the stairs running up the side of the dais in the great hall. They stopped to stand in the shadows on the side of the stage.

It felt like years, but it wasn't long ago that he'd stood in these shadows with Brokk, staring out at the crowd and dreading every second of the party to come. At the time, he hadn't known Lexi, but that night changed everything for him.

He turned her toward him and cupped her cheek. She leaned into his touch and smiled up at him. The swelling was gone from her face, and the bruises were fading fast, but not fast enough for his liking.

"You can stay here," he said.

She would hear their conversation, but he didn't care. There was nothing the council had to say that she couldn't hear. She would be safe here, but he hesitated to leave her.

"Go," she said and placed her hand over his on her cheek. "Go on; I'll be fine."

He turned his hand over in hers, squeezed it, and released her. "Let's go," he said to Brokk.

He didn't look back as he strode out and onto the dais. His and Brokk's boots thudded against the floor as his brother walked beside him.

Cole ignored the three thrones set out on the dais as he descended the steps to the large table the helots placed in the center of the room. He didn't care that while every council member was dressed impeccably in elaborately brocaded tunics and soft pants, he was still wearing Del's too small, human clothes. What these assholes thought of him didn't matter.

The six members of the council studied him as he approached. They were all the eldest and most powerful members of their extremely old and wealthy families. They were all purebloods, and they held power in the Gloaming; he should play nice with them, but he was not in the mood to do so.

If he decided not to go through the trials, he would have a seat on the council. The fact his father was king did not give him a right to the throne, but his father's line, and therefore his, was also one of the oldest in the Gloaming, and that gave him a right to a seat at this table.

Without a king, the council ruled the realm, but Cole needed more than a seat at this table to destroy the Lord. He required the power that came with being king too. His father was stronger than the other dark fae because he survived the trials.

"Where have you been?" Aelfdane demanded.

Cole didn't respond as he stopped behind the large chair situated at the head of the table. It was the chair his father always occupied during these meetings while he sat beside him. Brokk and, at one time, the rest of his brothers had always stood behind him.

He didn't know if it was out of respect for his dead father's memory, fear of him, or preferring not to fight amongst each other, but none of the council had seated themselves on the chair. He was aware that some, if not *all* of them, planned to stake a claim on it.

Cole pulled out the chair and settled himself onto it. It felt completely wrong to do so, but he was making it clear he had no intention of leaving this palace. Though he despised sitting in the chair, he settled casually back and stretched his legs out before him.

When Aelfdane started to pull out the chair beside him, Cole caught one of the legs with his foot and yanked it back. Aelfdane's eyebrows shot into his black hairline.

"That chair is for my brother," Cole said.

A thunderous expression crossed Aelfdane's face. "Who do you think you are?"

"Your future king, and I'm telling you to resume your normal seat at this table. I will have my father's chair, and my brother will assume the position *I* once held at this table."

The air around Aelfdane started to crackle as he drew on his powers.

"Unless you want your head on a stake beside that dragon, I'd rein your power in," Cole growled.

"Are you… threatening… *me*?" Aelfdane sputtered.

"Is that what you took it as?"

"Yes."

"Then you would be correct."

He thought Aelfdane was going to unleash on him, but Becca leaned over from where she stood beside him at the table and rested her hand on his arm. The older fae spun on her and opened his mouth to start shouting, but he seemed to think twice about unleashing on the council and bit back his words.

"Fighting amongst ourselves isn't going to solve our dilemma," Elvin said.

Elvin's black skin, hair, and eyes shone in the glow of the torches lining the walls. Though his words were meant to pacify, his eyes were as cold as one of the ice realms when they met Cole's. He wasn't a hothead like Aelfdane, but he also wasn't happy to see Cole sitting in his father's seat.

Cole smiled at him. Elvin's eyes narrowed, but he settled at the table with the others. Brokk settled into the chair beside him.

"I will undergo the trials as soon as possible," Cole stated.

"You really think you'll be king?" Durin demanded.

"Yes."

"Absolutely not!" Aelfdane declared. "That will never happen."

"My father was king."

"I don't care. No half-breed will sit on the dark fae throne."

"When I survive the trials, that throne will be mine," Cole said.

"You'll *never* survive them."

Cole shrugged as he leaned back and folded his hands on his belly. "I bet you considered it impossible for someone to kill a dragon with their bare hands, but I did, and I staked its head outside. I *will* survive them."

The men all exchanged glances while Becca licked her lips as she eyed him.

"Are you saying you killed that dragon?" Elvin asked.

"Who else do you think did it?" Cole replied.

"You could have found a dead dragon and cut off its head," Alston said.

"When was the last time you saw a dead dragon lying around?" Brokk inquired. "Oh, right, never," he continued when none of them replied.

"That dragon killed my father, and I killed it," Cole said. "I don't care if you believe me or not; your beliefs won't make any difference when I'm ruling over you."

All the council members exchanged a look. Most of them wisely remained silent.

"A single man can't kill a dragon," Finn stated. "That's impossible."

"No, it's not," Cole said. "But I'm not going to argue with you about it. I want to start the trials as soon as possible. The Lord of the Shadow Realms has promised to unleash his dragons on the Gloaming if I do not take the throne."

That quieted them for only a second before they exploded into conversation. He let them argue with each other while he watched. Brokk rolled his eyes before shifting his attention back to the bickering council.

CHAPTER TWELVE

LEXI REMAINED hidden in the shadows, but if she poked her head out a little, she could see most of the table. The dark fae council all looked like they were walking on thin ice, while Cole looked like he'd set up a chair and was casually catching fish on that ice.

She didn't know how he could remain so calm when she was on the verge of chewing off her fingernails to keep from screaming. She had no powers, and being half human, she wasn't as strong as any purebred immortal, but she wanted to go out there and protect him from them… somehow.

Instead, she remained standing in the shadows, spying as she used to when she was a little girl and her dad was in one of his meetings. She was always so scared he'd catch her, but he never did.

During those times, she'd never understood half of what she overheard. She understood all of it now, and most of these fae didn't want Cole in charge. The woman was the only one who didn't speak as she eyed Cole in a way that made Lexi feel as murderous as Godzilla on a rampage.

"Are you done?" Cole demanded in a voice commanding enough to silence them.

They would make it difficult for him to claim the throne, but these self-important assholes already obeyed him.

"The Lord cannot threaten us," one of the fae said.

"He can, and he has," Cole said calmly. "How soon can the trials start?"

Lexi leaned forward to make sure she didn't miss the response.

～

"I'M NOT SURE," Elvin said. "I will look into it and send word when I know."

"Good," Cole stated.

"A half-breed will not lead us," Aelfdane declared.

"Once I survive those trials, I will."

"My son will also endure the trials," Durin said.

"So will mine," Alston said.

Cole kept his face impassive while he inwardly seethed over these two assholes so gallantly offering their sons up for death. They were both too cowardly to endure the trials themselves, but if, by some miracle, one of their sons survived and he didn't, they planned to rule the Gloaming through them.

"I will endure the trials too," Aelfdane said.

At least he's not as cowardly as the other two.

"That's fine," Cole said as he stared at Aelfdane. "If anyone else survives the trials, I'll kill them when it's over, as custom dictates."

Aelfdane paled a little but didn't respond.

"You can all go now," Cole said.

Used to being dismissed in such a way by his father, they didn't question it until they were to the door. Once there, they hesitated before leaving the hall. Returning to the table now would only make them look more foolish.

"Now what?" Brokk asked.

"Now, I'm going to take Lexi to my rooms," Cole said. "She

wants to return home soon, and I need you to protect her in case Malakai returns."

"Of course," Brokk said. "But without me here, the palace will be open to the council's invasion."

"Do you think they'll try to move in?"

"Yes."

"So do I."

"How do we stop it?"

"Brokk can stay here," Lexi said as she slipped from the shadows. "I'll be fine at home with Sahira. I'm sure she's made plenty of skin-melting potion by now."

"That sounds lovely," Brokk said.

"Can I come out now?" she asked.

Cole smiled as he beckoned her forward. "You already are."

She chuckled as she descended the stairs with fluid grace. "That I am. I don't think the council likes you."

When she slid her hand into his, he squeezed it.

"I don't care if they like me. I intend for them to respect and obey me, and once the trials are over, they will. Now, as for Brokk staying here, that's not going to happen. I have to know you're safe during the trials, and having him with you will help with that."

"But what if they take over the palace?"

"Then I'll drive them out again."

He looked over her head to Brokk, who nodded his agreement.

Lexi glanced around the hall. "You can't lose this place."

"I won't."

"If they decide to move into the palace, I won't be able to keep them from it anyway," Brokk said. "There is no king, which means the council has a right to this place. Together, they rule the realms until a new king is crowned."

"Before my father was crowned, the council lived here for nearly a hundred years as many tried, and failed, to survive the trials," Cole said. "He evicted them afterward, and we will too."

CHAPTER THIRTEEN

LEXI KEPT her apprehension hidden as she stared at Cole and then around the room. Many tried and failed for a *hundred* years before Tove ascended the throne. And she would bet every last one of them was a purebred dark fae.

The dark fae designed the trials *for* a purebred dark fae. Would he be able to survive them?

She closed her eyes against the doubts churning in her mind. She couldn't do anything to keep him from the trials, and she wouldn't even if she could. He had to do this for himself and his father.

She would do the same.

"A hundred years without a king?" she whispered.

"That was many years ago," Cole said. "It won't be anywhere near that long this time."

She hoped he was right. She couldn't take losing him a second time.

"Now, if you're ready, I'd like to change," he said to her.

"Of course," she replied.

When he offered her his arm, she slipped hers through his. He locked it against his side before clasping Brokk's shoulder. "Thanks for having my back."

"Always," Brokk said.

Lexi walked with him through the double-wide doorway of the great hall and back into the main hallway. Her step faltered when she spotted the woman who sat in on the council meeting.

Her skin crawled as the woman's black eyes surveyed her. Then a smile twisted a mouth that would have been beautiful if not for the cruelty of it.

She'd seen the way this woman looked at Cole and didn't have to see the hostility in her eyes to know there was something between them. Lexi buried the knot of jealousy in her chest and pulled back her shoulders as the woman strode toward them.

"Cole," the woman purred in a voice meant for seduction.

Cole was rigid as he stared at the woman with a look of disdain that probably would have deterred many; the woman never hesitated.

"Becca," he greeted coldly.

"And who is this?" Becca asked as her eyes ran over Lexi. "I didn't see her during the meeting."

"That's because she wasn't there."

"Oh, really." Becca's eyes flicked pointedly toward the great hall. "But you both came from there."

"What is your point?" Cole demanded.

The lethal tone of his voice would dissuade most, but Becca was used to getting her way and rarely deterred from it. She smiled as her almond-shaped eyes narrowed on Lexi. Ciphers coiled around Becca's hands and wrists before vanishing beneath the sleeves of her tunic.

"No point, just an observation. The council wouldn't like it if our conversation was overheard by—" She paused as her gaze raked disdainfully over Lexi. "—a vampire? Witch? What *is* your newest play toy, Cole?"

Cole tried to pull her away from Becca, but Lexi refused to

budge. She wasn't as powerful as this woman, but she wouldn't back down from the bitch either.

"My name is Lexi," she said.

Some of Becca's amused derision vanished. "I never asked your fucking name."

Lexi didn't see Cole move before he was standing over Becca. She backed away from him until her foot connected with the wall and she couldn't go any further. Cole towered over her as he rested a hand on the wall beside her head.

"I'd watch what you say."

The hair on Lexi's nape rose at Cole's warning. For the first time, Becca didn't look smug as a glimmer of unease crossed her striking features.

"Before you speak again, think carefully, Becca. Do you understand?" he demanded.

A muscle in Becca's jaw twitched; she managed a small nod before Cole stepped away and clasped Lexi's hand. Becca looked like her head might explode, but she wisely chose not to say anything more.

"Get out of my home," Cole said.

Becca lifted her chin. "You don't want me as an enemy."

"You've got that wrong, Becca. *You* don't want *me* as an enemy. Now, get out."

She hesitated before giving Lexi another scathing glare. Then she turned and sauntered away as if the encounter never happened. Cole didn't relax until the door closed behind her.

"Are you okay?" he demanded of her.

"I'm fine," she assured him. "But I don't think she likes me very much."

"She doesn't matter."

"She doesn't agree."

"I don't care."

He didn't say anything more, and Lexi forced herself not to look back as she walked with him down the hall.

CHAPTER FOURTEEN

LEXI STOOD at the window of Cole's bedroom and stared down at the Gloaming. The overcast sky had given way to a clear one. The dark fae realm was beautiful in the glow of the four moons illuminating the rolling hills and residences. It reminded her of the hobbit's Shire.

Though the occupants of these residences were far taller than a hobbit, many of the fae built their homes into the verdant hills. Or at least they were in this area of the Gloaming. Just like the earth, things could be far different in another section of this realm.

Not many dark fae moved about at this time of night, but those who did glided like spirits across the land. Horses also roamed those hills. The animals foraged on grass as they moved freely amid the homes.

Behind her, the door creaked open, and she turned as Cole returned from seeing Brokk. Dressed in black, loose-fitting pants and the tunic of the fae, he was so handsome it made her heart ache.

And he might not be here for much longer.

"Cole."

His name was a mere whisper she hadn't realized was going to leave her lips until it did. The smile slid from his face, and he glided across the floor to her.

She didn't move away from the window as he stopped before her and, clasping her cheeks, he kissed her. The second his lips touched hers, she lost her breath, her head spun, and her bare toes dug into the stone floor.

He hadn't touched her like this since before he left, and she'd desperately missed it. His kiss made her feel like a plant denied the sun, and he was its rays.

Her body came alive beneath his hands as every part of her reacted to him. Her heart soared as his tongue caressed her lips before slipping past them. The wild taste of him seared itself onto her as his allspice scent flooded her nostrils. He tasted of power and life and love.

She clung to him as the demanding nature of his kiss eased, and he released her to roam his hands leisurely down her body. After he left, she'd slipped into the T-shirt she brought from home with her. She hadn't expected this when he returned, but she wasn't wearing any underwear.

He emitted a low growl when he discovered this, and his fingers gripped her bare ass. Lifting her, he set her on the windowsill. The cool stone against her ass doused some of her ardor as she recalled the fae below.

She tore her mouth away from his and twisted to look behind her. Though the fae were going about their business, one could look up and see them. She had no idea how much they could see with their excellent vision, but she suspected it was a lot.

The idea of someone watching them colored her cheeks. The dark fae probably didn't care about such things, but she did.

"They'll see," she whispered.

"You're mine, Lexi. I'll never allow anyone else to see you this way," he whispered.

Then he waved his hand across the window, drawing on the shadows hovering along the wall until they covered the opening. Once done with this, the shadows encircled his hand and slid up his wrist before releasing him.

Awe filled her as those shadows slid back to the walls while keeping the window blanketed. When she turned back to him, his eyes shone silver.

She rested her hand against his cheek and drew him down for another kiss. When he tugged her shirt up, she lifted her arms, and he broke the kiss so he could pull it over her head.

He tossed her shirt aside and, stepping back, drank her in with a leisurely perusal that caused her skin to prickle with anticipation. She leaned back and propped her hands behind her to give him a better view.

"You're so beautiful," he said as he brushed the hair back from her face.

His thumb ran over her cheekbone and the lump there. The silver in his eyes blazed brighter until she swore it would burn her. Grasping his hand, she sat up and pulled it away from her.

"He has no place here," she said.

Gripping his shirt, she pushed it up to reveal his chiseled abs. His skin was hard yet supple beneath her fingers; she traced the ridges and valleys of his stomach before gliding up to his chest. He tugged his tunic off and tossed it aside to expose the ciphers running from the tips of his fingers, around his arms, and across his shoulders.

Some of his ciphers licked at his chin, and though she couldn't see them, more ran down his back to his waist. The black markings hinted at his vast power and reminded her of flowing water, even if they looked like flames.

His broad shoulders blocked out most of the room as she deftly undid his button and tugged his pants down. She'd seen it before, but the length and thickness of his erection still amazed her.

Enclosing her hand around his cock, she stroked it and smiled when he swayed toward her. He rested his hands on the walls on either side of the window as his hips thrust toward her.

Lexi marveled at this magnificent man and how he desired her as badly as she did him. When sadness tugged at her heart, she shoved it aside. Now was not the time or place for the unknown and all its frightening possibilities. This was for them and them only.

There would be plenty of time for sadness later.

She slid off the windowsill to kneel before him. He watched her with the hunger of a wolf stalking its prey, and she was eager to be that prey. Bending, she licked the head of his erection and rejoiced when his breath sucked in.

"Fuck!" he hissed.

Lexi made her way slowly along the head of his dick before sliding her mouth over it to lick and suck his shaft. His muscles quivered as his hips rocked toward her. One of his hands fell to the back of her head to guide her up and down.

He tasted of salt and man, and as she drew him deeper into her mouth, she gripped his ass and relished the flex of his muscle beneath her hand. She was losing herself to the power she held over him when he pulled away from her, bent, and scooped her off the ground.

Lexi wrapped her legs around his waist as he returned her to the windowsill. The cool shadows at her back ran along him as he sank his shaft into her.

She gasped and buried her face in his neck. He held her for a moment before thrusting into her. They were together again, joined, *one,* and it was so unbelievably right she almost wept from the joy it brought her.

Her fingers dug into his back as his arms enveloped her in a warm cocoon while he plunged deeper. The shadows weaved around them as his power intensified, and she felt the pull of energy while he fed on their joining.

Resting her mouth against his shoulder, her fangs extended as she bit into him. She groaned as his blood filled her mouth, and she greedily swallowed the potent liquid.

The warmth spreading through her turned her bones to liquid. Her body bowed, and a rush of pleasure swept her as his cock pulsed deep within her.

CHAPTER FIFTEEN

LEXI LAY CURLED against his chest as the sun touched the horizon and its rays spread across the room. He'd tried to get her to sleep, but she refused. And Cole would not sleep while with her, not after what happened when she tried to wake him from a nightmare. And while she trusted him not to attack her again accidentally, he didn't.

So as the night sped by, they talked for a couple of hours, had sex again, and talked some more, but they'd both grown silent an hour ago.

"I'd like to learn how to fight," she finally said. "My father taught me how to throw a punch, and I'm scrappy, but he refused to teach me to do anything more. He believed fighting was unladylike, but I think it's necessary."

Knowing how to fight wouldn't help her much against a stronger supernatural, but she'd inflict as much damage on them as she could beforehand. And she would learn the best ways to attack Malakai if he ever tried to put his hands on her again.

"I'll teach you when the trials are over," he said. "There's still time for you to sleep."

"No."

"Lexi—"

"Our time together has gone by way too fast, and I might not see you for a while. I'll sleep when I return home."

"I'd prefer it if you'd stay here, away from Malakai."

"In a palace that the council is going to move into?"

"Brokk can take you somewhere safe."

"I'll be safe at home."

"You'd be safer here."

⁓

WHEN SHE TILTED her head back to look at him, he marveled at her beauty and how fast she'd healed. Sahira's potions worked magic on Brokk when he nearly died, and they were doing the same for her.

Almost all the bruising and swelling was gone from her face. Malakai's fingerprints had faded from her neck, as had the welts they left behind.

"Would I?" she asked. "I don't think Becca likes me very much."

He should have known that bitch would come up eventually.

"Her opinion doesn't matter," he said.

"Maybe not to you, but she is a member of the council, and I'm a half human, half vampire who doesn't belong here. I doubt she and the council would be happy if they discovered me somewhere in the Gloaming."

"I can keep you safe."

"Not while you're going through the trials."

"Brokk—"

"We agreed I was going to return home after this, and I *am* going home."

Cole contemplated it, but she may well be right; she might be safer at home than in the Gloaming. There were few he trusted here now that his father was dead. Things were calm, but he doubted they would stay that way.

The dark fae had lost a king they admired, and there was a lot of power up for grabs. And power made mortals and immortals do crazy things. They could never claim the throne without enduring the trials, but they could make it more complicated to keep the throne once he survived the trials.

"Were things serious between you and Becca?" she asked.

The last thing he wanted to discuss was Becca, but he wouldn't lie to her about the woman or try to deny their past. "No."

"But there was something between you?"

"There hasn't been anything between us in a long time."

When she looked to the window, he clasped her chin and turned her head back to him. Her sweeping lashes brushed her cheek before they lifted. For a second, he lost himself in the fathomless sea of her green eyes.

"The only thing Becca truly wants is power, and she mistakenly saw me as her way to gain more of it. What little there ever was between Becca and me is over, and there will *never* be anything between us again," he vowed.

"I don't think she agrees with that statement."

"I don't care what she thinks. You're it for me, Lexi, and I mean it."

Doubt swirled in her eyes. He caressed her cheek as he bent to kiss the tip of her nose. He had to tell her what she was to him; it would add pressure to her, but it would also ease her doubts about their relationship.

Everyone knew a lycan never betrayed their mate.

CHAPTER SIXTEEN

LEXI'S HEART swelled with love as she gazed at him. Words of love were on the tip of her tongue to utter, but she didn't get them out before he spoke again.

"You're my mate, Lexi."

Her words died as confusion, joy, and then a cold dread crept through her. His mate? His *lycan* mate?

That meant when he said she was *it* for him, she really was *it*. The bond he felt toward her wasn't complete in the lycan way, but he was bound to her.

That meant she wouldn't have to share him with anyone else. He would always be loyal to her as *no* lycan ever strayed from their mate. Her joy returned, but then a cold dose of reality doused it again.

It also meant he didn't want to be with her because he loved her as she loved him, but because his instincts told him to claim her.

The words she'd been about to utter withered away.

"You think I'm your lycan mate?" she asked.

"I don't think it; I *know* you are," he said.

~

SHE DIDN'T LOOK relieved as he'd expected. Instead, she appeared… annoyed. He frowned over this response, and his hackles rose. Did she look annoyed because she didn't want him for eternity?

They'd never spoken of love or their future, but he believed she cared for him. Was he wrong?

He retracted his claws when they lengthened, but he couldn't get his fangs under control. *She might not want forever.*

He believed it was forever for them, but she was young, and she didn't feel the pull of a bond between them like another lycan would or a full-blooded vampire toward their consort. She could walk away without consequence.

"You haven't completed the lycan bond with me," she said.

Was that it then? Was she afraid about how the bond was completed?

That would be a good possibility, but Lexi wasn't one for fear. She'd run toward the marketplace when the dragons destroyed it. She wasn't scared to go home, even if Malakai remained a threat and would until he died.

"Do you know how it's completed?" he asked.

"I've heard the lycan bite their mate while having sex, and that is how they claim them."

"Yes." That was some of it.

"They say a lycan loses control when it happens," she said.

"I won't hurt you."

"I know."

"I haven't completed the bond because I couldn't claim you without telling you about this first."

"And you waited this long because…?"

"Because I didn't think it was appropriate to dump it on you after I was called back to the Gloaming."

"But now that you're about to face the trials, it's fine."

The irritation in her voice was unmistakable. Gripping her chin again, he lifted her face to him once more.

"I *am* going to survive the trials," he said.

She nodded, but his words didn't ease the sorrow in her eyes.

"And I won't claim you before the trials," he said.

"Why not?"

"Because others cannot know what you are to me until the trials are over and I'm around to protect you. They'll see you as a weakness to me, and they'll go after you to get at me. And I will *not* let anything happen to you.

"When the trials are over, the throne is mine, and I can protect you better, I'll make sure every immortal knows what you are to me and that fucking with you will equate to a swift and brutal death. Until then, only Brokk can know what you are to me."

CHAPTER SEVENTEEN

LEXI WASN'T sure what to say. She would give anything for five minutes alone to think and maybe scream a little. Then she would sort this mess out.

She should be happy. He would never cheat on her or forsake her for another. They would be together forever, but she wanted him to love her for *her* and not because of his lycan biology.

And was eternity something *she* wanted? Yes, she loved him, but she was still young, and he was the only man and the only relationship she'd ever known.

Shouldn't she experience more?

She tipped her head back to gaze into his striking blue eyes. They pierced straight into her soul and caused her heart to race. Could she ever let another touch her in the same way as him?

Her stomach rolled at the possibility, and bile burned her throat. No. She could never touch another or be with another like she was with him.

She was young and inexperienced when it came to men, and she would always remain that way. Well, maybe not so inexperienced as he was always teaching her something new, but she would never know another man.

She loved him too much for that, and even if he didn't profess his love in return, he was as much *hers* as she was his.

"We can discuss the details of the bond when you survive the trials," she said.

A small smile curved his mouth, but it didn't sparkle in his eyes like it normally did.

"What about the Lord?" she whispered.

Cole stiffened against her. "What about him?"

"What...." She glanced nervously around though it was only the two of them here. "He killed your father, Cole. What do you plan to do about that?"

"I plan to kill him."

Lexi had suspected such a thing, but hearing it confirmed made her gulp.

"I'm not sure how, but that man *will* die," Cole vowed.

A knock on the door in the outer room pulled his attention away from her before she could respond.

"What?" he demanded.

"The council has sent word," Brokk's muffled voice barely carried through the wooden door and both rooms.

Cole hugged her close before reluctantly pulling away. Lexi rolled out the other side of the bed and lowered her feet onto the gray stone floor before rising. The stone was cool against her bare feet, and she wished for her slippers.

Near the fireplace was a fluffy white rug with the head of some monster she'd never seen before. She hadn't stepped fully onto the rug, it seemed wrong to step on dead things, but she did push on it with her toes and discovered it was soft and fluffy.

The gray stone walls of the room were bare and austere. Though it was luxurious with its massive, king-sized bed and bathroom with a tub big enough to swim in, there was no warmth to the room.

Cole strode over to a dark wood armoire, opened the doors, and pulled out a pair of lightweight, brown pants and a black tunic.

Lexi padded over to the corner of the room and the bag she left there last night.

She pulled out a pair of jeans, her T-shirt, and socks. She was tugging on the socks when Cole finished dressing. He held his hand out to her as she pulled on her last sock. Jumping up, she steadied the tremble in her hand when she claimed his.

She forgot all about her astonishment over discovering she was his mate as their hands joined. It was such a small thing to be upset about when he would soon be facing something that could kill him.

Lexi struggled to conceal her growing anxiety from him, but it felt like a fist had punched into her chest and squeezed her heart.

He released her hand to open the door. Brokk stood on the other side, and if the look on his face was any indication, she wasn't going to like what he had to say.

"What did they say?" Cole asked.

"The trials start tonight," Brokk said.

Lexi suppressed an urge to cry out, but she couldn't stop her hand from going to her heart before she lowered it. She wouldn't let Cole see her distress. He was the one facing death; she was the one...

She was the one who would wait to see if he survived.

And that sounded like Hell to her.

"Good," Cole said, which was the exact opposite of what she was thinking. "We'll be down in an hour, and I'll escort you both back to Lexi's manor."

Brokk bowed his head, but he looked about as thrilled as Lexi felt. Cole closed the door and, before she could speak, pulled her close and kissed her.

∼

THREE HOURS LATER, Lexi found herself in front of her manor once more. She couldn't recall why she'd been in such a rush to return now that they'd arrived.

So what if she was hiding Orin and the refugees? What did it matter when Cole would leave her here and she might never see him again?

He pulled the horse they'd rode from the Gloaming to a stop in front of the manor. The animal was a large, black stallion with an intriguing white stripe of hair in its mane. She'd spent most of the ride playing with that stripe as she tried not to think about the wait to come.

Cole could have created another portal that would have led them straight here, but since opening portals was draining to an immortal and he needed to be at his strongest for the trials, they came through one of the portals connecting the Gloaming to the human realm.

She'd made sure he fed on her again before they left the Gloaming. She hoped it would be enough to fuel him through the trials.

"How long will the trials last?" she asked as Sahira opened the front door. Her familiar, Shade, sat at her feet. The cat didn't move as it watched them.

"I don't know," Cole said, "but I'll return as soon as I can."

This time, she didn't doubt it.

She turned in the saddle and, resting her hand on his cheek, drew him down for a kiss. It was on the tip of her tongue to tell him that she loved him, but the words stuck in her throat.

Instead, she broke the kiss, and her forehead fell to his. "Be careful."

"Always," he promised. "I *will* return, Lexi."

"I know."

He slid from the saddle and, grasping her waist, lifted her from the horse. She slid down the length of him as he set her on the ground and held her close. Behind them, Brokk dismounted from his horse.

"Can I put him in the stable, Lexi?" he asked.

"Yes. There's an extra stall in there."

He led his stallion away, and Sahira closed the door.

"I should go," Cole said.

She didn't want to let him go, but she couldn't stand here clinging to him. Reluctantly, she released him and stepped back.

He kissed her again before clasping her cheeks in his palms. "Stay close to Brokk. If Malakai comes anywhere near you, scream, and he'll be by your side in an instant. He may only be half vampire, but he can transport, and he'll fuck Malakai up."

She managed a wan smile. "I know he will. Don't worry about *me*; just worry about *you*."

"There's no need to worry about me."

"Maybe not, but I still will. Be safe."

"Always."

He kissed her again before releasing her, gathering the reins, and mounting his horse. He nudged the horse into a walk and would be out of view in no time.

And he might be riding out of her life forever.

When he was a hundred feet away, her voice finally broke free.

"Cole!" she shouted.

She started running after him before she realized she'd commanded her legs to move. He turned in his saddle and, when he saw her coming, dismounted. He took two steps toward her before she flung herself into arms. He embraced her against his chest.

She buried her face in his neck and drew the scent of him into her. Leaning back, she clasped his face between her palms and kissed him.

"I love you," she whispered.

Shock registered on his face before a brilliant grin spread across his handsome features, and his eyes lit with happiness. She wriggled out of his arms and turned to run back to the manor before he could reply, but he caught her wrist and pulled her back into his arms.

"I love you too," he said before kissing her again.

CHAPTER EIGHTEEN

COLE STUDIED the Victorian-style manor as Torigon trotted up to it. Lexi's home showed signs of wear and tear in its chipped paint and sagging shutters. But the war and the lack of help she had to run it had taken its toll on the place. In contrast, this place remained pristine.

He didn't think it was because Malakai was doing the work himself. No, that asshole wouldn't know how to lift a hammer, never mind how to put a nail into wood. This place looked good because he had more money, power, and the ability to wield it more than Lexi did.

He'd told Brokk he was coming here, but not Lexi. She was anxious enough about the trials without adding this to it. However, he was not leaving for the trials without trying to find Malakai first.

If he was here, Cole would kill him, and Lexi would never have to worry about him again. He'd also feel a lot better about leaving her in the human realm if the vampire was dead.

He rode by the stables, but there were no animals in them. With their ability to transport, he didn't know many vampires who consistently rode enough to own horses.

He was almost to the front door before he pulled Torigon to a stop and dismounted. Torigon's ears twitched as he looked around before lowering his head to munch on the grass. Cole hoped he tore giant chunks out of the well-manicured lawn.

He studied the yard for a sign a vamp was near, but only the trilling birds and chattering squirrels disturbed the day. Certain Malakai wasn't hiding somewhere nearby, Cole ascended the stairs to the farmers' porch wrapping around the house.

If he was here, Malakai would see him coming, and he didn't care. He pounded the solid oak door and listened as the hollow thuds echoed throughout the home. He waited a second before banging on the door again.

From somewhere inside, the patter of footsteps approached the door. They were too light to be Malakai's, and he wasn't surprised when a thin, brunette woman opened the door a few seconds later.

She held a rag in her hand as she peered up at him from sunken eyes surrounded by dark shadows. The bites on her neck indicated she was here for more than cleaning. Judging by her too-thin frame and sunken cheeks, Malakai was taking too much.

"Can I help you?" she asked.

"Is Malakai here?"

"No."

When she started to close the door, he held his hand out to stop her. He pitied this poor, abused human, but nothing would deter him.

"Are you sure?" he demanded.

"He hasn't been here in days."

"Do you mind if I come in and look around?"

She started to reply, but Cole nudged the door open and slipped inside.

"You shouldn't be here," she whispered as he strode into the foyer and stopped before the sweeping staircase.

Malakai's coppery scent, tinged with hints of sandalwood,

hung heavily on the air, but it was his home. The staleness of the aroma led him to believe the woman was telling the truth. Malakai hadn't been here in a while.

Still, he would check every inch of this place before leaving. The woman trailed behind him as he climbed the stairs. He went through every room on the second floor, searched all the cabinets and closets before returning to the first floor.

If the woman wasn't here, he would have torn the place apart to make sure Malakai knew he'd been here. But the woman would only clean it up, and he wasn't going to make her life more difficult than it already was.

"He's really not here," she whispered as she trailed him into the kitchen. "I haven't seen him in days."

"Was he injured the last time you saw him?"

"He can be injured?" she breathed as she gazed at him with hope-filled eyes.

"Yes."

"No, he was perfectly fine the last time I saw him."

So, he hadn't returned home since their fight. Where would he have gone?

Cole pondered this as he studied the kitchen, but he doubted the piece of shit had any friends, and if he did, Cole didn't know them. Malakai had to be somewhere he believed safer than his home. Unfortunately, Cole didn't have time to figure out where.

"You should leave here," he said to the woman as she trailed him back through the home.

"I have nowhere else to go."

"There are plenty of other places to go. It's a big world."

He didn't wait to hear her reply before he walked out the front door and strode down the steps. The lycan part of him protested against leaving this realm without destroying Malakai first, but with no way of knowing where the vamp went, there was little he could do, and he had to return to the Gloaming for the trials.

Once in the Gloaming, he would send word to Brokk to tell him he hadn't located Malakai.

Cole mounted Torigon and turned him in the direction of the Gloaming portal. It was time to become a king.

CHAPTER NINETEEN

A LITTLE WHILE LATER, Lexi found Brokk in the stable. Under normal circumstances, she'd be floating on cloud nine—Cole loved her too; it wasn't just about the mate bond—but things were far from normal.

Brokk had removed his horse's saddle and set it in the tack room. He was filling a bucket with soap and water when she entered. It would be difficult for her to slip away to see Orin while he was here, but she would figure it out.

For a second, the memory of what occurred the last time she was here flitted through her mind before she pushed it away. She wouldn't let that twisted bastard ruin one of her favorite places on earth.

"Is Cole gone?" Brokk asked when he spotted her.

"Yes."

"He'll survive the trials. If anyone can, it's him."

"I want to believe that; I really do, but then I recall that he's only half fae, and they designed the trials *for* the fae."

"Even if he's only half, outside of my father, he's the strongest fae I've ever known. The only one who would be any competition for him is my brother Orin, but that will *never* happen."

Lexi somehow managed to keep her face impassive at the mention of Orin.

"The Lord would see Orin dead and the entire Gloaming leveled before Orin ever sat the throne," Brokk continued.

Fighting against her impulse to start fiddling with her hands or shifting uncomfortably, Lexi searched for a new topic of conversation as Brokk carried the bucket over to where his horse stood in the bath stall.

"Do you want to be here?" she asked.

He stopped in the middle of sponging his horse's back. "You and Sahira saved my life. I don't care what you are to Cole... no, that's not right, of course I care. But even if you weren't his mate, I would be here to help you both."

"You don't owe us anything."

"That's not true, but I also consider you and Sahira my friends, and I don't let *anything* happen to my friends."

Those words warmed her heart. "I consider you a friend too."

"Good."

"And as my friend, will you teach me how to fight? I'd like to learn how to kick some ass."

Brokk grinned at her. "Absolutely."

∾

COLE STUDIED the two young dark fae who were thrown into these trials, and most likely their deaths, by their greedy, cowardly fathers. Both Eoghan and Auberon had the slender builds, black hair, black eyes, and pointed ears of the fae. They both had ciphers encompassing their biceps, but those marks went no further. However, they could be hiding them.

And both were too young to be here; they had no chance of surviving the trials. Neither of them seemed to realize this as they talked about what they would do once they sat on the throne.

Apparently, no one had informed them that if they both

miraculously managed to survive, one would have to kill the other. He didn't think they would be so arrogant if they knew this.

They'd grown up in the lap of luxury, and neither of them fought in the war. This was a game to them. One they would lose.

He'd be amazed if either Eoghan or Auberon survived more than a day. Their fathers seemed to share in their delusions of grandeur as they spoke with their young sons.

"They're as good as dead," Aelfdane said.

Cole had been thinking the same thing, but he turned and looked down his nose at the dark fae. "So are you."

Aelfdane blinked in disbelief, and then anger clouded his face. "I'm not afraid of you. That throne will be *mine*."

Cole didn't bother to reply as he walked a few feet away to study the portal the council had summoned forth. He felt Becca's eyes burning into his back, but he ignored her.

"Where does it go?" he asked Elvin.

"To a distant outer realm," Elvin replied. "It's there that our ancestors created the trials with the help of the arachs. They put that magic into action thousands of years before our fathers roamed the Gloaming."

"Why were the arach involved?" Cole asked of the long-dead immortals who once controlled and ruled the dragons.

"I suppose our ancestors must have required more magic than they possessed to achieve their goal."

"How long ago was that?" Cole asked.

"The oldest record I've found of the trials is fifty thousand years old."

"And how did they choose a king before then?"

"Your guess is as good as mine. Perhaps the trials were around before then, or maybe they fought until only one man remained standing. Maybe they did it through birthright until they realized that being the son of a king does *not* make one a king, and they needed a better way to crown a leader."

"No, being born to a king does not make one a leader. Being a leader does that," Cole said.

Elvin stared at him but didn't reply.

"Shall we go?" Cole asked.

"I see no reason to put it off."

Elvin stepped through the portal first, and Cole followed. He'd been to some of the outer realms before but never one the dark fae and arach worked together to transform. The outer realms he visited were usually barren chunks of rock, but some held creatures no man wished to encounter.

Others were claimed by immortals who turned them into their little kingdoms though few lived there with them. Some couldn't be located unless someone knew the exact way there, and others were easily found.

As the portal fell away, Cole stepped into an outer realm the likes of which he'd never seen before.

CHAPTER TWENTY

IN THE DISTANCE, volcanoes spewed smoke and fire into the air as red lava oozed down their sides. What lay between him and those volcanoes, he didn't know as a hundred feet before him, another mountain blocked out the land.

A tunnel cut into the center of the mountain. Despite his excellent vision, he couldn't see more than a few feet into it. Shadows shifted and coiled over the entrance as they dipped low before retreating again.

"What do we do?" Eoghan asked.

The young fae didn't sound as confident anymore.

"You start the trials," Elvin said and waved a hand at the passageway. "What you do from there is up to you. I'm not sure what happens if you try to turn back, but once you start the trials, death or conquest are the only ways to escape."

Cole flexed his hands as he studied the shadows. He'd hoped to return to Lexi soon, but he had a feeling this was going to take longer than he'd anticipated.

Brokk will keep her safe.

"I'm assuming you'll know the way once you start," Elvin continued.

"Then it's time to start."

Cole didn't look back as he strode into the tunnel.

~

"HANDS UP," Brokk instructed as he danced around Lexi and jabbed at her.

Lexi ducked the punch, but he wouldn't have connected anyway. He was taking it easy on her. She understood why; he'd only been teaching her for half an hour, but she was impatient for more, and she wasn't in the mood to be babied.

"You're taking it easy on me," she said.

"You're just starting to learn, and if I hurt you, Cole will castrate me."

Lexi laughed, and when she did, he feigned a move and caught her face with the tips of his fingers. It could have been a lot worse, and would have been, if it were anyone else.

"Hands up," he reminded her.

Lexi lifted her hands and circled him as they moved around the yard. When he came at her again, she darted to the side and threw up her hand to block his blow.

"Cole said he would teach me how to fight, so I think he'd let you keep your nuts," she told him as they danced.

"Let's hope so."

As he watched her with a calculating eye, she realized he'd designed his moves to learn more about her.

"You're fast," he remarked. "And nimble. You're better off running from an attacker than fighting them."

"Sometimes, that's not an option."

"I know, but *you* should know that flight should be your first response."

Lexi stopped moving. "I'm tougher than I look."

Brokk stopped too and stood staring at her. "Yes, but so are most supernaturals, and, unfortunately, you aren't as strong as most of them. Like it or not, being half human makes you weaker than a full immortal."

She didn't like it, but she couldn't deny the truth.

"Okay, so I'll run first," she said.

Not likely, but she kept that to herself as Brokk wouldn't approve. The look on his face said he didn't believe her.

"Don't get yourself killed," he said.

The concern in his voice gave her pause. As Cole's mate, his life hinged on hers, and Brokk cared too much for his brother to risk seeing what would become of him if she died. Not all lycans perished when their mates did, but none of them were the same afterward.

She'd never seen a mateless lycan, but she'd heard they were nothing more than walking shadows of their former selves. Shadows that were better off dead.

Many lycans preferred death and embraced it when they lost their mate. She didn't know what they did to meet their end, and she didn't want to know. It sounded awful, and she did *not* want Cole to experience it.

Maybe, because he was also half fae, Cole wouldn't suffer as much as a purebred lycan if she died. She hoped he never learned the answer as she *really* liked her life.

"I'm going to stick around for a very long time," she assured him. "Now, show me what else to do."

She started moving around him again, and after a brief hesitation, he fell into step with her.

"We'll start building up your strength and endurance tomorrow," he said. "You work with the horses, so I'm sure you're already strong, but we'll make you stronger. Also, get ready to start running... a lot."

"I'm ready."

He feigned a punch to her head, and she slapped it aside before his fist tapped her stomach. If it were anyone else, the blow would have knocked her on her ass, but it was meant to reveal one of her weaknesses.

"Do you have the potion Sahira created?" he asked.

Lexi tapped her jeans pocket. The potion that would eat the skin from anything it touched was tucked securely away. Sahira had cast a spell over the bottle to keep it from breaking by accident.

She felt better having it on her, but she might not get it free in time to use it on someone, or something else could go wrong. She tried not to think about those possibilities; doubt wouldn't do her any good.

"We'll also start training with weapons. You'll be at a disadvantage strength and powers wise, but if we can find a weapon you excel at using, it will give you an advantage."

"I like that idea."

He smiled at her before disappearing. Lexi's hands lowered as she stared at the spot where he'd stood. Then fingers tapped her right shoulder. She spun to find him standing behind her. He tapped her cheek with the tips of his fingers.

"Hands up," he said.

She put her hands up and kicked out in the fast, crisp way he taught her earlier. He slapped her foot down before coming at her from the side again.

"What's going on here?"

Lexi spun at Sahira's question. She grinned at her aunt, who gazed between her and Brokk with open disapproval.

"Brokk is teaching me how to defend myself," she said.

"I don't think that's a good idea," Sahira replied.

"Why not?"

"It's not appropriate for women to fight."

"Maybe it wasn't appropriate a couple of hundred years ago, but times have changed, Sahira," Lexi said.

A muscle twitched in Sahira's cheek. "You could get hurt doing this."

"I could, but not being able to defend myself, especially if Malakai returns, *will* get me hurt."

Sahira didn't back down. "Your father wouldn't approve of this."

Lexi suppressed a wince as her words cut deep. Sahira always knew where to strike to get a response from her, but it didn't matter. She'd already made up her mind. She couldn't spend the rest of her life defenseless and hoping someone else would save her.

She got lucky Cole arrived when he did during Malakai's attack. She probably wouldn't be so fortunate next time.

"My dad is dead, and I refuse to have someone watching over me twenty-four seven. *Refuse*," she emphasized. "Besides, it's impossible for that to happen. Maybe my dad wouldn't approve of me learning to fight, but he'd approve less of me being raped, forced into marriage, or killed because I couldn't fend off an attacker."

Sahira's mouth closed, and her eyes narrowed, but she didn't protest any further. "Be careful."

"I will," Lexi promised, and Brokk's fingers brushed the side of her head, drawing her attention back to him.

"Hands up," he said, and they started their dance again.

Though she disapproved, Sahira crossed her arms over her chest while she watched them.

CHAPTER TWENTY-ONE

THE TUNNEL WAS SO black Cole couldn't see his hand in front of his face. There were no shadows here. For there to be shadows, there had to be light.

The lack of shadows had to be a test as the dark fae thrived in their presence. He missed the shadows and his ability to see.

For his entire six hundred and seventy-two years, he'd never been in a place as dark as this. Bringing his fingers to his face, he touched the corners of his eyes to make sure they were still there.

Without his eyes to guide him, he relied heavily on his other senses. Straining to hear, he tried to detect the presence of something else within the passageway, but the crunch of his footsteps against the rock was the only sound.

He didn't know if the others had entered behind him; he didn't bother to look back. It would be pointless. When he stopped to listen, he didn't hear their footsteps or breaths.

It wouldn't astound him to learn there were numerous tunnels and somehow the realm had made each of them traverse a separate one. Or that the trials were changing around them to accommodate their number.

He couldn't see, but his instincts guided him onward, and he didn't have to put out his hands to keep him from walking into the rocky walls. So far, they had guided him well as he made his way through twists and turns.

When he turned a corner, the sound became more muffled as the walls closed in around him. Jagged bits of stone brushed against his skin, tugged at his clothes, and scraped the top of his head as he bent to avoid smacking into a low-hanging rock.

Cole's steps slowed as he strained to hear more while his eyes darted uselessly back and forth. Stopping, he rested his hand against the cool stone.

Something dripped somewhere ahead of him. It was a low, hollow pinging sound barely discernible over his breaths.

Sensing something was coming, he edged cautiously forward. He didn't pick his feet up off the ground as he shuffled into the darkness. The wall curved beneath his fingertips, a stone grazed his temple, and with his next shuffling step forward, the rock changed.

Cole paused as his fingers slid over the smooth surface. He hadn't expected this smooth surface after the jagged roughness of the rocks. His fingers dipped into two holes before sliding lower.

His hand fumbled over another open hole before brushing over something small and rigid. He froze, and the hair on his nape rose as he realized they were teeth and the other two cavities were eye sockets.

Cole yanked his hand away and scented the air. The potent aromas of mildew, stone, and earth permeated the air, but he didn't detect any rot. But if these were the remains of a long-dead fae who failed in the trials, there would be no aroma of decay.

Shuffling forward, he kept his hand away from the walls, but something brushed his fingers, and when he reached out, he grasped the skeletal remains of another hand stretching out of the ground.

Curiosity won out over his disgust, and he followed that hand to a boney forearm and on to the solid rock the upper arm protruded from. There was nothing else of the skeleton, only that arm stretching out of the stone.

What the fuck?

In all his years, throughout all his travels and countless battles, he'd never experienced anything like this before. What was going on? What happened to this thing? How had it become trapped in the rock?

And how many of them surrounded him?

He suspected the answer to that was a lot. Rising away from the arm, he wiped his hands on his pants, but it did nothing to remove the feel of those smooth bones against his palms.

He was standing in the middle of a tomb, and if he wasn't careful, it was going to swallow him too, strip the flesh from his bones, and leave him trapped within the stone.

The walls closed further in on him, and though they continued to brush against him, he didn't touch them again. He knew all he needed to know about his surroundings without becoming more friendly with the dead surrounding him... watching him.

When he turned another corner, the ground gave way beneath him. One second, he was standing on solid stone, and the next, he was plummeting into a freefall.

Shit!

The air ripped at his clothes and battered him. His arms spun as he sought some purchase to slow his fall, but whereas the walls above had been steadily closing in on him, his hands connected with nothing as he fell further and further into an endless pit.

Was it endless, or would he soon find himself crashing into the ground and shattering every bone in his body? Once there, would the stone cover him until he became another skeleton reaching out of the earth?

And there was the possibility there was no end to this pit and he would fall for eternity. He wouldn't put it past the dark fae and arach to design an endless pit that immortals never escaped.

How many dark fae had fallen in before him and were still

falling beneath him? How many were trapped in here, rotting in this place as they wasted away from years of starvation?

He'd fallen into the first trial, and he had to figure out how to defeat it if he was going to survive.

Realizing that it was pointless, Cole stopped searching for a hand or foothold. There wouldn't be any. The only way out of this place was himself and his abilities.

He shut down the endless possibilities of what lay below and concentrated on the currents of air battering him. Focused on those currents, he drew strength from the power of the air.

The air danced across his fingertips, flowed up his arms, and over his shoulders like faeries flitting across lily pads. It hummed against his ears until it vibrated his eardrums and filled his lungs with its life-giving properties.

The power of it seeped into his veins until it suffused his entire being. Feeling as if he were one with the air, he spread his fingers out beneath him and held his palms out. Air pushed against his palms until it felt as solid as the walls above.

As those air currents built, his plunge eased until it stopped. Hovering in the air, he used its currents to keep him afloat as he stared into the darkness.

From somewhere deep within the cavern, an agonized scream rebounded off the walls and spiraled into the pit until it echoed around him. Despite the fact it came from a distance, it sounded as if he could touch the owner of that scream.

There would be no touching or saving the owner as the scream abruptly cut off. Cole recognized a death scream when he heard one and knew it had come from one of the two kids. Either Eoghan or Auberon had met their end in this place.

Bowing his head, he closed his eyes in a moment of silence for the lost fae before opening them again. It was sad they'd died when they didn't have to, but it was time to get out of this place.

He could use the air currents to lower himself, but he was unwilling to go any further down. While he could hover, he couldn't fly out of here and could only use the currents to lift himself a little.

Wiggling his fingers, he shifted the air beneath him and used its currents to push him toward the side of the pit. It was farther away than he'd anticipated, but eventually, his fingers and feet found rock.

He shut down the image of skulls and hands grasping for him as he climbed, but his fingers found holes in eye sockets and gripped teeth far too often. They sliced into his fingers and cut through the material of his soft boots to gash his feet.

Blood dripped from his wounds. In the beginning, they healed almost as fast as they happened, but as he steadily ascended, they stopped healing as quickly. The blood coating his fingers and toes made the rocks slippery and climbing more difficult. When it caught on a tooth, one of his fingernails tore away completely.

"I hate this place," he muttered.

He estimated himself to be about halfway up the wall and a couple of thousand feet into the climb when he realized it was also testing his strength and endurance as his arms and legs ached. He'd spent far too much time in battle, but he hadn't done much climbing, and his body let him know it didn't like it.

And as he climbed onward, it dawned on him that this would be the easiest trial. They would only get more difficult after this.

When he finally made it to the top, he slid his hands onto the rocky surface and ignored the tremble in his arms as he pulled himself out of the pit. His legs wobbled, but he pushed to his feet and staggered into the wall.

He disliked touching the wall but required its support as he rested his shoulder against it. He wiped the sweat from his brow and gave himself a chance to recover.

Every part of him hurt, but strength was also returning. Feeding on Lexi earlier had infused him with a lot of power, healing him faster than normal.

When he felt a lot stronger, he pushed away from the wall and started down the passage. After another turn and a hundred feet, a golden glow emerged at the end of it.

One trial down. Unknown number left to go.

And after the tunnel, he could only imagine what those other trials would entail. Glad to be free of the unending darkness, Cole stepped into a desert wasteland stretching as far as he could see.

Lifting a hand to his forehead, he shaded his eyes against the sun as Auberon and Aelfdane emerged from two other tunnels. Cole stood in the middle of the other two dark fae who looked to him before turning their attention to the desolate land before them.

There was no sign of Eoghan, but there wouldn't be. The young fae had met his end in the tunnel. His remains were probably already infused into the rock.

Cole studied the sand rolling out before him like a rolling sea as it swept over dunes while dipping and rising endlessly. A red sun baked the earth and roasted his skin. Though his shadow fell across the sand, there were no others here.

Just like in the tunnel, the desert would deny him the power of the shadows.

CHAPTER TWENTY-TWO

LEXI HELD her breath as she crept down the stairs. When one of the steps creaked, she winced and stopped with her other foot still in the air. From below, the grandfather clock ticked away the seconds as she waited for someone to leap out and demand to know what she was doing.

But no one emerged to ask her why she was sneaking downstairs in the middle of the night. When she was certain no one was going to tackle her, she carefully put her foot down and snuck the rest of the way down the stairs.

Once on the first floor, she scurried like a mouse hunting for cheese into the library. With her heart pounding, she leaned against one of the open doors resting against the wall.

She bit her lip as she contemplated closing the doors, but that would only draw more questions if someone woke to discover them locked. If she wasn't here to open the doors and answer those questions, it would be worse.

And she couldn't leave the manor to enter the tunnels from one of the other locations. If Sahira or Brokk saw her sneaking across the lawn, they might try to follow her, and she couldn't have that.

At least now she knew they weren't aware of her being up and moving around the manor. She had to enter the tunnels through the library; she could always stroll back across the grounds later. If someone saw her then, she would tell them she couldn't sleep and went for a walk… in the middle of the night.

It was perfectly normal.

Even if it wasn't perfectly normal, and even *if* they would be mad at her for taking such a risk after what happened with Malakai, she didn't have any other options. She *had* to tell Orin that Brokk was here, and though she dreaded being the one to do it, he should know about his father.

Leaning around the wall, she glanced toward the stairs, but no one was coming after her. She pushed herself away from the open door and hurried across the room to the gray, stone fireplace.

It took her less than a second to find the stone that opened the entrance to the tunnel. She glanced back to make sure she remained alone before slipping inside and closing it again.

The tension eased from her shoulders as she lifted the flashlight hanging near the entrance and clicked it on. The dim glow barely chased away the shadows, and it did nothing to chase away the damp, mildew scent of the earth hanging heavily on the air.

Despite her relief over making it into the passageway undetected, a growing sense of dread escalated inside her with every step she took. Maybe Orin already knew his father was dead.

He didn't stay locked up in the tunnels because he needed to search for more refugees and bring food back for them. Although, he would have to be a *lot* more careful about his travels now. He couldn't let Brokk catch him.

She had to be the one to tell Cole about Orin being here. If Brokk discovered him first, she would never get the chance. She couldn't imagine the betrayal they would feel if they uncovered her secret before she revealed it.

She shoved aside the ugly possibility as she descended further beneath the ground. Between the trials, Malakai, Orin, and the refugees, she already had enough to worry about without heaping something that may never happen onto her plate.

She made her way deeper into the tunnels and toward where the others normally slept. Over the past couple of weeks, Orin had gathered more refugees seeking asylum from the Lord and his lackeys.

She knew where they all were. However, Orin could be anywhere down here. Unlike the others, he liked to wander.

After he came to her with the refugees, she allowed Orin more access to the tunnels in case they needed to flee. She'd told him to stay away from the entrance into the manor unless it was absolutely necessary, and to her amazement, he'd listened to her... so far.

A minuscule flicker in the shadows alerted her to Orin's presence a second before he emerged like a ghost from a wall. The first dozen or so times he did this to her, she jumped, squeaked like a rat, and nearly pissed herself.

She'd gotten so she could almost always see the slight shift before he emerged. He still occasionally startled her, but it wasn't as often as in the beginning. He enjoyed scaring her, and when he did, she had to resist trying to kick him in the nuts.

However, it wouldn't go over well if she did rearrange his privates as badly as she would like to. As much as he exasperated her, she wasn't looking to fight with him. They were reluctant allies in this, and fighting would only make it worse.

His eyes and hair were as black as the shadows surrounding him and created a strange illusion as they blended into the dark while his skin and clothes remained visible.

"What are you doing here at this time of night, Kitten?" he asked.

Her teeth clenched as he called her the nickname he started using before Cole returned. She'd made the mistake of revealing how much she disliked it in the beginning.

"I'm not a kitten!" she'd retorted, and he laughed.

Now, she tried to act indifferent every time he said it, but the amused gleam in his eyes told her that she'd failed.

"How do you know what time of night it is when you're down here?" she retorted.

"I know all," he murmured in that smug way he had.

She restrained herself from rolling her eyes; even if he didn't know it yet, his father was dead.

"What are you doing here?" he asked.

"We have to talk."

His eyes flicked to the shadows behind her. She spun to play the flashlight over the walls behind her. For a second, she feared someone followed her, but the glow didn't reveal anyone standing there.

"What about?" Orin asked, drawing her attention back to him.

She twirled her fingers as she tried to think of where to start and what to say. They were in this together, but they weren't friends, and they certainly weren't close. No one wanted to hear about the death of a loved one from a stranger.

And then she realized it didn't matter who delivered the news; loved one or stranger, nothing made the blow any easier.

"Brokk's in the manor," she said.

She might as well tell him this first; he probably wouldn't be in the mood to talk after he learned of his dad's death, and he *had* to know to be more careful while coming and going from the tunnels.

"Why?" Orin demanded.

"Cole asked him to stay here."

Orin's eyebrows drew sharply together over the bridge of his hawkish nose. "You've seen my brother again?"

"Yes."

Surprise crossed his features before he covered it. "And why would Cole ask Brokk to stay here?"

"He thinks I need protection."

"Do you?"

She shrugged. "There was an incident, but I'm fine."

Orin's eyes coldly surveyed her. When they lingered on the barely visible bruises on her neck, she lifted her chin.

"Who attacked you?" he asked.

"That's none of your business."

He released a small snort of laughter. "Okay then, tell me why Cole cares about any incident involving you... or why he cares about *you*?" he asked.

Cole didn't want anyone to know she was his mate because they would use it against him, and she would *not* give Orin that weapon. He was Cole's brother, but they were as close as the north and south poles.

"I guess I'm a really good lay," she replied with a casual indifference she didn't feel.

"There are plenty of those in the world, and he's had many of them. He wouldn't protect a single one of them. So, why *you*?"

Lexi somehow managed to keep herself from wincing over his words, but she didn't keep her reaction completely hidden from him. This conversation wasn't going how she'd planned, but then, she hadn't planned any of this. She had no idea what she was going to say or do when she came here tonight.

"And if Cole is so concerned about you, where is he that he can't protect you himself?"

Lexi gulped; she would have to tell him about his father now. "He's going through the trials."

CHAPTER TWENTY-THREE

ORIN OPENED his mouth to respond before closing it. His forehead furrowed, and he shook his head before looking to her again. His shock and confusion were evident, but there was also a growing understanding in his eyes.

An understanding he sought to deny if his next question was any indication.

"What trials?" he asked.

"The dark fae trials to become king. Orin, your father is dead," Lexi whispered. "I'm sorry. I didn't mean to tell you like this…. I don't know how…. I… I… meant to tell you, but…."

Her voice trailed off as she realized she was talking in pointless circles and sounding like an idiot. Orin stared at a spot over her shoulder. She had no idea what the look on his face was—grief, confusion, denial, anger?

"I'm sorry," she whispered. "I know how difficult it is to lose your dad."

"That can't be true," Orin said. "He can't be dead."

Lexi had thought the same thing when word of her father's death arrived. It was easy to deny something when you didn't witness it.

"Cole was there," she said. "He saw it happen."

He finally blinked. "Cole was there? *He* told you this?"

"Yes."

When his gaze ran over her again, his interest was much keener. Lexi refused to fidget beneath his scrutiny.

"What happened to my father?" he demanded.

Lexi took a deep breath before telling him how the Lord of the Shadow Realms ordered the death of the king of the dark fae... and why. She contemplated telling him that Cole wasn't on the Lord's side anymore and planned to fight against the evil monster, but she kept the words to herself.

She already felt like she was betraying Cole by keeping *this* secret from him. If he wanted Orin to know he planned to kill the Lord, he would tell him once he found out Orin was here.

When she finished, Orin's only reaction was a slow blink. Lexi stared at her feet as she dug the toe of her sneaker into the ground; he had to understand he was a big part of the reason his father was dead. That wasn't a burden anyone should have to bear, not even an asshole like Orin.

"I have to go," Lexi said. "I'll leave through one of the exits in the woods. That way, if someone sees me returning to the manor, I can claim I couldn't sleep and went for a walk."

"Who goes out for a walk in the middle of the night?"

"I do... on occasion. It's peaceful at night, no one is around to bother me, and I love the song of the crickets and tree frogs. Besides, it's better than me emerging from the tunnels and into the manor. Brokk doesn't know the tunnels exist, and Sahira would have endless questions for me. You're going to have to be more careful; I don't know how long Brokk is staying here."

"Cole intends to be the next dark fae king."

It wasn't a question, but Lexi answered him anyway. "Yes. He didn't have a choice. And now, he's already started them. If he doesn't do as the Lord commands, the Lord has promised to level the Gloaming."

Orin showed no reaction to her words. The man was as emotional as the shadows surrounding him, but she sensed a wealth of sorrow and confusion inside him—or maybe she was just hoping it was there.

No one should be this cold after learning about their father's death. She'd agreed to help him, and their lives depended on each other, but she trusted Orin about as much as a pissed-off rattlesnake.

Still, she preferred to believe the man whose life had become so entwined with hers wasn't this callous when he learned about the death of his father. He had to be this emotionless because he was a dark fae and good at keeping his emotions locked away.

She had no doubt he would save his ass before anyone else here, but she'd seen signs of kindness in him too. He wouldn't be rescuing refugees and bringing them here if he didn't possess some compassion. He claimed saving those refugees benefited him, but she believed there was more to it than that.

Or maybe she was trying to see something that wasn't there. They depended on each other after all, and she preferred to think she hadn't thrown herself in with a man-eating shark.

"If something comes up or if Cole returns, I'll try to drop a note to you through the stable or library entrance." She had planned to stay away from that entrance after Malakai, but they would be the easiest two entrances for her to access. "George has also been around the manor and the stables more often. Look for notes there, but *don't* come out through there."

Orin gave her a barely discernible nod.

"I have to go," Lexi said.

She started to turn away, but his words stopped her. "Cole's not pure dark fae."

"I know."

"The dark fae won't accept him as their king."

"They won't have a choice once he survives the trials," she said.

Orin snorted with laughter. "Do you think someone who *isn't* a pure dark fae can survive?"

She hated that his words caused doubts to creep in. She was afraid, if she doubted it for a second, that somehow it would cause him to die. It was stupid to think that way, but she couldn't help it.

"Cole can and *will* survive."

"You have a lot of faith in my older brother."

"I do."

"And if he does survive, what then?"

"What do you mean?"

"You're a fool if you've allowed yourself to fall in love with him."

"Then I'm a fool."

Orin's lips compressed into a thin line, and a muscle twitched in his cheek. "He won't survive."

"I'm not going to argue with you about this. I only came to tell you about your father, that Brokk was at the manor, and to be careful. I won't be able to come back as often."

"Understood."

"Okay. I have to go."

She strode past him and deeper into the passageways. She was about to turn left when she stopped to look back at him. He remained where she left him with his head slightly bowed. He struggled to keep it hidden, but she sensed the anguish emanating from him as his shoulders hunched up.

"Orin." It took a few seconds, but eventually, his head turned toward her. "I'm truly sorry about your father. He was a good man."

She started to walk away again but stopped when he said, "Andi."

Andi was the name she gave to the refugees when Orin first came to her with them; it was what they knew her as down here.

"You'll let me know if Cole survives," he said.

"I will."

He didn't say another word before stepping back and blending seamlessly into the shadows once more.

CHAPTER TWENTY-FOUR

THE SUN BAKED Cole's flesh until it blistered before splitting open. Sand caked his swollen, dry eyes, but he'd given up trying to wipe it away. It was impossible to keep the small grains out of them.

Sometimes the particles drifted up over his ankles; at other times, the sand was hardpacked beneath his feet and crunched with every step. The blood trickling from his swollen and broken lips dripped off his chin. He didn't bother trying to stop it.

Dried blood caked on his arms as more of his flesh split open beneath the onslaught of the unrelenting sun. His head throbbed so much that each beat of his heart pounded in his temples and blurred his vision.

He had no idea where he was in this land, if he was going the right way, or wandering in circles. He kept going because the alternative was death.

He'd long ago lost sight of Aelfdane and Auberon. Maybe they were still out there baking and blistering beneath the sun, or perhaps they succumbed to it days ago. He didn't care either way.

As the hours and what he assumed were days passed, there was no end in view from the sea of golden brown surrounding him. His body tried to heal with every passing step, but it was becoming more beat down by his growing hunger and thirst.

In the beginning, he briefly considered turning into the wolf so he could traverse the land faster, but these were trials for the dark fae. A lycan wouldn't pass them; there was no way the magic at work here would let that happen. Besides, running through this wasteland with a heavy coat on him probably wouldn't help with the heat.

One of the blisters on his neck popped and sizzled when the liquid oozing from it baked on his flesh. He didn't dare touch his skin. It hurt bad enough without feeling the pressure of his fingers against it.

He pondered taking his shirt off to cool himself a tiny bit more as sweat and blood cleaved it to his body. However, he refused to give the sun one more centimeter of exposed flesh to destroy.

Dust and sand clogged his nostrils and choked his mouth. He would gladly kill someone for a sip of water, as the sand in his throat made it feel as if he'd eaten razor blades.

When he came over the top of a hill, the sand rose almost to his knees, and he staggered and nearly went down. He caught himself before he toppled into the sand. If he went down, he wasn't sure he would make it up again.

Occasionally, he glimpsed bones in the distance but never went to explore. Sometimes, he believed those bones were dragging themselves through the sand, but it was impossible to tell reality from fiction anymore.

Stopping, he bent his head as he tried to find some reprieve from the unrelenting sun. There was none.

The sun never set in this hellhole.

He craved the cool nights of the Gloaming and the silvery rays of its four moons. He longed to wrap the cool embrace of shadows around him.

Imagining them encompassing his body helped ease some of his misery, but no matter how clearly he pictured the coolness of the shadows in his mind, it wasn't enough to chase away the heat.

He considered taking a small break but didn't know if he would have the energy to get up again. He hadn't stopped in days, and he was so exhausted he swore he fell asleep on his feet.

The imaginings of Lexi kept him moving. Forcing one foot in front of the other, he focused on her as he trudged through the sand sucking at his legs. He recalled her strawberry scent and how the sun brought out deep, vibrant red and gold strands in her auburn hair.

The taste of her kiss replaced the grainy sand on his lips. Her laughter drowned out the rush of blood in his ears as she gazed up at him with amusement in her twinkling, hunter green eyes. In his mind, he traced every one of the freckles sprinkled across the bridge of her nose.

The image of her was so real she drew him onward as she beckoned to him with the crook of her finger. A dim part of him realized he was lost to delirium, and the rest of him didn't care.

She was here. He was almost to her. If he could just touch her, then....

When a whirling, crashing, sucking sound drowned out the sound of her laughter, Cole stopped. Lexi continued to shimmer before him until a sound like nails raking a chalkboard pushed her out of his mind.

It sounded like the land was tearing itself apart as the ground beneath his feet quaked. And when Lexi vanished, her absence revealed the wave of earth cascading toward him. Cole's nostrils flared as the barren wasteland suddenly became a crashing ocean of sand.

Unable to trust what he was seeing, Cole lifted his blistered and bloodied hands to wipe away the sand caking his eyes. The movement caused more of his flesh to rip open, and a mixture of more blood and ooze spilled down him.

Once he cleaned his eyes the best he could, Cole lowered his arms again and focused on the desert. The waves of sand were still rushing toward him, but when he glanced over his shoulder, only serene desert remained.

He was not hallucinating this sudden change of events or the shrieking noise threatening to rupture his eardrums.

He could turn and flee back into the desert, but if he did, he would spend an eternity roaming this land. He would continue to burn and bleed until the sun and sand eroded the skin from his muscles and then the muscles from his bones.

If he turned back, he wouldn't get the chance to face whatever this was again. And he suspected this was the key to defeating this trial. If he turned back, it was only a matter of time before he became nothing more than a skeleton, dragging itself across the earth in search of escape.

The bones he'd glimpsed before weren't an illusion created by a mind rotting from the sun. *That* was what would become of him if he ran from this sea of sand.

How many dark fae are out there, crawling through the desert, dead but still living an existence far worse than death?

It wasn't a question he wanted an answer to, and it was a fate he wouldn't allow to befall him, no matter how thirsty, exhausted, burnt, and pain-filled he was.

The waves were only a hundred yards away now and rising higher before crashing into the sand. The earth quaked more violently, and the shrieking noise drowned out all other sounds.

Cole gathered what little strength remained and ran toward the waves.

CHAPTER TWENTY-FIVE

THE FIRST WAVE of sand threw him off his feet when it hit him. However, the crushing impact that knocked the wind out of him and cracked a rib was not only filled with pain; it was also welcome.

The pain meant it was *real.*

And if it was real, then maybe it meant he was coming to the end of this trial. And even if it meant death, he would meet the end of this place head-on.

He landed on his ass, and sand plowed up around him as he skidded across it. Before he could regain his feet, a wave buried him. As more waves descended over him, they rolled him and battered him until his bones ached.

Desperate to break out from beneath the punishing weight of the sand, he clawed at it as he sought to break free. Sand burrowed its way into his cracked flesh and dug into him like a mole burrowing into the earth.

It shredded the skin from his body, stripped him to the muscle, and exposed his nerve endings. It worked its way into those endings until every one of them was covered and rubbed at by sand.

Then, from the endless sea of golden brown, a skeletal face emerged. Unlike the skeletons in the tunnel, this one was very much alive as its teeth nearly took off the tip of his nose before the sand tore them apart.

Cole strained to see anything beyond the endless brown, but it was impossible. When another wave crashed over him, he had to close his eyes or risk losing them.

Sand clogged his nostrils and choked his mouth until it shoved its way down his throat. Deprived of oxygen, his lungs burned, but he resisted inhaling until it became impossible to fight the instinct.

With an inhalation that he knew wouldn't bring any relief but he was unable to stop, he drew sand into his lungs until they felt like balloons about to burst from being stuffed so full.

Despite his inability to breathe, he continued to claw his way toward the surface while the sand worked to bury him. He could only hope he was digging in the right direction and wasn't working his way *deeper* into the earth.

Using his ability to manipulate the Earth, he pushed the sand away from his palms the best he could, but as he moved it away, more took its place. The relentless weight of it was close to crushing him beneath its punishing onslaught.

Something grabbed his ankle. He almost looked down to see it, but doing so would be completely useless. Until he was free of this mess, he wouldn't see again.

Judging by the feel of it, one of those skeletal things held his ankle. The waves had caught those things up with him, and they would do everything they could to make sure he didn't survive.

Cole kicked at the hand digging into his ankle and managed to knock it away as another set of fingers started clawing at his back. Those fingers entangled in his hair and drew his head back. Before he could stop it, teeth sank into his shoulder.

Clenching his jaw against his increasing agony and growing urge to pass out from lack of oxygen, Cole ignored the creature gnawing on him as he struggled toward the surface. He'd had enough of this place, these things, and all the *fucking* sand.

He *refused* to die in this place or to have one of these *things* bring him down. He would not fail here. Between Lexi and his determination to bring the Lord down, he had far too much to live for.

With renewed vigor, he clawed, kicked, and swam his way toward the surface as he continued to use his powers to shove the sand away from him. Just when he was sure he *was* digging his way deeper into the sand instead of out, his hand broke the surface.

For a second, he couldn't believe it was real, but as his hand twisted above the sea of sand, the sun warmed his fingers. Cole shoved his other hand through and rested his palms on the surface.

With a mighty heave, he pulled himself free of the crushing sand. It poured off his head and fell around him as he collapsed onto the ground and tried to gasp in air. Though sand poured from his mouth, no air passed his lips.

As if he didn't have enough things keeping him from breathing, bony arms encircled his neck and squeezed. The bones dug into his tendons, but there was no air to choke from him.

Another wave of sand smashed into him, and he toppled back onto the skeletal being. When its teeth clamped harder onto his shoulder, it released a strange, guttural cry that his muscles muffled. Lying on his back, Cole cracked an eye open to discover a wave of sand cresting over him again.

No!

He threw his palms up, and released a blast of power to take control of the Earth and keep the sand away. He would *not* be buried again.

Blinking against the particles caking his eyes, his vision finally cleared enough to reveal a ceiling of sand cascading over his head. In the unrelenting sun, the different grains and rocks sparkled and shone with a rainbow of colors. Cole sneered at those colors.

The creature tore a hunk of sinew from his shoulder as the wave ended. As the sun beat down on him once more, Cole expected another wave to follow, but it didn't.

Twisting to the side, he managed to tear himself free of the creature's hold. He rolled away from it as more skeletal hands erupted from the sand. They pawed at the air and patted the now calm earth as they searched for him.

Pushing himself to his feet, Cole staggered and nearly went down before catching himself. More sand spilled from his mouth, but he still couldn't breathe. His vision blurred and went out again as lack of oxygen caused him to sway.

However, he couldn't stop moving. Stopping meant death; it meant losing, and he *would* claim the dark fae throne.

He tried to cough the sand out of his lungs, but there was no air in him to do so. As he staggered forward, he clawed at his mouth and pulled handfuls of sand from it. He dug deeper until his fingers were pulling sand out of his throat.

When he couldn't get any deeper, he clasped his hands together and placed them against his belly. He shoved upward to push more of the sand out of him. Eventually, he loosened enough earth from inside him to work some air into his lungs.

Once those first breaths entered him, a bone-wracking wave of coughing swept his frame. Bending over, he rested his hands on his knees as he hacked up clumps of bloody sand. The intensity of the coughing cracked a couple more ribs and caused a fiery, stabbing pain in his side and back.

It took some time, but he finally wheezed in air. His lungs felt like someone had taken a baseball bat to them, but they were functioning again.

With trembling fingers deprived of their skin, he wiped away the sand sticking to his eyes and blinked against the fiery sun. In the distance, skeletal creatures dragged themselves across the sand toward him. They were so far away he didn't pay them any attention.

The barren wasteland spread out before him once more, but this time, a hundred feet away, the desert ended in a wall of dark. He couldn't see what lay within that dark and didn't care.

If it meant escaping this place, that shadowed land could lead straight to Hell, and he would be happy about it. Rising, he staggered into the darkness.

CHAPTER TWENTY-SIX

THE BLESSED COLD air of the darkness enveloped him as he lurched forward like a zombie in pursuit of brains—and those creatures were ruthless when tracking a meal.

Except, he didn't smell brains or food as he stumbled forward. Instead, the crisp scent of water filled his nostrils. If he'd possessed an ounce of moisture in his body, saliva would have flooded his mouth, but though he felt like drooling, he couldn't.

His stressed heart beat so rapidly it pulsed in his eardrums as he tracked the scent. He became so focused on the smell of water and the prospect of drinking *all of it* that his vision tunneled.

He didn't see the world around him and had no idea if an enemy loomed nearby as he searched for water. The cool rocks beneath his bare, skeletal feet were a welcome respite as he shuffled around a set of boulders that blocked his view of whatever lay beyond.

And then, he saw the water.

An unrecognizable sound issued from him, and his legs became so weak that he nearly went down. Somehow, he managed to stay on his feet as he staggered toward the pristine lake. Not a single ripple disturbed its glassy surface.

He was almost to the shore and could already taste the cool liquid slipping down his throat to eradicate what remained of the sand coating the insides of his cheeks and tongue when warning bells went off in his head.

He planned to trudge straight into the water and consume as much of it as he could while washing away the sand sticking to his muscles, but something inside his head screamed at him to stop when he arrived at the water's edge.

Falling to his knees, he stared at the water. It was so crystal clear he could see every one of the stones making up its bed. Hovering over the water, he shook as he restrained himself from gulping water from the lake.

These were the trials. And so far, he'd endured a trial by air, another by earth, and now he was staring at water.

The trials are the elements.

The knowledge was sluggish in coming as most of his brain continued to scream at him to *drink, drink, drink!*

But he couldn't drink. He'd defeated air and earth, so that only left water and fire. It couldn't be a coincidence that after leaving that wasteland behind, he was now facing this lake with all its delicious, life-giving water.

His entire body quaked as the aroma of the water intensified. Like a siren beckoning to the sailors, he couldn't resist its temptation as he leaned over the water. He hadn't realized he'd cupped his hands until he spotted himself hovering over the water with them.

The vision of himself—or at least he believed it was him, as he was barely recognizable—staring into that water shocked some reality back into him. He had no skin left on his face, and little remained on his body. It had been stripped away and replaced by the sand sticking to his bloody tendons.

One of his eyes protruded oddly. It took him a second to realize that was because part of his eyelid was missing. He'd lost his boots; skeletons and the sand had torn away his shirt and shredded most of his pants.

Only the waistband of his pants and some shredded fabric covered his upper thighs. The remnants of his pants shielded his only remaining flesh.

His ears were nearly gone; he couldn't tell if his hair remained or if it had been sheared away too. At first, he thought he still had some tissue on his face, but then it sloughed downward, and a ball of sand plopped into the water. It caused a circle of ripples to radiate across the surface.

Despite his lack of skin, he didn't feel any pain. He suspected that was because his nerve endings were so damaged, they didn't detect the sensation. He recalled the suffering he endured while trapped beneath the sand and knew it would return as his body healed.

Leaning away from the water, Cole tried to wipe away the sand. Without something to wash it from him, all his actions did was cause it to abrade his muscle further.

His hands fell to the rocky ground as he stared at the water and willed himself to get away from it. He didn't move. It was easier for him to kill a dragon than it was to find the strength to push himself away from the water.

Finally, and with a will he hadn't known he possessed, he placed his hands against the gray rocks and shoved himself to his feet and away from the lake. He staggered, lurched, and fell as he tried to get away from the relentless pull of the liquid he craved.

Lacking the strength to get back to his feet, he crawled a hundred feet away from the shoreline. There, he found an outcropping of rocks that created a small cave. He crawled inside the shelter and took some solace in the shadows enveloping him, but the water still called to him.

He leaned his back against the wall and positioned himself so he could see the water. Maybe he was wrong; maybe he'd denied himself much-needed hydration that would help him heal a lot faster and wash away the sand for no reason.

But he couldn't chance drinking that water in this condition. He was so weak and battered that if there was something wrong, he wouldn't withstand it.

He would wait to see if any of his competition survived. If they had, he didn't doubt they would go for the water. But would they also resist like him, or would they give in and drink it?

As he watched and waited, his body started to heal. Cole gritted his teeth against screaming as his nerve endings fired back to life. When they did, it felt like someone had taken his entire body and dipped it into a vat of boiling oil.

Quaking all over, he closed his eyes while his body gradually regrew the skin it lost. When this was over, this maddening agony would be one more thing he made the Lord pay for.

CHAPTER TWENTY-SEVEN

"KNEES TO CHEST!" Brokk commanded.

Lexi did everything she could to get her knees to her chest as she ran, but she felt like an idiot as her knees nearly hit her boobs. She didn't exactly love running, and she'd already run around the lake three times. However, this added knees-to-chest thing was making it almost impossible to keep going.

"Knees to chest!" Brokk yelled like a drill sergeant.

Lexi stopped running, turned to face him, and planted her hands on her hips. "I'm trying!"

"Not hard enough," Brokk retorted. "You're the one who asked to learn how to fight."

"What does me hitting my knees against my chest have to do with fighting?"

"Nothing," he said with a smile. "I'm just entertaining myself."

Lexi gawked as she resisted hurling a bunch of curses at him. Bending, she picked up a handful of dirt and threw it at him. Brokk laughed as he danced away from it.

"Come on," he said. "Get back to running."

Lexi was beginning to regret her decision to ask him for help with this, but at least his drill-sergeant-like ways were a distraction from her thoughts because none of her thoughts were good.

Cole had been gone for five days. Five days in which there was no word from anyone on what was happening. Five days in which Brokk hadn't given her much time to sit and wallow, but the night-time was different.

At night, she tossed and turned before giving up and rising from bed. She'd pace from the window to her bed and back again. She'd stare at the moon and search for crows while praying Cole returned to her.

Sometimes, she would creep down to the library and try to read, but she could never concentrate on the words. For the first time in her life, reading didn't bring her solace from the world.

The other night, she returned to the tunnels to deliver what little food they could spare. Orin wasn't there, but she found Nessie and the other refugees in the section where they had taken to living.

Nessie was a pretty brunette with gray eyes and a timid smile. Behind that smile was a spine of steel. The woman was determined to keep her four-year-old nephew, Jayden, safe no matter what it took.

When she first met them, Jayden looked so much like Nessie that she assumed he was her son, but his mother, a mortal, died during childbirth. Nessie stepped in to help care for him afterward and loved him like he was her own.

Jayden's father was a vampire who fought against the Lord during the war. Because of that, the Lord would ruthlessly hunt his child.

While Lexi hated keeping this secret from Cole, when she looked at Nessie and Jayden, she knew she'd made the right choice. They deserved better, and she would do whatever she could to make sure they got it.

Nessie didn't know where Orin had gone, but that wasn't unusual. There were times he slipped away for a day or two, but he always returned. She hoped he was extra careful about his comings and goings.

Since that night, she hadn't returned to the tunnel, but they should be set for food still, and Orin should have come back by now. She would have to go below again soon to make sure. If they got hungry, they might try to leave, which could be disastrous for all involved.

Until then, she concentrated on running, lifting, punching, kicking, and trying not to lose her mind. Brokk must have sensed this as every free moment she had, he used it to drill her into exhaustion.

Every night she fell into bed, certain she would pass out; every night, she was proven wrong. That didn't mean she wasn't tired. Every muscle she had ached, she was covered in bruises, and she'd come to despise running.

But every day, she dragged herself back outside to care for the animals before training with him again. He'd started training her on how to use a sword he took out of her father's armory, but the weapon was awkward and cumbersome.

She was much better with a short sword. However, Brokk didn't know how well she would do with using it in battle. Things were pretty up close and personal with a sword no matter what, but they were a lot more so with a short sword.

He didn't think she could handle being that close to an enemy and watching them die. She would do whatever she could to survive, and she excelled with the short sword compared to the longer one.

She was also pretty good with throwing stars and getting better. Brokk focused her on these as she could hit an enemy with them without ever getting close. Which meant, she could inflict damage against what would probably be a stronger immortal without putting herself in too much danger.

And as he drilled it into her head every day, once she inflicted that damage, she should run fast. Outrunning a vampire who could transport was impossible, but she was fast enough to outrun other immortals.

She just loathed the idea of running.

Sometimes, as they trained, Sahira would stand nearby scowling, wincing in sympathy, and sometimes pumping her fist when Lexi got in a solid blow against Brokk. Often, after those signs of encouragement, she would smooth down her shirt and pants and walk away.

She would never admit it, but Lexi saw her aunt's pride in what she was doing, even if Sahira was determined to hide it. Today, Sahira never left her garden.

As the sun started to set, they ended her training with a sparring match by the lake. Lexi ignored the sweat trickling down her neck and sticking her hair to her nape as the late June sun beat down on her.

She couldn't help feeling some pride as she traded jabs with Brokk. She was getting better at this. She would still get her ass handed to her by a trained, full-blooded immortal, but she might be able to take down one who had no fighting experience.

"Good, good," Brokk said as he danced before her.

If Malakai ever attacked her again, she might not be able to kill him, but she would make him regret it. She would tear him apart before he killed her.

CHAPTER TWENTY-EIGHT

BROKK SLIPPED through the shadows of the woods as he pursued the deer making its way through the trees ahead of him. Normally, he was content with feasting on the blood bags Lexi stashed in her fridge, but it had been a long time since he hunted in any way, and his darker nature sought an outlet.

His dark fae side and vampire side had both been denied since he'd taken over watching Lexi. He didn't resent it; he would do anything for his brothers—or, at least, he would have done anything for *all* his brothers before the war.

Now, he would still do anything for his brothers... within reason. He would do anything for Cole. They'd chosen the same side and stood by their father; they had shared many of the same losses and defeats and grown closer because of it.

He now considered Cole his best friend, but they were never close growing up or as young adults because of their age difference. They were friendly, joked with each other, and shared experiences, but not in the same way he had with his brothers who were closer in age.

Five of those brothers chose to fight against their father, and the other two, who remained on their side, perished during the war.

That only left him and Cole, and they'd bonded during their many days of endless battles and strategy planning. They also spent many nights drinking and prowling for women while they blew off steam.

He had no doubt Cole would die for him, and he would do the same. Cole could be dying for him and the rest of the fae right now, and he would have no way of knowing. The last time he heard from his brother was when Cole sent him a crow to let him know he couldn't find Malakai.

He couldn't think about Cole not surviving the trials. The two of them had done things neither of them expected or enjoyed doing. They'd fought for the bastard who killed their father, all while trying to figure out how to destroy him, and they'd failed.

They both lived with the guilt of that failure. But they also lived with the knowledge that while the Lord wasn't hunting them, they could do more than either of their brothers to destroy him.

A part of him hated Orin and Varo as much as he loved them. If he found them, he would protect them as his father would have, but he'd prefer to have nothing to do with them. They chose to break off when they could have stayed, and they were a big part of the reason his father was dead.

Taking a break from hunting the deer, Brokk leaned against a tree and drew the shadows around him. So far, there had been no threat to Lexi and Sahira, but he didn't know how long that would last. Once Cole got through the trials, Lexi would become a much bigger target for all those who would seek to bring down his brother.

And he would not let anything happen to her. He'd already lost too many of his brothers; he would not lose another.

Besides, Lexi was his friend, and despite having been alive for six hundred years, he didn't have any remaining friends outside his family.

He had considered her father a friend and was glad to call the daughter one too.

Closing his eyes, Brokk tipped his head back and welcomed the warmth of the sun beating down on him. Ever since he learned of his father's death, a chill had seeped into his bones that he couldn't quite eradicate.

The chill was more than grief; he hated to admit it, but it was also fear—fear of the unknown, for his brother, and all of them.

The Lord was crazier than they'd all believed. There wasn't anything that monster wouldn't do. Which meant all bets were off. Before, there were at least some rules and boundaries.

They were obliterated when the Lord killed the king of the dark fae.

Brokk's eyes burned as he strove to suppress his sorrow. It was nearly impossible as he recalled the coolness of his father's fingers brushing the hair back from his forehead before he pulled the covers around him. Once tucked in, his dad would pitch his voice low to regale him with whatever new story he made up.

The stories often consisted of pirates and dragons needing to be slain. The adventures made Brokk giggle. Sometimes, his mother came to visit him, but she was content to live mostly child-free.

Brokk was fine with that. They got along well enough when he saw her, but his father was his rock, and though the king was feared by many, he doted on his sons.

And he also had his brothers. Even without the constant presence of his mother in his life, Brokk felt surrounded by love growing up. Yes, there was a big age difference between him and some of his brothers, but there was always love there.

And now, almost all the love he experienced as a child was gone.

Varo and Orin still lived, but if they did defeat the Lord and somehow regain control of their lives, he wasn't sure he could forgive them for their role in his father's death—or Cole's, if his brother didn't survive the trials. He was there because of his brothers.

And if something happened to Lexi under his watch, he'd

never forgive himself either. While Lexi remained alive, Cole wouldn't become the cruel, vicious monstrosity Brokk sensed slithering beneath the surface.

If something happened to her, he suspected Cole would become as much of a menace to the realms as the Lord. He'd killed a dragon for their father; what would he do for her?

A roar in the distance drew his attention to the sky. A dragon soared above, tilted its wings, and swooped back toward the smoldering remains of the city in the distance. The dragons only did as the Lord commanded them, but still, he loathed all of them.

Stepping away from the tree, he was about to resume his hunt when the jingle of bits and the stomp of hooves stopped him. He took a step forward as riders approached the manor. The rider at the end flew the Lord's colors.

"Shit," he hissed and teleported behind the house.

CHAPTER TWENTY-NINE

COLE DIDN'T KNOW how much time passed before he woke. At first, it was an effort to open his eyes, but his grogginess vanished when he recalled where he was. He pushed himself up against the cool stone and winced when the rocks abraded his regenerating skin.

He couldn't believe he'd fallen asleep; he was lucky to wake again. There were countless horrors in this place—and competitors who would gladly kill him while he slept.

But then, it had been days and possibly weeks since the last time he slept. It was only a matter of time before exhaustion took over, and with as battered as he'd been, his body required the healing comfort of sleep.

Lifting his hands, he inspected the sand cleaving to the fresh, tender flesh forming over his muscles. It was as soft as a newborn's and every bit as sensitive when he prodded at it.

His nerve endings were also healing, and they were not happy about it, but then, neither was he. Every move he made caused pins and needles to stab those endings. And once they stabbed, they also twisted and ground around in there for a while.

Despite the fiery agony working its way over his body, he had to figure out how to defeat this trial, if it *was* a trial. Sleep had helped him heal, but it did nothing to ease his ravenous thirst.

He was about to crawl out of his shelter when the padding sound of footsteps caught his attention. The steps drew nearer until Auberon appeared. The young dark fae ran for the water.

Cole almost shouted a warning to the kid but stopped himself. If he warned Auberon away from the water now, he would have to kill him in the end. No matter what, there could only be one survivor. As determined as he was to win, Cole wasn't eager to take the life of the young fae.

Besides, he wasn't positive there was something wrong with the water. He might learn *he* was the fool and he could have consumed it.

Kneeling at the side of the lake, Auberon held his hands out, and Cole winced. From the tips of his fingers to his wrist, only bone remained on the one hand, and the other was bone to his elbow.

The kid was strong enough to have made it this far—which was a lot farther than Cole assumed he would—but the desert wasn't kind to him. When Auberon turned his head left and right to take in his surroundings, he revealed that half his face was gone and only bone remained. Somehow, the eye on that side was still in place, but it bulged disconcertingly from its socket.

From his position inside his shelter, Cole didn't think Auberon could see him, but he suspected he could walk out in the open, and the panicked, brutalized kid still wouldn't see him. His father never should have volunteered Auberon for this; Cole would make him pay for it when he returned to the Gloaming.

Auberon cupped his skeletal fingers and dipped them into the lake. Cole's teeth ground back and forth as the young man consumed the lake with the enthusiasm of a dog. Water spilled down his fingers and forearms to splatter on the ground. It must have been taking too long as he gave up drinking from his hands and plunged his face into the lake.

Unlike Cole, nothing of Auberon's clothes remained. The flesh had been stripped from most of his body, but some remained on his upper thighs and ass. Glimpses of bone peeked through the bloody remains of Auberon's legs.

Cole swallowed the sand still clogging his mouth as Auberon lifted his head from the lake. Water poured down his face and washed away the sand. Had he denied himself when he could be slurping down water like this kid?

Resting his hand against the cool rocks, Cole drew on the shadows and used them to cloak himself as he slipped from the shelter. Auberon dipped his hands into the water again, but he didn't bring the liquid to his mouth this time.

Instead, he froze as a shake started in his hands and ran into his arms before racking the rest of his lean frame. Cole frowned as he tried to understand what was happening. Had the kid consumed too much water too fast after not getting any for so long and was having convulsions?

And then, Auberon began to scream—or, at least, Cole assumed it was a scream. The sounds issuing from him were unlike anything Cole ever heard before, and he'd fought in the war. He'd seen the dying, listened to their screams, and done things he'd never believed himself capable of doing, but he'd never heard anything like this.

It was a gurgled, shrill, shrieking sound that brought to mind a bird being plucked of its feathers while the poor creature was still alive. Auberon jerked as he held his hands up before him.

Beneath the glow of the moon that rose while Cole slept, the water glistened on the tips of Auberon's bony fingers and slid down his arms. Cole didn't understand what was wrong until bubbles started foaming on the ends of those figures.

Like a sandcastle crumbling beneath the incoming tide, Auberon's fingers started dissolving at the fingertips. After the tips were gone, the first knuckles crumpled and then onward down to his second knuckles.

With what remained of his fingers, Auberon started clawing at his throat. The skin peeled back from his mouth, and bloody bubbles pooled from his lips before spilling down his chin.

Acid, Cole realized. *The water contains acid.*

And not just any acid, but an acid that ate whoever consumed it. Disgust and fury churned in Cole's gut as he watched Auberon melting like he was the wicked witch someone threw water on. He wanted to look away; he didn't.

He could never report the exact details of what happened here, but later, when he told Durin of his son's death, he would make sure the man knew his son suffered a horrible fate. He wasn't sure it would matter to Durin, but it mattered to him.

He watched until all that remained of Auberon was a foaming pile of loose bubbles sliding toward the water. Oh yes, Durin would suffer for his cowardice more than his son, as would Alston for volunteering Eoghan for this.

First he had to figure out a way around the lake, and he didn't think that would be as easy as taking a stroll around it. He suspected he would find no end to this lake.

Keeping himself cloaked in the shadows, Cole walked to the edge of the lake. If Aelfdane was nearby, he might sense his presence, but he wouldn't see him.

A more powerful dark fae than him would see him, but Aelfdane was not more powerful, and Cole didn't see or sense him anywhere nearby.

Maybe the sand had taken care of Aelfdane, or perhaps he was ahead of Cole in the trials. Either way, Cole had to figure out how to cross the lake without becoming the Wicked Witch of the West.

Kneeling at the shore, he ignored Auberon's puddle of remains still seeping toward the water as he studied the pristine surface. He crept his fingertips toward the water but kept them away from the deadly liquid. He didn't know how much it would take to turn him into a puddle, and he wasn't taking the chance.

Cole concentrated on the water as he drew on the strength

thrumming through his veins. The rocks vibrated beneath his fingers as he focused his power on the water. As the vibrations grew stronger, they created ripples across the lake's smooth surface.

He'd just woken, but he was still exhausted. And it was a bone-deep exhaustion that would take weeks of sleep to eradicate. He was also starving and needed to feed, but this land would never provide him the opportunity to do so.

Despite those growing weaknesses, he shoved his power forward and seized control of the water. The ripples on its surface intensified as he took control over it and started to push it apart. A lightning bolt crack zigzagged across the water's surface until it vanished.

Lifting his hands, he placed the backs of them against each other before pushing them apart. The crack widened, and the water peeled back until two walls rose twenty feet into the air on each side of him.

His muscles quivered as the water exerted its force against him, but it held firm... for now.

He had no idea how far he'd have to go until he reached the other side of the lake. He'd have to move fast as he also didn't know how long he could keep the water apart.

Rising, Cole stepped onto the damp rocks lining the bottom of the lake. He could only hope that dampness wasn't enough to dissolve him as there was no way he could keep the water parted long enough for the rocks to dry.

Keeping his hands out at his sides, Cole sprinted across the stones. As he ran, the water crashed down behind him, but he moved fast enough that it didn't touch him.

He had to block the pathway behind him; he couldn't take the chance that Aelfdane would follow him through here. If Aelfdane lived, he would have to find his own way across the lake.

Ahead of him, the walls of water trembled as the weight of them tested his strength. His feet slapped against the rocks as he ran and ran and ran. The bottoms of his feet burned, and Cole suspected he was losing some of his newly formed flesh, but he wasn't starting to melt away onto the rocks, so he took that as a good sign.

As the minutes stretched into what felt like hours, he was beginning to think there wasn't an end and, eventually, the water would win, but then a wavering light rose out of the darkness ahead of him.

Reinvigorated by that light, Cole poured on the speed as the crashing water cut off all chance of an escape behind him.

He sprinted out of the lake and into the fire.

CHAPTER THIRTY

FROM INSIDE THE BARN, Lexi heard the plodding thump of horses' hooves as riders approached. A feeling of dread descended over her; they rarely got riders here, and when they did, they were never as many as what she heard out there.

Anyone who came to the manor was usually on foot, and most of the time, it was a human seeking food. Few of them ever rode horses.

This can't be good.

She closed her eyes, took a deep breath, and braced herself for what was about to come. She petted the neck of the gelding she was brushing before leading him over to his stall and closing the door.

He poked his head out, and his ears flicked as the horses came to a stop outside the open barn door. Lexi didn't recognize any of the voices drifting into the barn. She wasn't sure if that was good or bad.

Lexi wiped her hands on her jeans and threw back her shoulders. She was a lot more on edge in the barn since Malakai's attack, but she refused to let him ruin her happy place.

However, she couldn't keep the tremble from her hands as she strode toward the open doors. She didn't hear him out there, but had Malakai returned with help who would force her to go with him?

The possibility caused nausea to churn in her stomach, and her hand flitted to the small dagger she now wore strapped to her hip. It would do little against him, but she wouldn't go without a fight.

When she stepped outside the door, a glimmer of motion caught her attention as Brokk materialized behind the manor. He strode toward her as her attention shifted to the five riders only ten feet away.

They sat on their mounts, with their shoulders back and their chins raised high. They wore brown pants, black boots laced up to almost mid-calf, and brown shirts that clung to their broad frames.

Judging by the size of them, they were lycans. Given the dour expressions on their faces, they weren't exactly thrilled to be here.

The rider at the back of the group held a white flag with a bright red, fire-breathing dragon. She recognized the dragon as the Lord's symbol. She gulped but kept her face perfectly composed as she clasped her hands before her.

She had no idea why they were here; they could be searching for Orin, they could be here for her, or maybe Brokk. The Lord had killed his father after all; perhaps they were here to destroy more of his family.

She almost touched the dagger again but restrained herself. There was no reason to make any threatening moves before learning why they were here, but she wouldn't let them take Brokk without a fight.

The creak of a door drew her attention as Sahira stepped outside the manor. She used her hand to shade her amber eyes against the sun, and her gaze met Lexi's before shifting to their newest arrivals.

"Hello," Lexi greeted the men. "Can I help you?"

She assumed the lycan in the front was a leader, but he didn't respond. The horse's tack jangled as the animals shifted but didn't relax.

"Hello," Brokk said as he stopped a few feet away from her.

The lead lycan's eyes flicked to him. "Brokk of the house of the dark fae?"

"Yes," Brokk replied. "What is the meaning of this?"

Before anyone could reply, a dragon swooped low overhead. Lexi instinctively ducked as the creature blocked out the sun and its enormous wings kicked up dust. The pitiless soldiers tried to remain impassive, but some of them flinched, and a couple of their horses pranced backward.

Brokk didn't react, but Sahira stepped back toward the open doorway. Lexi dared to peek up at the sky as the giant beast soared across it. When that shadow fell across the road, the humans on it screamed and dove for cover.

The dragon bellowed but didn't unleash its fire upon the land. It wasn't hungry, or maybe it was tired of tormenting the mortals.

Once it was gone, Lexi's attention shifted back to the Lord's men. They remained focused on Brokk as the lead lycan dismounted.

"We have orders from the Lord to search every house in the area for your brothers and any other rebels," the head lycan said.

Lexi's mouth went dry, but she somehow managed to keep her face perfectly composed as his words sank in. They were searching *every* house?

The war destroyed many of them, but there were still hundreds, if not thousands, in the area, depending on how big that area was.

How many houses were they going to search? How many had they already searched? How long had they been doing this?

Her fingers tightened until they dug painfully into her palms. When her father first built the tunnels, Sahira cast a spell to keep them hidden. These men were lycans, but they shouldn't be able to detect the aroma of those refugees.

Even knowing this, a clammy sweat broke out on her body. She tried not to let her rising panic show, but she suddenly felt like the word *guilty* was stamped across her forehead in vivid red letters.

"Is this going to create an issue?" the lycan asked.

"Of course not," Lexi said and hoped her voice didn't sound as strained as it felt. "We have nothing to hide here."

They had *everything* to hide here, but she couldn't stop them from doing this. If she tried, then she really would have guilty stamped all over her.

They won't find the tunnels.

Her father carefully crafted each entrance, so it was impossible to detect even if you knew it was there. However, she couldn't stop her rising terror over the possibility they would somehow uncover them.

And if they discovered them, then everyone inside was as good as dead. She compelled herself not to look at Brokk again. Would the Lord kill him too if they discovered Orin here?

No, she wouldn't let that happen. She would gladly throw herself on that sword before she let Brokk and Sahira pay the price for her choices.

"Right this way," she said to the lead lycan.

The others dismounted before following her inside.

CHAPTER THIRTY-ONE

Only five feet of rocky land separated the lake from the fire beyond it. Cole almost reeled backward when the fire hit him. For a second, the idea of the acid water was far more pleasing than the flames jumping and snapping all around him.

Then he realized that if he kept running, the fire burned but didn't devour him. He sprinted forward as the flames rolled over the top of him, beat against his sides, and roared so loud he couldn't hear his rapid breathing.

And then, just when he believed the fire was going to devour him, it eased up. Smoke and heat didn't blast his lungs as he inhaled crisp, fresher air into their brutalized depths.

The blisters covering his freshly grown skin from head to toe popped. Their ooze sizzled against his red flesh. The bottoms of his feet, already burned from the wet rocks, were nothing more than tendons and bone again.

Exhaustion and hunger had become heavy, draining weights, but he pushed onward. He'd made it this far; he would *not* stop now.

Flames crackled around him as the towering volcanoes spewed

black smoke into the air. The red lava sliding toward him bubbled and popped as it consumed everything in its path.

Was he supposed to climb up through those volcanoes? He studied the rocky terrain and oozing lava as he tried to figure out where to go from here.

From the corner of his eye, he caught a flash of movement a second before a creature rushed out of the flames. Cole danced back from the lumbering monster and ducked the massive, rocky arm it swung at him.

It's a cherufe!

He'd never thought to see one of the hideous, man-eating creatures in his lifetime. He'd believed they were all extinct, but the eight-foot-tall monster was very real and made up entirely of rocks and magma. Flames encompassed its colossal frame and rolled from its eye sockets.

When it opened its gnarled mouth, it bellowed smoke and ran toward him with the wide step of a charging gorilla. It would have been comical if it wasn't for the monster's determination to bash him to pieces.

Cole ducked when it swung a fist the size of a wheelbarrow at his head. If one of this thing's punches connected with him, it would flatten his skull.

Despite its size, the cherufe was fast as it spun toward him. Cole darted to the side as its rocky fingers gouged his back.

He ducked as its arms came down like it was trying to embrace him in a giant bear hug. Except this bear hug would crack his spine and tear him in two.

He danced back from the creature as he tried to figure out how to defeat it. He was no match for its strength, and with the flames enveloping its body, it would engulf him in fire if he launched himself at it. He also couldn't use those flames against the monster as it was part of the fire surrounding them.

The best he could do was stay free of its grasp, but he couldn't do that forever. This thing consisted of rocks and was in its element. If it tired, it wouldn't be for a while, and he was already exhausted and battered.

The ground shook as the thing ran at him with more speed than something that easily weighed a ton should exhibit. The impact of its steps caused rocks to break away from the side of a volcano. They clattered down the side and bounced across the ground.

Fresh smoke belched into the air from one of the volcanoes. A whistling sound followed a couple of seconds later. Cole chanced a glance at the sky as a black, flaming pile of debris soared toward him.

He threw himself to the ground and rolled away as it hit the place where he'd stood only seconds before. Smoke coiled from the three-foot dent it left in the earth.

As if shit wasn't bad enough, now the volcanoes were spewing lava bombs at him. Rocks clattered down the side of the nearest volcano, and fresh smoke billowed into the air when more bombs launched at him.

CHAPTER THIRTY-TWO

LEXI STOOD by the open doorway of the library as the lycans filed into her home. The large men took up far too much space and heated her manor more than the midafternoon sun. She had to resist pulling at the collar of her shirt as it became increasingly difficult to breathe.

"Can I get you something to eat or drink?" Sahira asked the men.

"No, thank you," the head lycan said. "We won't be long."

Brokk leaned casually in the manor's open doorway, but the tension emanating from him was anything but casual. He crossed his legs and folded his arms over his chest as the lycans made their way upstairs.

Sahira stood in the doorway across from Lexi. She kept her eyes on the stairs as doors opened and closed above. The bang of drawers shutting, closets opening, and the squeak of beds moving drifted down.

Lexi didn't know if they really thought a rebel might fit inside their dresser drawers or if they were going through everything to make it clear they had the right to do so, but resentment was starting to replace her dread.

They had no right to come into her home like this and go through her things. The Lord had no right to invade her privacy, but there was nothing they could do about it, and that monster and these men knew it.

The Lord had taken control and now wielded his power over all of them. And like a guillotine about to fall, Lexi felt the deadly blade of that control poised over her neck.

The lycans spent ten minutes upstairs before appearing at the top of the stairs again. Lexi hid her apprehension as they descended the stairs. She almost smiled to show she had no cares in the world but stopped herself.

Did she want to smile at the men who just pawed through her underwear? Was that the normal reaction to have?

No, it was not.

Besides, there wasn't anything to smile about. While she hated the idea of them upstairs going through her things, there was nothing to find up there. The entrance to one of the tunnels was behind her, and though it wasn't true, she suddenly felt its cool air brushing against her neck.

The lycans didn't acknowledge them as they split up to search the rest of the house. When one of them swept by her to enter the library, she waited a couple of seconds before turning to watch as he examined the shelves.

He pulled books free before sliding them back into place with too much force. She winced when a book tumbled from his fingers to hit the ground with a loud bang. He muttered a curse before bending to pick it up. At least he returned it to the right spot.

He removed more books and examined them before shoving them back into place. She almost asked him to be more careful but worried it would only invite destruction.

When he finally finished examining the precious tomes, he turned his attention to the fireplace. The burning in her lungs alerted her that she'd stopped breathing. She inhaled as he examined the gray stones before bending to look into the hearth.

Rising, he slapped his hand on the mantle and walked back to her. His arm brushed hers as he swept past her, and Lexi turned back to the hall. Brokk remained in the doorway, but the scowl on his face deepened.

Sahira had taken a couple of steps toward the kitchen as drawers opened and shut in there. The bottles holding her potions rattled as large hands handled them, but nothing broke. Lexi suspected they were probably scared to break any of those bottles.

The head lycan reemerged from the direction of the kitchen and strode down the hall toward them. "We'll search the barn next."

"Of course," Lexi murmured, but her heart raced.

They hadn't found the passageway in the fireplace, but would they find the one in the barn? And if they spread out around the property, would they find the one in the shed?

Brokk stepped out of their way as the rest of the lycans filed out of her home. They descended the stairs and stalked toward the stable.

～

COLE DODGED another lava bomb and, throwing himself to the ground, rolled away from the fire that erupted when it hit the ground. Flames ate at his skin as he moved, but he had to keep going.

Launching himself to his feet, he dashed away when the cherufe lunged at him again. Its hands clacked together when it missed him. Spinning, Cole kicked out and caught the back of its rocky knee.

The thing didn't react to the blow, but fiery pain lanced up his leg as the bones in his foot fractured and the cherufe's fire burned him.

Shit!

He danced back again, but his broken foot slowed him. With no other options, he ignored the discomfort as he kept moving.

He darted, danced, and spun away as he steadily led the creature down the side of the mountain, through the flames, and toward the water. His flesh slid to the side as it started to slough off him and blisters covered what remained of his skin. Not even the sand was as agonizing as this, but he didn't stop.

Bombs erupted into the sky and whistled as they soared through the air. As they crashed around him, they churned up chunks of earth and splattered him with their fiery remnants.

The bits and pieces adhering to him sizzled as they burrowed through his muscle and embedded in his bones. The sweat pouring down his body and dripping off his chin sizzled when it hit the ground.

With an image of Lexi rooted firmly in his mind, he drew the creature onward. The ground quaked beneath its feet as it chased him, and when it charged again, Cole barely avoided being embraced in a fiery hug.

Finally, the flames gave way, and he spotted the pristine water of the lake once more. Even knowing what they did, Cole found it almost impossible to resist plunging into those cool waters and finding some relief for his crisp-fried body.

When the cherufe ran at him again, he stepped to the side. The creature didn't run into the water, but it got close enough that Cole, drawing on what little remained of his power, lifted a ball of water from the surface and flung it at the fiery beast.

The cherufe sizzled and popped as the water doused its flames. Before it could recover, Cole raced at the creature.

CHAPTER THIRTY-THREE

LEXI DIDN'T KNOW if she should follow the lycans out the door or remain inside. What would a completely innocent person do in this situation?

She got her answer when Brokk followed them out the door. Sahira went after him, and Lexi trailed them. She wanted to shove past them and bolt out to the barn to see what the lycans were doing, but she kept herself restrained enough to stroll behind the others.

Or at least she hoped she was strolling; that was the look she was going for anyway. She suspected she looked like a marionette and her puppet master was drunk.

She'd grown up here and was a simple person; she was not an immortal built for a life of crime and fighting.

But that's exactly what she was now, and she was going to have to figure out how to be a good criminal.

Lifting her chin, she resolved not to focus on her walk and to act completely normal. This was all in her head; she was perfectly fine. They didn't suspect a thing, or at least that's what she told herself, and she hoped she was right.

By the time she arrived at the barn, the lycans were already exiting it. Four of them climbed onto their mounts, but the leader hung back to speak with Brokk.

"I heard about your father," the man said.

Brokk stiffened, and hostility radiated from him. Sahira's eyebrows lifted as Lexi's gaze shot between the two men before shifting to the other lycans. These behemoths would take her down with ease, but she wouldn't let Brokk fight alone.

"King Tove was a good man," the lycan continued, and Brokk's hostility ebbed. The lycan pitched his voice low as he kept his gaze on his men. "And I'm sorry for your loss."

Lexi's shoulders relaxed as the lycan strode toward his mount. Grasping the reins, he swung himself onto his horse without touching the stirrups.

"It's only going to get worse," Sahira said when the riders were out of view. "The Lord has complete control over all the realms, and with the dragons on his side, there's no way to stop him."

"*Fucking* Orin," Brokk hissed.

"How many times do you think they'll come back?" Lexi asked.

"They won't stop until the Lord is convinced he's crushed the rebellion," Sahira said.

"He'll never be convinced of that," Lexi replied.

"No, he won't," Brokk said. "And even if he does crush it, he won't stop."

Before either of them could reply, he stalked away. Lexi started to follow him, but Sahira grasped her arm.

"Let him go," Sahira said.

Brokk stopped at the edge of the lake and stood gazing across the water. Lexi had no idea what to do for him or anyone else. She'd been lucky here today, but how long would that luck last?

~

LEXI PACED the confines of her room until she felt ready to scream. At 3:00 a.m., she wandered over to the window to gaze at the moon.

The bright, full orb lit the night sky as its rays cascaded across the land. Beneath its silvery glow, the world didn't look as devastated as it did in the daytime. It seemed almost peaceful. She yearned for looks not to be deceiving, but there was no changing the past.

Gazing at the moon reminded her of the time she'd stood in the moon room with Cole. The memory was so vivid she felt his breath on her nape as he introduced her to the four moons of the Gloaming.

She hadn't known what to make of him then, but he'd awakened something inside her that night, and it refused to be caged again. Then the memory of him vanished, and she was once again alone in her room. And she was colder than she'd ever been in her life.

What would she do if he didn't return?

Dropping her head into her hands, she rubbed her temples before turning away from the moon. She would survive without him; she had no other choice, but she would make a stand against the Lord.

She may not be a powerful immortal, but she would be another enemy of that madman. And if Cole died, she would find a way to make him pay for his death.

Turning away from the window, she retrieved her thick, white robe from where it lay on the end of her bed and left the room. Lexi had no idea where she was going as she descended the stairs, but she couldn't stay in her room.

Light filtered out of the library. She was usually the one awake and roaming around in the middle of the night, but when she stepped into the doorway, she spotted Brokk sitting in one of the chairs, staring at the fireplace. She stood uncertainly for a minute before padding toward him.

For a minute, she suspected he'd fallen asleep in the chair, but as she came around the side of it, she saw he was awake. *Harry Potter and the Order of the Phoenix* sat on his lap.

"Couldn't sleep?" he asked.

"No." She settled onto the cushion of her overstuffed love seat and tucked her feet beneath her. "You couldn't either?"

"No."

"He's been gone for over a week."

"For all we know, the trials could take a year."

"A year?" she squeaked.

"They won't. I'm pretty sure we would have heard if it took my father that long to complete them, but it could still be a while."

Though he spoke to her, he continued to stare straight ahead.

"Are you okay?" she asked.

A small smile curved his lips before he leaned back in the chair and relaxed a little. "Yeah, I'm fine."

"Do you have to feed?"

"I hunted a deer after the lycans left earlier."

"What about... what about... ah... you know the, ah... dark fae side of you?"

She fought the blush burning its way up her neck as she asked the question. She felt like an idiot for blushing over this conversation, but it wasn't one she wanted to have with him.

"I mean," she said, "I don't know about the dark fae... well, I *do* know about the dark fae, but I don't know about you since you're only half, but it's been a week... and... and...."

It took everything she had not to bolt from the room as Brokk grinned at her.

"And as a dark fae, I must be ready to go insane?" he asked.

Was her face on *fire?* It took all she had not to try to cover her burning cheeks.

"I'm fine," he assured her.

"If you have to... if you have to go somewhere for a little bit, we'll be fine here."

"I can control my deviant ways for a little longer."

His teasing only caused her to blush more, something she wouldn't have believed possible until her face burned hotter. Shifting her attention to the fireplace, she tried not to think about Orin down there.

She didn't have many friends, but she considered Brokk one, and she didn't want to lose him. For a second, the urge to tell him was so strong she almost blurted her secret, but she clamped her lips together.

She couldn't tell him before Cole. Cole was already going to be pretty pissed at her for this; if she spilled everything to Brokk first, he'd only feel more betrayed. No, her guilt was her penance, and she would have to live with it until she could unburden herself.

"Besides, Cole would kill me if I left you here unprotected," Brokk said.

"I'm sure he would understand. He is half dark fae himself."

"No, he wouldn't."

Lexi didn't argue with him, but they both knew he would eventually have to go somewhere for the dark fae to feed.

"How do you like the book?" she asked.

He shrugged and fiddled with the book's binding. "I haven't been able to pay much attention to it."

"You miss your father."

"I miss my whole family. I once had eight other brothers and my father. Now, it's just Cole and me."

She hadn't lost as much as Brokk and Cole during the war, but she knew what it was like to feel almost entirely alone in this world. Before Cole entered her life, she only had Sahira. And though she tried to remain optimistic he would survive the trials, she couldn't stop the niggling doubt festering in the back of her mind.

The war had already stripped so much from them; it couldn't take Cole too.

"He's coming back," she whispered.

"He is," Brokk said. "After my father, he is the most powerful being I know. He killed a dragon, Lexi. By himself and with no weapons. I've *never* heard of anyone accomplishing such a feat."

"He killed a dragon," she murmured more to herself than to him.

Right now, she needed the reminder.

"I know this is going to sound cliché, but your father does live on in you," she said. "He always will. My father lives on in me too. Sometimes, I open my mouth, and my dad comes out. One day, when I have children, the same thing will happen to them. Except, they'll think it's *me* coming out of them, but it's really my dad. It makes you wonder how many generations of our family, that we never met, influence our lives and actions."

When Brokk didn't say anything, the tick of the grandfather clock in the sitting room filled the silence. The passing of those seconds was a constant reminder of time marching steadily onward.

As an immortal, she still had plenty of time left to her, but she also resented those passing seconds. Each one of them was another second without her dad and Cole.

Each one of them was one more tick toward her forgetting more about her dad. And it would happen; she did not doubt it. No matter how many times she replayed her memories of him in her head, it was impossible to remember everything, and some of them were slipping away.

The memory that mattered most, the one of his unconditional, enduring love for her, would never fade. That love lived in the center of her soul and always would.

"It's an interesting concept," Brokk finally said. "Some of our habits could be those of a being who lived thousands of years before us, and we don't even know it."

"I like to think at least a few of our habits are. We may be immortal, but we can die, and this way, at least a part of us truly does live on forever."

"I had some insane ancestors then."

Lexi laughed and rested her head against the back of her chair. "Me too."

They fell into a companionable silence, and as she listened to the ticking clock, her eyes closed, and she finally slept.

CHAPTER THIRTY-FOUR

As HE RAN, Cole gathered the air rushing over his fingers and pulled it around him. The water had put out the cherufe's flames, but it hadn't dissolved the creature. It had taken time to kill Auberon. Unfortunately, Cole didn't have time.

He didn't dare touch the cherufe again as his broken foot continued to throb. Touching it might get him killed. Instead, he pushed the air ahead of him until it became a wall of pulsing, unseen fury building before him.

When the creature turned toward him, Cole lifted his hands and held them up in front of him as he pushed the air forward. He bellowed as the wall of air slammed into the creature. The impact lifted the cherufe and flung it backward.

It flew twenty feet into the lake and came up sputtering as its rocky arms slapped at the surface. It splashed its way forward but only made it five feet before it stopped. Without the flames in its eyes, its sockets were empty.

It remained frozen for nearly a minute before it started to howl. All around it, the water began to bubble and churn like a thousand piranhas were feasting on the most delicious meat they'd ever encountered.

The cherufe's arms flailed in the air, and its hands smashed the surface. It thrashed like it was trying to swim back to shore, but the more it flailed, the lower it sank in the water.

A side of its rocky face slumped downward before breaking away and splashing into the lake. When it lifted its hands to hit the surface again, they splintered apart on the downward swing. The broken fragments fell beneath the roiling water.

The cherufe's cries echoed across the lake until it finally fell silent. Bubbles and foam continued to disturb the pristine surface for a few minutes after the monster disappeared as the water continued to devour its prey.

Finally, when the lake quieted, Cole turned and hobbled a few feet away. When he did, he spotted Aelfdane emerging from a walkway the dark fae had created in the lake. The dark fae was a couple of hundred feet away, but when their eyes met, Cole knew this was it.

Aelfdane wasn't anywhere near as battered as him, but he hadn't been through the fires or battled a cherufe yet. And Cole was certain more of those lumbering beasts lurked within the fires.

He could turn and walk back into the fire and hope one of the remaining cherufes or the flames destroyed Aelfdane, but he wasn't one to rely on hope. Besides, Aelfdane wouldn't let him get away that easily. At least not while Cole was more battered than him.

Aelfdane bore the marks of the battle in the desert like Cole had. However, Cole suspected he'd also taken some time to rest as his wounds were healing.

Aelfdane would see him as an easy target right now as his flesh bubbled and popped; he still limped on his broken foot, and blood seeped down to coat his skin. Cole could slip into the flames and hope to lose the dark fae there, but he'd never walked away from a battle before, and he wasn't about to hide from this arrogant prick.

They stared at each other until Aelfdane smiled. At first, he sauntered toward Cole as if he had all the time in the world and was closing in on a guaranteed kill. But as he drew closer and Cole didn't move, Aelfdane charged across the distance separating them.

When the dark fae held his hands out at his sides, Cole knew Aelfdane intended to do exactly what he'd done to the cherufe he plunged into the water. After everything he'd endured, there was no way he was going in that lake.

Aelfdane was fifty feet away, and Cole felt the pulse of the air coming toward him when he knelt by the water's edge. He rested his fingers near the lake, and drawing on its power, he pulled forth some of the water.

It rose in a wave that hovered in front of him before he twisted his wrist and flipped his fingers at Aelfdane. The water whipped through the air and around the wall of air coming toward him.

With no other choice, Aelfdane had to spin toward the serpentine water and use the air he'd planned to hammer Cole with to deflect it away. Before Aelfdane could turn back toward him, Cole launched to his feet and, ignoring his throbbing foot, sprinted toward the dark fae.

He would tear this motherfucker apart and shove his broken arms up his ass before he finished with him. Aelfdane, and everyone else who stood in his way of Lexi and revenge, would meet the same deadly fate, and *nothing* was going to stop him.

When Aelfdane turned toward the wall of flames, he flicked his fingers, and a ball of fire launched at Cole. The flames crackled as the ball shot through the air like a comet across the sky.

Cole threw up his arms, but not in time to deflect the fire. It crashed into his forearms before spiraling away and crashing into the ground behind him. The flames left a hole in his forearm, but they also cauterized the wound, so no blood seeped free.

Lowering his arms, Cole sprinted at Aelfdane. The dark fae stumbled a step back before recovering. For some reason, he hadn't expected Cole to attack, and that underestimation of his opponent would be his downfall.

Aelfdane was starting to recover when Cole hit him. The pure dark fae weighed less than Cole and was not as seasoned in battle, but Aelfdane knew this was a fight to the death, which fueled his strength.

As they hit the ground, Aelfdane's fingers dug into Cole's cheeks and tore away chunks of skin. The blood spilling down his face splattered Aelfdane as Cole wrapped his hands around the dark fae's throat.

He pressed his thumbs up and under Aelfdane's chin and pushed up as he sought to tear his head from his shoulders. A lava bomb crashed into the ground only feet away. Bits of debris flew off and splattered them.

The burning remnants of the bomb seared through Cole's flesh as Aelfdane waved one of his hands through the air. A hammer of air hit Cole so hard in his back that his ribs cracked.

He thought his spine might have broken too, but he didn't lose feeling in his legs, and he could still move. If Aelfdane hit him like that again, he wouldn't continue to move for much longer.

Keeping hold of Aelfdane's throat, Cole flipped over, so Aelfdane was on top. Before the fae could recover, Cole rolled with him toward the water. It was a risky move; he could end up in the lake as easily as Aelfdane, but it was a chance Cole was willing to take.

Blood seeped around his fingers as they sank deeper into Aelfdane's throat. He rolled again as another fist of air hammered one of his legs. He was sure the blow was meant for his back or maybe his head, but his constant movement had thrown off Aelfdane's aim.

Still, he bit back a vicious curse as the blow wrenched his knee out of place. Pulling back his fist, he battered Aelfdane's face.

The dark fae's nose flattened beneath the impact, as did one of his cheeks. From the broken remnants of his face, Aelfdane's eyes bulged grotesquely, but it didn't slow the dark fae as more blows of air battered Cole.

They were near the edge of the water when another lava bomb crashed into the ground. It was so close it skimmed Cole's arm and tore away a chunk of sinew. The loss of muscle weakened his grip on Aelfdane, and the dark fae squirmed as he nearly broke free.

If Cole didn't do something soon, he could lose his battle. Unable to keep a firm hold on Aelfdane's neck, he bashed his forehead into Aelfdane's already shattered nose. The dark fae howled as his face caved in further and bits of his broken teeth fell to the ground.

Cole didn't let up as he slammed his forehead into Aelfdane again and again. Aelfdane's movements became more sluggish, and the next blast of air to hit Cole was little more than a glancing blow.

Gathering his strength, Cole fumbled to lift his nearly useless arm and grip Aelfdane's head. He seized the top of Aelfdane's skull and snapped his head to the side with his other hand. Cole gritted his teeth and twisted as Aelfdane battered him with his hands.

Despite the blows and Cole's weakness, cartilage and bone popped, muscle gave way, and he succeeded in tearing Aelfdane's head from his body. Cole slumped forward over the bloody remains before resting his good hand on the ground and pushing himself to his feet.

He swayed before steadying himself and bending to lift the head. His fingers slid through Aelfdane's black hair as he plucked it off the ground and limped toward the water.

He didn't look down at the head before tossing it into the lake. Then he returned for the body, and lifting it over his shoulder, he carried it to the water and threw it in. As it had done with the cherufe, the water churned and bubbled as it devoured the dark fae.

Cole watched until no ripples marked the water before limping back toward the fire. Using his hands, he deflected the flames away from him the best he could as he pushed through the inferno.

With no other choice and no other way to go, he started

climbing the closest volcano. As he climbed, he occasionally glimpsed shadowy figures moving through the fire and smoke, but none of them came after him again.

He didn't know if the cherufes left him alone because they were trying to avoid the same fate as the one he killed, or if it was because he'd successfully navigated the trials, but even the lava bombs stopped soaring.

When he arrived at the top of the volcano, he made his way around the rim. Smoke continued to billow from inside, and lava churned, bubbled, and popped from deep within the volcano's lethal pit, but he ignored it as he walked, and none of it soared up to hit him.

Once on the other side of the volcano, he discovered a wall of pure black waiting for him. When he glanced in either direction, more volcanoes decorated the burning land, but behind them, there was only this blackness.

Unsure of what lay ahead, and with no other way to go, Cole descended into the dark.

CHAPTER THIRTY-FIVE

As Cole traveled further through the darkness, he realized it wasn't darkness but a hive of shadows that drew apart before coalescing around him again. They slid over him and slipped into the countless wounds tearing apart his flesh.

Though they crept through his body like termites through walls, he didn't try to stop them. He'd always welcomed the shadows, they'd always been a part of him, and there was no way to avoid their entrance into his body.

He'd have to retreat to the volcanoes, and like with the desert, there was no turning back. This was another test, and he suspected it was one of trust as more of them entered his body and stopped him from walking.

If he resisted them, they would retreat, but if he welcomed them... he had no idea what would happen then, but he expected to find out.

Giving himself over to the shadows, he spread his arms out at his sides with his palms facing forward, tilted back his head, and opened his mouth. The second he did so, a cluster of shadows rose over the top of him. They hovered for a second before pouring into him.

Unlike the desert sand, the shadows didn't choke him or block his lungs as they spread throughout his body. They clogged his mouth, his chest, and his extremities, but he could still breathe while they worked on healing him from the inside.

It was the oddest sensation but one he welcomed as they dove into his muscles, entered his veins, and slid into his heart to pump through him with every beat. The shadows outside him encompassed his entire body.

He welcomed their embrace as they cooled what little remained of his burnt skin. The chunk of sinew the lava bomb cleaved from him stopped bleeding, and his blisters ceased oozing as new tissue formed over his tendons.

His ears reformed, and hair once again tickled his nape. The shadows rubbed against him, and the cool tendrils caressing his face healed his nose and returned his eyebrows. His unrelenting thirst finally eased as moisture filled his body once more.

They whispered secrets to him as they slid into his ears and wove their way across his brain. From their point of view, he saw the black seeping across his mind, burying itself in his synapses and becoming a part of him.

Their power swelled within him as they told him to keep their secret. What was happening here and what each trial entailed could never be revealed.

He was the sole guardian of the secrets they shared and would remain so until someone else succeeded in the trials, but unless he was already dead, they would still have to get through him.

He would *never* allow that to happen. These shadows were his, and so was the Gloaming. His enemies would have to tear it from his cold, dead fingers.

The shadows loosened their grip on him enough for him to start walking again. As he descended the hill, they continued to become a part of him.

Though he was always careful to keep most of his ciphers hidden, the shadows set them free. He looked down to discover all his ciphers on display. The black, flame-like markings had always covered him from head to toe, but with the shadows inside him, the ciphers pulsed and shifted with their power.

The swell of strength building inside him almost made him laugh from the rush of it, but there was no laughter to be found here. He'd become the guardian of something powerful and deadly, and he would take care of it.

Gradually, the shadows started pulling back. They retreated from his mind and slid out of his nose and mouth with every exhalation. As they exited the wounds they entered, the injuries closed, and most of his ciphers vanished. All that remained were the ones he always kept on display.

While he walked, the shadows continued to move around and embrace him, but they'd stopped entering him. They didn't have to. He'd passed the final test, and soon he would be free of this place, but he would never be free of the power that thrived here.

He'd always been a part of the shadows, but now *they* were also a part of *him*.

CHAPTER THIRTY-SIX

COLE WAS ALMOST to the bottom of the hill when the darkness eased and the shadows finally gave way. He emerged onto a rocky plane similar to the one he stood on before entering the tunnel.

And when he glanced to his right, he saw the tunnel opening. He'd somehow managed to come full circle, and the remaining members of the council were there to greet him. The five of them stood before the open portal to the Gloaming.

His Gloaming now.

He didn't bother to shield his nudity as he walked toward them. He'd never cared about nudity before; he cared less now.

"Have you all been standing here, waiting this whole time?" he asked them.

"No," Elvin replied. "We have taken turns keeping watch. I sent back word something was happening when the volcanoes stopped erupting."

When Cole looked over the tunnel, he saw that the volcanoes had stopped spewing smoke and lava.

"Where are the others?" Durin asked.

"Are you going to pretend to be concerned about your son now?" Cole inquired.

Durin's jaw clenched, but he wisely kept his mouth shut.

"Eoghan didn't survive the tunnel," he shot a pointed look at Alston, who had the sense to find his feet fascinating. "Your son, Auberon, screamed as he died an excruciating death," Cole said to Durin. "And *I* killed Aelfdane."

They exchanged looks as he let his revelations sink in. When they looked to him again, he saw the wariness in their eyes.

"I am your king," he stated. "And if one or *all* of you intend to fight me on it, then I'll kill you too."

"That's not necessary," Elvin said. "You have survived the trials and, as the law dictates, have earned the throne. But more than that, the trials have proven you are strong enough to protect the Gloaming."

Durin made a sound that caused Cole's eyes to narrow on him, but the coward wouldn't look at him. One day, Cole would make him pay, but today was not the day.

Even with all his newfound power coursing through him and the backing of the dark fae throne behind him, he still needed the council on his side. They held a lot of sway over the dark fae realm.

"Yes, you are," Becca purred.

She seemed to have forgotten her irritation with him as she lustfully eyed his body. When Cole scowled at her, she smiled. Becca was something he would also deal with later, but all he wanted now was to return home to Lexi.

She had to be worried about him, and not only did he need to ease her apprehension, but he also had to hold her. He missed the feel of her in his arms more than he'd missed water while in the desert.

"I expect all of you to meet me in the palace in one hour," he said. "We have much to discuss."

"Of course," Finn murmured.

He didn't look back at them as he strode toward the portal and entered it. He would never look back on the trials or the realm that nearly destroyed him.

It was time to move on to a throne he never wanted but would fight to the death to protect.

As he stalked through the portal, the shadows twisted around him, and he felt their movement in his soul. He wasn't sure he would ever get used to the strange sensation, but he welcomed it.

When he emerged from the portal, he was only fifty feet away from the palace gates. A crow cawed as it soared toward one of the open palace windows and slipped inside. As soon as he got inside, he would send crows to Lexi and Brokk.

He hoped she would agree to join him here for a little while. He would have preferred to go to her, but he couldn't leave until he secured the throne.

Grasping one of the gates, Cole felt the familiar warmth beneath his hand as it recognized him before opening. He ignored the rotting dragon's head and Sindri's body as he strolled through the gate.

For the first time in years, he admired the palace as he stopped. Its endless rooms and numerous mysteries had always fascinated him, but sometime over his many years here, he stopped appreciating it as much.

He didn't make that mistake again today. This towering, magical structure with a personality all its own was *his* now, and he would make sure the palace deemed him worthy of such a claim.

These fae, moving about the inner courtyard, going about their lives, were his to rule and protect now. Like the palace, he would make sure they also deemed him worthy.

He would not always be kind, he would not tolerate disobedience, but he would be just and fair. And he would fight and die for them if it became necessary.

This was his land, these were his people, and he was glad to be their king.

Taking a deep breath, he smiled as he examined the buildings and the fae before walking up the stairs to the palace. One of the double doors swung open before he reached it, but as he entered the hall beyond, he discovered no one there.

Then the helot Adham emerged from one of the hallways.

"Milord!" he greeted as he rushed toward Cole. He came to a stop a few feet away. "Milord... Your Highness. You've returned."

"I've returned," Cole said. "How long was I gone?"

"Ten days."

Ten days of pure, unadulterated hell.

"It is good to see you," Adham said as he fell into step beside Cole.

"You too, Adham. I need some paper, a pen, and two crows. When that is done, I want any members of the council who have taken up residence here removed."

"No one has moved in, milord."

Adham stared at the door like a dog at a bone.

"The council didn't try to move in?" Cole asked.

"They tried, but they were unsuccessful."

Cole had intended for the crows to be the first thing he did, but those words caused him to stop and face Adham. "Explain."

The helot stopped in front of him. "Your entrance through the doors was the first time they've opened since you and master Brokk left."

Cole gazed around the hall before chuckling. "I love this place."

CHAPTER THIRTY-SEVEN

LEXI WAS in the middle of sparring with Brokk when the loud caw of a crow pierced the day. She stopped so abruptly that she never saw Brokk's next move until he swept her feet out from under her and her ass hit the ground.

Despite having the air knocked out of her and an aching tailbone, she gazed hopefully at the sky as the crow soared toward them. Her hands flattened on the ground, her heart hammered, and her mouth went dry in anticipation.

But there was only one crow, and as it swooped toward Brokk, her hope shriveled. No one from the dark fae realm would write to tell her if Cole died, but they *would* send a note to Brokk.

And Cole wouldn't write to Brokk and not her, would he?

He was new to this whole relationship thing; he might not understand she was desperate to hear from him too. She had to believe that was what happened, and it wasn't a notice of Cole's death heading toward Brokk.

Or maybe a friend was sending a note to Brokk. Why was she instantly jumping to Cole? Brokk was a dark fae prince; of course, someone from the Gloaming would seek to communicate with him.

Then why was she still unable to breathe? She sucked in a

breath as the crow landed on Brokk's shoulder and released the note into his waiting hands. The bird flew off as another crow swooped out of the trees and soared toward her.

An unexpected sob escaped Lexi as the bird landed on her shoulder. Its beautiful black eyes surveyed her before it dropped the note in her hand and brushed its head against her cheek. The soothing caress caused a tear to slide down her face as she rubbed the bird's head in unspoken thanks.

It released a small caw before spreading its wings and flying away. Lexi snatched the paper up and almost tore it as she unfolded it. The tears in her eyes caused the words to blur, and she had to blink them into focus.

I'm back. I cannot leave the Gloaming right now. Please join me here.

Love, Cole.

Her tears landed on the paper before she clutched it against her chest and sobbed. All this time, she tried to maintain the faith he would return, but each passing day and every endless night had eroded some of her faith.

And now, he was back, and he wanted her with him.

She didn't realize Brokk was kneeling at her side until he rested his hand on her shoulder. "I'll take you now," he said.

Unable to form words, she simply nodded as joy filled her to the point of bursting. Cole was alive!

She hadn't realized what an emotional mess these past ten days had made her until she couldn't suppress her sobs while Brokk helped her rise. When she lifted her eyes to his, he grinned at her.

"You're a mess," he said.

Lexi laughed as her tears continued to fall. "I am! But I'm so happy. I have to tell Sahira about this."

Despite the tears blurring her vision, she ran toward the manor to tell Sahira the good news.

CHAPTER THIRTY-EIGHT

LEXI TOOK A QUICK SHOWER, packed a small bag of supplies, made an excuse to see the horses, and went out to the barn. She pushed open the barn door and stepped into the shadowed interior.

Though the sun still shone, it was near nightfall, and she'd brought the horses in before she started sparring with Brokk. Two of them had already been removed from their stalls and saddled to ride to the Gloaming portal. She was impatient to get to the Gloaming, but Brokk preferred to ride to the portal rather than open one.

Small bangs and crunches filled the barn as the horses pulled hay from their feedbags. She entered the feed room, collected a handful of carrots, and strolled out again.

As she moved down the row of stalls, they poked their heads out to greet her. She patted each of the horses on the neck and gave them a carrot while she searched the shadows.

Once convinced no one was around, she poked her head out the door. Brokk and Sahira stood by the stairs of the manor, waiting for her, but they were staring at the road while they talked.

She only had a few minutes at most to get this done. Ducking back inside, she rushed into the feed room, moved aside a couple of bags of feed, and exposed the trapdoor securely hidden in the floor there.

She lifted it only far enough to slip a piece of paper inside. On that paper, she'd hastily scrawled, Cole has returned. I'm going to the Gloaming. I will return soon.

She covered the trapdoor again, wiped her hands on her jeans, and left the room. "Goodbye, girls and boys," she called to the horses. "I love you, and I'll be back soon."

The sound of them munching on their hay was her only response. At the barn door, she glanced back, but they were all busy eating their dinner. George would come to help with them, but Lexi still hated to say goodbye.

Apprehension gnawed at Lexi's gut as she approached her aunt. She wouldn't stay in the Gloaming long; she couldn't leave Sahira here alone and clueless about Orin's whereabouts, but she had to see Cole.

Sahira and Brokk turned toward her. Her aunt gave a wan smile as she opened her arms to Lexi. She wasn't Cole's biggest fan, but Sahira had jumped for joy and clapped her hands when Lexi delivered word of his survival.

They'd danced around the kitchen together as they hugged each other. Now, some of that joy had faded from Sahira.

"Please come with us," Lexi said as they embraced.

"I can't," Sahira said. "I have potions to make, and I promised to deliver them to Eliza tomorrow. We can't turn that money down."

Lexi hated the idea of leaving her here alone. However, Sahira was right, they needed the money from her potions.

The newly forming marketplace was off to a slow start. It wasn't easy to get immortals and humans to sell and shop there when dragons leveled the last marketplace.

Eliza, a witch who had decided to try her hand at making money in the human world, was eager to get a vast array of supplies into her shop. She was determined to become the place all immortals and humans went to when they needed something.

Because of that, she wanted a lot of goods available and had agreed to sell some of Sahira's potions. Sahira was excited to bring more income into their home. They could certainly use it.

"I won't be gone long," Lexi said.

Sahira grasped Lexi's hands and squeezed them. "If you think you'll be gone for more than a few days, contact me. I'll join you then."

Lexi didn't think she'd be gone for that long. Under normal conditions, she wouldn't be in a rush to return, but these weren't normal conditions. There was far too much that could go wrong here for her to stay away.

"I'll contact you," Lexi promised. "And Brokk will leave a crow here in case you have to contact us. If Malakai or the Lord's men return, let me know right away."

"Don't worry about either of those things. I'll take care of everything. Make sure you have your birth control," Sahira said.

"Sahira," she hissed, and Brokk chuckled.

Lexi's face burned. Damn it, one of these days she would stop blushing so easily!

Sahira laughed. "Did you remember to pack it?"

"Yes," Lexi muttered.

"Good."

"I love you," Lexi whispered as she embraced her aunt again.

"I love you too. Be careful."

"You too."

Lexi reluctantly released Sahira, lifted her bag of supplies from where she'd left it on the ground, and turned to Brokk.

"Are you ready?" he asked.

"Yes."

A leaden weight settled in the pit of her stomach as she walked away from her aunt. *She'll be okay, and you'll be home soon.*

Lexi slipped her bag onto her back, grabbed the reins of her horse, and swung herself onto its back. Brokk climbed onto his mount and turned his horse in the direction of the closest Gloaming portal.

Brokk had assured her the horses would be safe in the Gloaming. Otherwise, she would have insisted on walking. She couldn't wait to see Cole, but she wouldn't risk the animals' lives.

The ride to the portal only took twenty minutes, but it seemed to take forever. When she followed Brokk into the shifting darkness, the shadows enveloped her, and her heart raced with excitement and trepidation.

During the ride, she'd had far too much time to think. And thinking was not a good thing as it resulted in far too much anxiety. She had no idea what Cole endured during the trials, if they had changed him, or what would be expected of him once he became king.

She doubted the dark fae would be thrilled to know about her existence. She doubted they would embrace the idea of their half-breed king having a half-human mate. And she already knew Becca hated her.

It was another problem to heap onto her growing list of them.

When they emerged from the portal and into the Gloaming, some of Lexi's tension eased when she spotted the palace in the distance. She had no idea what the future held for them, but Cole was in the palace, waiting for her, and knowing that eased all her other anxieties.

As they rode toward the colossal structure, she couldn't stop herself from being awed by it. She suspected she could spend the rest of her life here and still be amazed every time she looked upon the sprawling spectacle with its peaked towers, dark façade, and spiked fence surrounding it.

As they drew closer, the dragon head drew her eyes. It was huge, and the monstrous beast had teeth that could squash a car. Still, she couldn't stop a twinge of pity for it.

Once inside the palace gates, they dismounted. When a dark

fae boy slipped from the shadows, she jumped a little, but Brokk didn't react.

"Take the horses to the stables," Brokk commanded the child. "And make sure they're taken care of."

"Yes, milord," the boy murmured as he took the horses' reins.

Lexi watched him lead the horses away before she shifted her attention to the palace doors. Despite her excitement to see Cole, apprehension built inside her.

What would he be like after the trials? Had they changed him? She loved him, but what would become of *them*? Would the dark fae accept him as their king?

"Come on," Brokk said.

Lexi followed him up the stairs. Before they reached the doors, one of them opened to reveal a beautiful dark fae woman on the other side. The woman bowed her head to Brokk before turning to stare questioningly at Lexi.

"Where's my brother?" Brokk inquired.

"He's meeting with the council in the great hall," the woman replied. "I'll let him know you're here."

"No," Brokk said. "Don't disrupt them. We'll wait."

"As you wish, milord," the woman demurred before slipping away.

Lexi gazed longingly at the entrance of the great hall. She was impatient to see Cole again, but she wanted nothing to do with that council.

CHAPTER THIRTY-NINE

"WE WILL HAVE the memorial for my father tomorrow," Cole stated.

He rested the tips of his fingers on the table and studied the remaining council members. After sending the crows to Lexi and Brokk, he'd taken the time to shower, eat, and dress before meeting with them in the hall.

"There may not be a body, but the residents of the Gloaming should have a chance to say goodbye to him. I will take care of the details," Cole continued.

"As you command, milord," Elvin said.

"My coronation will be the following day."

"Why so soon afterward?" Finn asked.

"The Lord threatened to destroy the Gloaming if I do not ascend to the throne. I don't think there's any reason to make him wait."

"And what do you plan to do about the Lord?" Alston asked.

"What do you mean?"

"He killed our king," Becca said. "He must pay for that."

"And how do you propose to make him pay?" Cole asked.

"Many of the dark fae fought on his side during the war. Some split off to join the rebellion, but we lost a lot of our soldiers during the war. We don't have the forces to fight him… or the allies. Besides, our loyalty lies with the Lord."

Cole didn't care about any of that. However, he didn't trust anyone at this table not to run back to the Lord and reveal everything he said here. They might act like they were eager to avenge his father's death, but that didn't mean it was true.

"He killed our king," Durin said.

"And he'll kill all of us too if we try to go against him, and I will not allow the dark fae to suffer any more than they already have."

A couple of them exchanged a look while Becca batted her eyes like a teenager on her first date.

"There are many in the Gloaming who want revenge for our king's death," Finn said. "Tove was beloved in this land."

"And I bet every single one of them would prefer to live," Cole said. "And unless they want to unleash the wrath of the dragons on this land, they will accept that my father is dead, and we must move on."

Alston scowled at him, but Elvin teepeed his fingers and rested his chin on them. His black eyes shone in the sputtering torchlight. He looked about to say something but refrained from speaking.

"The dark fae seek vengeance when wronged," Alston said.

Cole's flesh rippled as he gazed at the man. Alston was correct, and not declaring his goal to avenge his father's death would make him appear weak and could create a rebellion, but if he *did* announce those intentions, the Lord would unleash his dragons on the realm.

He was sure the Lord was well aware of the situation he'd placed Cole in when he killed his father and commanded Cole to take the throne. The almost certain infighting to follow was one more way for the man to maintain his control.

The dark fae could not turn on the Lord when they were too busy turning on each other. Cole would do his best to avoid such a fate, but it was going to take him time to learn who he could and could not trust in this realm to help him form a rebellion against the Lord.

"We will not be seeking vengeance this time, but you are free to start your own rebellion. I'll let the Lord deal with you. And I'm sure he'll be glad to feed more of us to his dragons."

Alston paled visibly and pulled his hands off the table to rest them in his lap.

"We will hunt down the traitors, and we will destroy them," Cole continued. "That is why the Lord killed my father, so we will get our revenge for his death by destroying those who deserve it."

"You plan to destroy your brothers?" Becca inquired.

"Yes," Cole said.

The hideousness of that word burnt his throat as the lust in Becca's eyes deepened. He hadn't believed it was possible, but she repulsed him more every time they encountered each other.

He opened his mouth to speak again, but a current running through the palace walls stopped him. Cole leaned heavily on his fingers and frowned at the strange sensation. He'd spent his entire life inside these walls and never experienced anything like it.

It was as if the palace was... happy?

But how was that possible? And how could he feel it?

And then the faint scent of strawberries drifted to him, and his heart lurched. *Lexi* was here, and the palace was happy about her presence, or Brokk's return, or maybe both.

This strange connection he felt to these walls was a little disturbing but also exciting. It must be some new ability from the trials. Had his father experienced this?

If he had, he'd never mentioned it, but then, he wouldn't. Like all dark fae, he'd kept many of his abilities hidden. It was the best way to stay alive in this world where friends and sons could become enemies, and one small misstep might destroy you.

It was possible his father never felt this connection to the palace after the trials. Unlike Cole, Tove didn't grow up in the palace. Cole was born here; it had always been his home, and he'd always felt bonded to it.

Tove moved in after surviving the trials. He'd claimed the throne, but had the palace claimed him too?

Like many of the other secrets the palace held, Cole doubted he'd ever get the answer to his questions. He felt the connection now, and that was what mattered.

Despite this new, deeper connection, there were still rooms here that wouldn't open to him. Curious to see if the locked rooms would grant access to the new king, he'd tried a couple of them when he returned. The doors refused to yield their secrets.

Maybe some of those locked rooms would open to him now, but he could spend a lifetime trying all the doors here and still never know. When a new ripple went through the walls, Cole stepped away from the table and strode toward the hall.

CHAPTER FORTY

"ARE WE DONE HERE?" Durin inquired.

"No," Cole said. "Stay where you are."

Upon returning to the Gloaming, he'd dressed in the normal attire of the dark fae. The soft leather of his boots was silent against the floor as his pace increased.

Lexi is here!

When he entered the hall, he spotted her and Brokk by the double doors at the end. In the flicker of the torches lining the walls, her hair shone and shimmered with color. The torch flames emphasized the smattering of freckles on her sun-kissed skin and her striking beauty.

They also emphasized the dark circles under her eyes. She hadn't been sleeping well.

Because of me.

He wanted to tell her she would never have to worry again, but he couldn't lie to her. Things were *not* going to get easier now that he was king.

Seeing her was like a punch to the gut, and for a second, he couldn't breathe as he simply stood and drank her in. He would gladly endure a hundred more trials to have her by his side.

When Lexi spotted him, her mouth parted, and she took a few stumbling steps forward before catching herself and stopping. As if afraid someone had seen her, she glanced nervously around.

He didn't care who saw them or what they thought about his relationship with her. Striding toward her, Cole opened his arms wide. She released a small cry before bolting past Brokk and closing the distance between them.

Her bag fell from her shoulders a second before she flung herself into his arms. Cole crushed her against him and lifted her off the ground. Her sweet scent enveloped him as his fingers threaded through her silken hair to grasp the back of her head.

Relief descended, and the lycan within him stirred. During the trials, he repressed the lycan part of himself, but it had made its demands for its mate known since returning to the Gloaming.

He cradled her face in the hollow of his shoulder. When her tears wet his neck, he pulled back to gaze down at her. The water glistening in her enchanting green eyes made them shine brighter.

"Don't cry," he told her.

"I can't help it." She clasped his face between her palms and rested her forehead against his. "I'm so happy. I knew you would survive, but… but… I was so scared."

"There's no reason to be scared now. I'm back."

More tears slid down her cheeks as she grinned at him. "You're back."

When he claimed her mouth, the kiss quieted the lycan as the heat of her scorched him to the center of his soul. The taste of her was sweetly familiar and all the more exciting because of it.

Each time he kissed her was as exciting as the first time. She made him feel like he was drowning and she was his safe harbor. Every time their mouths touched, he lost a piece of himself to her, and he didn't care.

As their tongues entwined and his cock hardened, he knew he should break away, but he couldn't bring himself to part with her yet. He was ravenous; both the dark fae and lycan were clamoring to be sated, and she was the only one who could do it.

It was only the fact they were out in the open, with his brother somewhere nearby, that stopped him from taking her. There was a time when he wouldn't have cared who or how many others watched him with a woman, but *no* one, other than him, would ever see or hear *her* in such a way.

Reluctantly, he broke away from her. Her dazed eyes blinked up at him as she searched his. Her swollen lips were far too enticing; he had to set her down, or he would finish what he started.

He stepped a little away from her but couldn't bring himself to release her completely. He kept a hand at the small of her back as he held her against his side.

"Are you okay?" she whispered.

"Yes."

Her brow furrowed as she studied him, but she didn't push him any further.

"Are *you* okay?" he asked.

"I'm fine," she assured him.

"Were there any problems at the manor?"

"Some of the Lord's men came to search it, but they didn't cause any problems."

Her words caused his skin to prickle. Did the Lord already know about her? It was only a matter of time. And once the Lord learned of her, her life would be in a lot more danger.

"Why did they search it?" he asked.

"They're searching all the residences for rebels, but we know who they're really after," Brokk answered.

Cole scowled. "Orin and Varo."

"Yes."

"They really didn't cause any problems?"

"No." Lexi rested her hand on his arm. "They were fine, and they didn't stay long. Everything else was quiet."

Cole glanced at Brokk. His brother's face didn't reveal

anything, but the set of his jaw said he wasn't thrilled by the experience.

"Is there anything else I should know?" Cole asked.

"I asked Brokk to teach me how to fight," Lexi said.

"And did he?"

"We're working on it," Brokk said. "But she shows promise and has improved."

"Good," Cole stated. "That's something we'll continue to work on."

Lexi grinned at him.

"I have to finish with the council," he told her. "I'll be back soon."

"We'll be here."

He kissed her cheek and started to turn away before stopping. Between his imprisonment in the Lord's tower and the trials, they'd been away far too often. He didn't want to leave her so soon after finally holding her again.

He'd intended to keep the knowledge of what she was to him a secret from others for longer, but he wanted her by his side for the memorial service and his coronation. The dark fae wouldn't be thrilled to learn his mate wasn't one of them, but they would have to accept it.

He held his hand out to her. "Come with me."

She stared at his hand before shifting her gaze to the hall behind him. "They don't want me in there."

"They're going to have to get used to seeing you by my side. Besides, we're not discussing anything that others can't hear. We're finalizing the details of my father's memorial and my coronation. You can be there for that."

She wrung her hands before her. "I'm happy to wait here."

"I want you with me."

CHAPTER FORTY-ONE

LEXI STARED at Cole's hand as those words sank in. He wanted her with him.

As much as she'd prefer *not* to see the council, and especially Becca again, she couldn't say no to that. He looked much the same as he had before he left. His face was thinner, and his clothes were baggier, but she didn't see so much as a scratch on him.

She sensed looks were extremely deceiving as the tiredness in his eyes wasn't there before. Those eyes also held a knowledge that spoke of things she couldn't imagine. New lines marked them, and there was a pinched set to his mouth.

He also emanated a *lot* more power.

He'd always been one of the most powerful beings she'd ever encountered; she'd sensed that from their first encounter, but there was so much more here now.

The strength of his newfound power caused the hair on her arms to rise and left a metallic taste in her mouth. When she first met the dark fae king, she'd sensed Tove's power, and at the time, it was more than Cole's.

That wasn't true anymore, and this was so much *more* than Tove once possessed.

She didn't know if it was because this power was still so new in Cole or if surviving the trials somehow caused it to manifest stronger in him than in his father. She didn't know how that was possible.

Did the others sense it as well?

They must. The beings in this palace were full-blooded immortals, whereas she wasn't. If she felt it this strongly, then what did it feel like to them?

Goose bumps broke out on Lexi's arms as she pondered this. And if they sensed it more strongly than her, would it make it so they wouldn't fuck with him, or would they see him as a challenge to take down?

Either way, she would be by his side, fighting for him.

She slipped her hand into his and squeezed it as she sought to convey her love to him. The dark fae intimidated—no, she couldn't lie to herself, they unnerved her, and she did *not* want to see Becca again, but she would stand by his side… for as long as he would have her there.

He might change his mind when he learned about Orin. Until then, she would do everything she could for him.

"You should come too," Cole said to Brokk.

Brokk fell in to walk on the other side of Cole. They entered the great hall together. The first time Lexi was here, it was packed with immortals and lit up with a beautiful night sky of shifting constellations.

Now, the dome-shaped ceiling was completely black, and only the torches on the walls lit the room. She suspected the night sky wouldn't return until the mourning period for King Tove was over.

The dark fae at the table watched their approach with a mixture of curiosity and confusion. Becca looked like a cat sharpening its claws as she eyed Lexi like she was a goldfish in a bowl.

When Cole stopped at the head of the table, she expected him to release her hand, but he kept it.

"You all know my brother, Brokk," Cole said. "And I'd like for you to meet Elexiandra Harper."

The council members exchanged a look.

"You'll be seeing her often around the palace," Cole continued.

The man with the dark brown skin rose and bowed his head before extending his hand to her. "It is a pleasure to meet you, Ms. Harper. I am Elvin."

She clasped his fine-boned hand, and he gave it a small squeeze before releasing her. The other men at the table rose and introduced themselves, but they didn't extend their hands to her. Becca remained seated.

When Elvin turned toward her, Becca crossed her legs and kicked her foot as she twirled a strand of hair.

"I've already met the half human," Becca said.

They lifted their eyebrows, and Cole glared at Becca. She ignored him.

"We will start my father's memorial service at noon tomorrow," Cole stated. "It will be a subdued affair as will my coronation, which will be the following day. I will invite all of the Gloaming to attend both events," Cole said.

"We'll make sure to spread the word," Elvin said.

Lexi couldn't decide if she liked him or not. The others were openly disapproving of her, but he took her presence here well. Was it too well? Was he as helpful as he seemed, or was it all a ruse?

"What about Aelfdane's seat at the table?" Durin asked.

"He had no children," Alston said.

"His brother can take it, and if he decides he doesn't want it, then it will remain empty until we can agree on a suitable replacement," Cole said. "That is enough for tonight."

Having been dismissed, the dark fae rose from their chairs. Most of them wouldn't look at her, but Elvin didn't hide his curiosity. She met and held his black eyes as he studied her.

"Until tomorrow then, milord," Alston murmured before turning and walking out of the room.

When the others followed, no one spoke again until the sound of the front door closing drifted down the hall.

"Can you have the servants ready the hall for the memorial tomorrow, Brokk?" Cole asked.

"Yes," Brokk replied.

"We'll have a glass coffin and place some of father's things inside."

"I'll have them take care of it."

"Thank you."

"I'll see you in the morning."

With that, Brokk walked away. He slipped out the double doors and into the hall. Left alone with Cole, Lexi didn't know what to say or do. It had been a while since she felt shy or uncertain around him, but he was different from the Cole who left her, and she wasn't sure what to make of him.

Cole clasped her chin and lifted her face to him. "Will you stay here, with me, for the next couple of days?"

"Will that cause problems for you?"

"No."

"Cole, these are your followers, and you're going to need their support. If I'm going to be a problem—"

"You're my mate, which means you will *never* be a problem. They will have to get used to seeing you by my side because that is where you belong."

The vibrant, Persian blue of his eyes held her captive as she stared into their penetrating depths. "I'll always be here for you, but don't put yourself at risk for me."

"I would die for you, Elexiandra; do not doubt that."

His words stole her breath. She knew she was in love with him, but right then, the depth of her love for him hit her like a punch to the gut.

"I'll stay," she whispered.
He smiled before kissing her.

CHAPTER FORTY-TWO

ONCE MORE GROWING AROUSED by her kiss, Cole pulled away before he lost himself to her. "Come with me," he said.

Taking her hand, he led her out of the room and into the main hallway. Her hand was the perfect fit in his, and as his thumb stroked her silken skin, his cock swelled.

He needed to touch her and taste her. He had to be inside her as he listened to her sounds of ecstasy while she moved against him.

Walking became more difficult, and before they made it to the stairs, he drew her into the shadows, turned her into the wall, and threaded his fingers through her hair. When her head tipped back, her lips parted, and she gazed breathlessly up at him.

She was a beautiful temptation he could no more resist than the tides on earth could resist the moon. Bending, he kissed her as he pinned her against the wall.

When his tongue claimed her mouth, the taste of her seared itself onto him. That sweet taste burned away the lingering fire and sand still clinging to his tastebuds. It pushed the memory of the trials from his mind as she became the only thing he could sense and feel.

He settled his other hand on her hip and slid it around to slip it under her shirt. He rested his palm against the small of her back; her breath caught when his erection pressed into her belly.

Sliding his hand up her back, he slid it around to brush against the bottom of her lacy bra. Normally, she wore simple undergarments.

He craved seeing and touching more of her, but though they were alone, he wouldn't take her in this hallway. Not when there was a chance someone might come across them.

Retracting his hand from her shirt, he kept the other firmly on her hip as he stretched a hand to his right. His finger fumbled over the door before seizing the handle. He twisted the knob and pushed the door open. Lifting her, he carried her into the room and kicked the door shut behind them.

Setting her down, he released her to lock the door. When he turned back, the spectacle of a dozen moons shining back at him froze his hand in the air between them.

As he gazed at those moons reflecting all around them, he realized what room he'd entered. He smiled, and excitement thundered through his veins at all the delicious possibilities. He couldn't have planned this more perfectly if he'd tried.

He couldn't recall the last time he entered this room; it had to have been hundreds of years ago. Until tonight, he'd forgotten about its existence.

He would never forget again as he planned to use it to watch as he teased her until she climaxed. And he would drink in her reaction to everything he did in all the mirrors lining the walls.

Through the skylights in the ceiling, two of the four moons of the Gloaming, Orius and Carpton, hung heavily in the sky. They were the source of the moons reflecting all around him.

"What is this place?" Lexi whispered as she stepped away from him.

"A dance studio a past king built for his wife," Cole said.

Resting his hands on her hips, he pulled her a step closer as she gazed at the mirrors in awe. The multiple reflections of the moons made the room nearly as bright as day. Their silvery glow shone in her hair and eyes as her attention returned to him.

"It's beautiful," she murmured.

"Yes," he said, but he wasn't talking about the room.

When she ducked her head, a slight blush colored her cheeks before she glanced at him from under the thick fringe of her sweeping, black lashes. Moving his hands up her sides, his fingers grazed her as he lifted her black shirt.

Lexi's arms rose, and he tugged the shirt over her head before tossing it aside. His mouth watered when he caught sight of her red, lacy bra.

He traced the sexy pattern that revealed hints of her creamy skin through the delicate material. "Is this new?"

"It is," she confirmed. "I bought it from a witch in the marketplace."

"And what were you thinking about when you bought it?"

"You."

He smiled as his hands fell to the button of her jeans. "And what were you thinking about me?"

"That I hoped you'd like it. So, do you?"

"Oh, I do. And what do you have under here?" He gave the waistband of her jeans a small tug.

"You're going to have to take them off to find out."

The sexy smile she gave him caused his already hardened dick to swell further. He loved her growing confidence around him and found it sexy as hell.

"I guess I will," he said.

He reclaimed her mouth and nipped at her lip as he slid the button on her jeans free. She kicked off her sneakers as he tugged the jeans down her hips.

Breaking the kiss, he leaned back and smiled when he discovered her lacy red underwear matched the bra. He knelt before her and pulled her jeans down over her feet. He tossed aside her socks and clasped her thighs as he drank in the enticing curves of her slender body.

It took everything he had to resist the water during the trials, but he could never resist her.

"You are the sexiest woman I've ever seen," he said. "I could stare at you for hours."

Sliding his other hand up the inside of her thigh, he nudged her legs further apart before his fingers slipped inside her underwear. She trembled as she rested her hands on his shoulders.

He spread her wetness with his fingers before leisurely teasing her clit. He relished the familiar way her body reacted to his touch.

She was made for him; he did not doubt it. She was his, he was hers, and he would possess her in every way possible.

The lycan prowled beneath the surface as it sought to claim its mate while the ravenous dark fae part of him clamored to be sated. He teased her until her hips swayed into his touch and her head fell back.

Her auburn hair grazed the tips of his fingers as her breath came faster. Everything inside him demanded he take her, but he couldn't stop watching as she rode his hand. Her nipples stood against the lace as her fingers dug into his shoulders.

Then, with a cry that rebounded off the mirrors, she came. He pulled his hand slowly away from her. Claws extended from the tips of his fingers, and he sliced her underwear. It fell to the floor in a whisper of cloth before he clasped her ass with his hands and drew her close.

The muscles of her sheath were still contracting from her orgasm when he placed his mouth against her. She tasted as good as she smelled, and though she'd been coming down from her climax, he pushed her back over the edge as he greedily fucked her with his tongue.

The tremors from her second orgasm were still shaking her when he rose. Unable to resist her any longer, he yanked off his shirt before kicking aside his boots.

He undressed faster than he ever had in his life. Despite his growing need to be inside her, when she reached for him, he grasped her hands and turned her around.

He unclasped the bra and tossed it aside before guiding her toward the mirrors. At the wall of glass, he placed her hands on the bar lining the mirrors as he stepped behind her.

In the glass, her eyes were a deeper, more vibrant shade of green when they met his.

CHAPTER FORTY-THREE

LEXI COULDN'T TEAR her eyes away from Cole's silver ones reflecting at her in the mirror. Did he realize how much his control had slipped?

Even if he didn't, she did as those silver eyes glowed like a fire burned behind them and his claws skimmed up her belly and between her breasts. When he loosely clasped her throat, she sensed the possessive lycan beneath his surface.

He pulled her head back and whispered in her ear, "You're mine, Elexiandra Harper, and you're going to watch me fuck you."

A shiver of anticipation ran down her spine. He kept hold of her throat as he pulled her hips back. Though it was strange and a little unnerving to watch herself and him in the mirrors, it was also unbelievably erotic.

Lexi couldn't get enough of seeing him from all angles and watching as the muscles of his ass flexed. Yes, he was thinner than the last time she saw him, but he was still magnificent. She hadn't imagined she would ever enjoy something like this, but not only had she never been so aroused, she was also fascinated.

He held her gaze as he guided his cock into her before grasping her hips, pulling her back, and thrusting deep. She gasped at the breathtaking sensation of having him filling her again.

When they were together, nothing else mattered and everything was right. He made her forget all the horror and sadness in the world as he gave her only love, joy, and pleasure.

It had been too long since she'd experienced this wonder, and though she could never forget what it was like to be with him, it was still as amazing as the first time.

Once inside her, he didn't move as their eyes remained locked in the mirror. He kept one hand on her throat while the other flattened against her lower belly. They simply stared at each other until he pulled slowly back before plunging deep again.

Despite the obvious emergence of his lycan side, her skin prickled when his dark fae power seeped out around them. It crackled the air as his muscles swelled.

She'd experienced this sensation before as he fed on the energy their joining created, but it was far more potent now. Shadows rose to dance and swell around them.

Cole pulled the shadows closer until they slid over her as well as him. Like phantoms seeping through walls, more of them appeared around Cole.

It was magnificent and frightening, and though she couldn't feel the shadows gliding over her, they concealed parts of them before revealing more when they moved. It unnerved her a little, but she couldn't deny she liked seeing how much he enjoyed this.

In response, her fangs lengthened and reflected in the mirror as a new hunger awoke inside her. Cole must have spotted those fangs as he growled.

He pulled her away from the bar and guided her to the floor. When she was on all fours, he wrapped his arm around her waist to hold her up. In the mirror, his face contorted strangely before returning to normal.

He's losing control of the lycan.

The moons beating down on them wasn't helping him to keep

control. A lycan didn't require a full moon to change, but they had a connection to the moon and its cycles.

Before, being around a lycan on the edge would have terrified her. An out-of-control lycan was one of the most dangerous creatures in all the realms.

Now, seeing him this way only titillated her. She wanted him out of control.

~

COLE TURNED his face into Lexi's shoulder and breathed deep. Though it normally calmed him, the scent of her only provoked the lycan more while the dark fae feasted on the power their joining emanated.

The fae was being sated while the lycan was growing increasingly out of control. He fought it even as the lycan howled to claim its mate. The moons weren't helping; he shouldn't have stayed in this room with her.

He should pull away, but he couldn't let her go. His mind spun as his thoughts became more chaotic.

Claim her. Claim her. Claim her.

He tried to reassert control over the wolf for fear it would injure her, but his fangs lengthened as his body swelled. The shadows retreated when the lycan shoved aside the dark fae to take control. When he met Lexi's eyes in the mirror again, he barely recognized himself.

He'd expected to see terror or revulsion staring back at him from her, but instead, he saw only love and desire. Between the shadows and the lycan, she should be petrified, but she wasn't.

She accepted him completely, and she would not run from him, no matter what happened.

That realization caused the last of his restraint to shatter. He wasn't in control; the beast was.

When he sank his fangs into her shoulder, she jerked beneath him as he claimed her in *every* way possible. The throbbing in his fangs intensified as they filled with the serum a lycan used to mark their mate.

And then, it released. As the serum filled her, she cried out as she came. He thrust into her again and emitted a sound that was completely animalistic as he found his release.

∿

WARMTH SPREAD from Cole's bite to fill her veins and pulse through the rest of her body. It wasn't an unpleasant sensation; not even the bite felt bad. In fact, it felt good as the heat entwined around her heart before slipping into her stomach.

He's claimed me.

She'd heard that lycans bit their mates when they claimed them, but he'd also released something into her.

His eyes still burned with silver fire in the mirror, and he didn't release his bite on her. She couldn't tear her gaze away from his as he started to move inside her again. He'd already fucked her harder than he ever had before, but she suspected he was just getting started.

The lycan was unleashed, and it was an insatiable beast.

CHAPTER FORTY-FOUR

LEXI HAD NEVER BEEN MORE exhausted in her life. She didn't think she would ever move again, and it was more than being tired as every one of her muscles was limp and useless. She wasn't sure she had bones anymore.

But her brain would *not* shut off. Cole had claimed her as his mate. Ever since he told her what she was to him, Lexi had known it was only a matter of time before it happened, and she'd wanted it, but she should have told him about Orin first.

Now, he could not take the claiming bite back, and he had no idea of this giant secret she harbored from him. Would he see it as a big betrayal?

There was a good possibility he would, and she couldn't blame him if he did. She would be *pissed* if their roles were reversed, but she hadn't expected him to claim her tonight. She'd assumed there would be a warning before it happened.

She should have known that one day, he wouldn't be able to control himself. If he decided to have nothing to do with her when he learned the truth, he would regret this claim.

She opened her mouth to tell him everything before closing it again. His father's memorial service was tomorrow, and his coronation was the following day. It was already too late to change anything, and he had enough to deal with over the next two days.

Unburdening herself now would only ease her guilt, but it would do nothing to make anything better for him. It would only make it worse as there was nothing he could do about Orin until the memorial and coronation were over.

She would tell him after the coronation and deal with the consequences then. Until then, she would do her best to be here for him.

Cole ran his fingers through her hair before caressing the edge of his bite. "Does it hurt?"

"No," she said.

"I'm sorry I was so rough with you."

Lifting her head, she propped it on her hand and smiled at him. "It's not anything I couldn't handle, and did you hear me complaining?"

He quirked an eyebrow as he let her hair fall from his fingers and settle against her back.

"Besides," she said as she kissed his nose, "I liked it."

His blue eyes flashed with silver. After everything he'd done to her, she hadn't considered it possible for him to feel desire again so soon; she was wrong.

"Is that so?" he murmured as he ran a finger over her bottom lip.

She didn't respond as her pulse quickened. She hadn't believed it possible for her to feel desire again so soon either, but he was proving her wrong.

However, she couldn't stifle a yawn as the moons dipped lower in the sky.

"You're exhausted," he said.

"I am," she admitted.

He settled his hand on the small of her back and turned onto his back. Planting his feet, he rose in a fluid motion she would have considered impossible. She marveled at his strength and grace as he lowered her to the ground.

She shivered when he stepped away. Wrapping her arms around herself, she couldn't suppress a yawn as he retrieved her clothes and handed them to her.

Taking her jeans, she pulled them on and shoved her ruined underwear into her pocket before slipping on her bra. She was about to pull on her shirt, but she paused when she glimpsed her reflection in the mirror.

Her hands froze and her mouth parted as she gazed at his bite on her shoulder. Only two of his fang marks were visible, but she assumed the two on her back were doing the same thing as the ones on her front.

And that thing was *glowing* a brilliant silver that matched the color of the moons.

"Oh," she whispered as her fingers brushed the bite.

Cole came to stand behind her. His hands slid around to clasp her fingers as they settled on the edge of the bite.

"Is that normal?" she asked.

"Yes. When a lycan claims their mate, they inject a serum into them that marks them as theirs. The wounds will take longer than normal to heal too."

"I didn't know that."

"Does it bother you?"

"No." And it didn't. "But it's... really strange. I mean, I'm *glowing.*"

"The glow will fade once you're away from the moonlight. But beneath the moon, my bite will be evident on you."

She liked that idea. The bite was ethereal but also beautiful.

"Do you wish I hadn't claimed you? I should have asked first, but I...."

His words trailed off. She knew it would be difficult, if not impossible, for him to admit he lost control.

"I'm glad you did," she assured him.

She just hoped *he* didn't come to regret it.

Lexi pushed her morose ruminations aside and rested her palm against his cheek. "I love you."

He bent to kiss his mark. "I love you too."

His warm breath against the bite caused her toes to curl. Then he pulled away, kissed her cheek, and stepped back. When he turned away, she glimpsed his ribs through his skin. She'd never seen them before.

"Cole?" When he looked back to her, his eyes shone with love, and a small smile curved his lips. "How bad were the trials?"

The emotion instantly left his face, and a callousness settled over his eyes. When he turned away, she grasped his arm.

"Talk to me," she whispered.

"I cannot reveal much about them. The survivors are the only ones who know what the trials entail, and it is our secret to keep."

"You mean your burden to bear."

He didn't reply.

"Maybe so, but you can still tell me something," she said. "You look good, but you've lost weight, and I can tell the trials have changed you."

He pulled his arm away, retrieved his pants, tugged them on, and buttoned them before looking at her with the emotion of a shark.

"They were difficult, but I survived, and I came out stronger because of it."

"I can tell," she murmured as she studied him. "I can feel the increase of your power from here, but how bad was it?"

"They are not something easily survived."

She suspected that was probably a huge understatement as she pulled on her shirt. "You look well."

"I look this way because I survived. The shadows healed me before I left the trials behind. I never would have let you see me otherwise."

Lexi bit her lip at this revelation. She had no doubt he'd been as eager to see her as she was him, but if he would have kept her away, then he must have looked *really* bad.

What happened in there?

No matter how badly she craved the answer, she would never get it. Walking over, she wrapped her arms around his waist and rested her head on his chest. Beneath her ear, she listened to the solid, reassuring beat of his heart as his arms enveloped her.

"Come on," he said. "Let's get you up to my rooms and in bed. You need to rest."

"So do you."

"I'm fine."

"Maybe I should stay in a guestroom or something."

"No," he bit out.

"You have to sleep, Cole."

"And I will. But I just got you back, and I'm not going to part with you again."

Lexi sighed, but in truth, she didn't want to be apart from him either.

Before she could say anything more, he swept her into his arms and carried her across the room. She draped her arms around his shoulders and settled her head in the hollow of his neck. As the warmth and strength of him enveloped her, she closed her eyes.

When he opened the door and stepped into the hall, she recalled the bag she brought with her. "Oh," she said as she lifted her head from his shoulder. "My bag. I forgot all about it. I left it in the main hall."

"I'm sure one of the helots has discovered it and taken it to my room. If not, I will locate it in the morning."

"Okay," she murmured and rested her head against him once more.

He didn't seem to feel the weight of her in his arms as he strode down the hallway and up a set of stone stairs that twisted as they rose higher. His breathing never increased though the added burden of her in his arms had to be tiring.

When they arrived at his rooms, she wasn't sure what floor they were on, but he'd never broken a sweat. He opened the door and kicked it shut behind him before carrying her into his bedroom. Her bag sat on his bed.

CHAPTER FORTY-FIVE

A KISS on her shoulder woke Lexi the next morning. She cracked her eyes open to discover Cole leaning over her. The first rays of the sun shining through the open window made his eyes sparkle and his hair shine.

The dark stubble lining his jaw made him impossibly sexier, and she lifted her hand to run her fingers over the hairs. She relished the feel of them beneath her fingers. It made him more real.

"You're really back," she whispered.

"If you think you imagined what we did last night, then I have failed you and will have to remedy that later."

She chuckled as she sank deeper into the luxurious pillows and the sheets fell back a little to reveal the upper swell of her breasts. "I do *not* have that good of an imagination."

His ravenous gaze raked over her, and he propped himself on his elbow before running his fingers across her forehead.

"I have to go help with the arrangements for today," he said. "I'm not sure how long I'll be gone, but I'll return before the memorial starts. I'd like for you to be by my side throughout the day."

Those words caused her stomach to lurch. Cole leaned back as she wiggled up from the pillows and tugged the sheet around her.

"They'll talk," she said.

"What are they going to say? That I had my mate at my side throughout my father's memorial service and coronation? Good. There is no hiding what's between us anymore, Lexi. I have marked you, you are in my rooms, and my bed... again. *No* woman can claim such a thing. This is my personal space; I've never brought another here. They're already talking, and they have yet to see my mark on you."

Her eyes widened at this revelation. He'd never brought another here? She didn't question him further about it because she'd prefer not to have any more details of his past relationships, but it was intriguing.

"Are you sure about this? It's going to be difficult enough for you to take over as king without having a half human, half vampire standing by your side. I'm not exactly a combination that speaks of power."

"I don't care. The sooner they come to accept you will be my queen, the easier it will be on all of them."

Lexi gulped. He was so confident in his power and ability to rule. So confident he could make them accept her, and after surviving the trials, he had every right to his confidence, but she was not so sure.

"I didn't bring anything to wear to events like that," she said. "I doubt jeans and T-shirts are appropriate for either thing."

"I'll send a couple of helots up to make sure you're attired properly."

"Can they do that on such short notice?"

He kissed the tip of her nose. "This is the Gloaming. It's a land filled with magic."

He rolled off the bed and walked over to the window to stand next to the chair there. Before falling asleep, she last saw him sitting in that chair, staring at the moons.

Too worried he might fall asleep while holding her, he refused to lie in bed with her last night. She'd missed him, but she understood. His nightmares endangered her before the trials; she couldn't imagine what his sleep would be like now.

Pushing herself up, she rested her back against the headboard. "Did you sleep at all?"

"Yes."

"Cole…." She let the admonishing tone of her voice trail off.

"I got a couple of hours of sleep. It was more than enough."

She had no idea if that was true or not, but he did look better than yesterday. The lines around his eyes and mouth weren't as noticeable, and his eyes weren't as remorseless.

"The Gloaming is waking," he said.

Lexi's gaze drifted to the window, but she couldn't see the dark fae realm beyond. Then he turned away and strode back to her. Bending, he kissed her forehead.

"I'll have breakfast and the helots sent up right away," he said. "Do you need blood?"

Her mouth watered at the mention of blood, not because she was hungry for it, but because he was so close. She managed to lock away her yearning as she smiled at him.

"No, I'm fine," she said.

He leaned closer and rested his thumb on her bottom lip. Pulling it gently down, he revealed the tips of her elongated fangs. When he did, his eyes sparked with silver.

"You're hungry," he stated.

"I'm not," she said. "It's just when you said blood…." Her words trailed off as her gaze fell to his neck. "I'm not hungry, but your words made me think of *your* blood," she admitted.

He slid his arms around her and lifted her from the bed to settle her on his lap. "I fed on you last night but never gave you the chance to feed on me."

She wanted to continue arguing with him, but she couldn't when he was so close and so tantalizing. The sounds of the morning faded away as the pulse of his heart pounded in her ears. She licked her lips as the lure of that blood beckoned to her.

Sliding her arms around him, she lowered her mouth to his neck and bit deep. The hot rush of blood filling her mouth made her groan. He tasted of fire and power. It was different than before, but the potent combination had her yearning for more.

His fingers dug into her back as he held her closer. Beneath her ass, his rigid erection poked against her. Her breathing came faster as his blood and arousal battered her senses.

Half out of her mind with desire, she clawed at the button on his pants, pulled it open, and freed his cock. Shifting, she continued to feed on him as she straddled his lap and took him into her.

She clawed at his back as his shaft and blood filled her, and she rode them both to completion.

CHAPTER FORTY-SIX

As Cole promised, he sent up breakfast and four women to make her a dress. The women were kind to her and talked while they worked, but she suspected there was a lot they weren't saying.

Their curious glances at her and the covert looks they exchanged with each other spoke volumes, but they didn't ask her anything. For now, they were content to silently speculate about her relationship with Cole as they all worked on sewing her dress. They told her their names but revealed nothing else to her.

Lexi tried to help them, but they shooed her away. Feeling helpless and out of place, she stood awkwardly by as she watched their hands and needles fly over the shiny, black material spread out before them. She didn't know if it was fae magic or years of practice that made them so adept, but they had a dress taking shape in no time.

When they finished, Lexi tried to slip into the other room to put the dress on, but Amaris stopped her with a hand on Lexi's arm. "You'll need our help getting it on and with the buttons."

"Oh, ah, yes, okay," Lexi said.

She tried not to let her semi-nudity bother her as she shed her clothes and stood before them in her simple black bra and underwear. These women were dark fae, and nudity and sex were a part of life for them.

As the women gathered around her, they got some of the answers to their unspoken questions when they spotted Cole's bite on her shoulder. All four of them froze while they gazed at the mark. One stretched out a hand as if she were going to touch it before snatching it back.

Finally, Amaris cleared her throat, and they all went to work again. They pulled the dress over her head and settled it into place. The sleek black dress, with its flowing skirt, demure bodice, and long sleeves, fit like a second skin.

One of the women worked on the buttons in the back while the others hemmed and hawed while making last-minute adjustments. When they finished, they all stood back and nodded their approval.

"We'll work on the dress for the coronation today," Amaris said. She seemed to be the one in charge of the women. "It will be ready for you by tomorrow."

"Thank you," Lexi said.

The door opened, and they all turned as Cole entered the main sitting room. He stopped walking when he spotted them, and his gaze landed on Lexi. The women waited as he stared at her.

"You're beautiful," he finally said.

"They did an amazing job on the dress," Lexi said.

Cole didn't acknowledge any of the women as his attention remained on her. The women exchanged more looks but didn't speak as they edged away from her.

When Cole held his arm out to her, Lexi slipped her feet into the black slippers the women had made her. She walked over and hooked her arm through his.

"Thank you," she said over her shoulder to the women, who all grinned at her.

"Anytime, miss," Amaris replied.

Cole led her from the room and down the hall to where they descended the spiral staircase.

"How are you doing?" Lexi asked when they reached the bottom.

"Fine."

His clipped tone said he was the opposite of fine, but she didn't push him on it. In just this past month, he'd been locked away by the Lord, watched his father die, killed a dragon, and survived the trials. Now he faced his father's memorial and his own coronation.

He was probably the opposite of fine, but he was doing better than most would in his situation.

When they were almost to the main hall, Brokk slipped from the shadows to join them. Cole led her into the main hall that was as black as it was yesterday.

A glass coffin sat on a golden stand before the stairs of the dais. On top of the coffin was the crown Tove wore the first time she saw him. Inside the coffin sat a set of black clothes and a pair of black boots.

Beside the coffin was a portrait of Tove. He looked stoic and handsome with his chin raised high, his crown on, and a sword in hand. The tip of the blade rested on the ground.

Though they both remained impassive, her eyes burned for Cole and Brokk's loss. Her hand tightened on his arm as she sought to offer him comfort.

She ascended the stairs with Cole and almost balked when she saw the small, delicate throne set to the right of the throne he was sitting in the first time she saw him. His father's throne remained in the center of his and Brokk's thrones, but that smaller throne was a new addition, and it was meant for *her*.

Cole stopped in front of the throne and gestured for her to sit, but she didn't move. "You want me to sit on a *throne*?"

"One day, you'll be my queen, Lexi. Now that the trials are over, it's best to establish your presence at my side."

Her head spun as she stared at the throne. This was all happening so fast. She'd barely had time to process being his mate, and now she had to figure out how to be the queen of a realm she'd only ever entered three times in her life.

He expected her to help lead a land that was not her own and she knew little about. And the dark fae were known for their cruelty and indifference. How well would they take to an outsider marrying their new king?

She wasn't ready for this, but then, Cole hadn't been prepared to become king, and neither he nor Brokk were ready to lose their father. This had never been a part of her plans, but she could do it.

Lifting her skirt, she settled onto the throne that was more comfortable than it appeared. Lexi adjusted her skirts the best she could while trying to act like she belonged here. Inwardly, she rebelled against it.

She was a simple girl who led a simple life until the war. Now, she was sitting in the dark fae palace, staring at the elaborate and awing dark fae hall, while the most powerful fae in existence and one of the most powerful beings in all the realms sat beside her.

And that being had claimed *her* as his mate and intended to make her his queen. Which meant he planned to marry her. They hadn't discussed such a thing, but she should have known it would be the next logical step once he claimed her as his mate.

Of course, he would have to ask, and she would have to accept, but she couldn't imagine anything more wonderful than being married to Cole. Not even her uneasiness over this place and her role in it could dim her happiness, but it was going to be an incredibly difficult road ahead of them.

She hoped she was strong enough to endure it.

From somewhere in the palace, a clock struck twelve, and Cole rested his hand over hers. As soon as the chimes stopped ringing, a line of dark fae materialized in the doorway. The line snaked around the room and poured into the hall as an endless sea of dark fae came to say goodbye to their king.

And while they bowed their heads over his coffin, many of

them cast surreptitious glances at her and Cole. The others were not so covert in their curiosity, and a few openly gawked at them.

Some were clearly *not* pleased. She suspected more than *some* of them weren't pleased; they were just a lot better at hiding it.

Cole didn't release her hand as the dark fae continued to arrive throughout the day. Even after the sun set and moonlight streamed through the windows set high up in the wall, they came.

When the clock struck midnight, her stomach rumbled, but she didn't complain as the mourners continued. She had no idea what time it was before the last of them finally left, but as soon as the doors closed, her shoulders slumped in exhaustion, and it took all she had not to slide out of the chair like a limp noodle.

Her ass had fallen asleep; her bladder had stopped screaming hours ago and now ached, as did her cramped, empty stomach. She wasn't sure her feet would support her, but when Cole stood and lifted her hand to help her from the throne, she rose.

The rising did *not* help the bladder situation, and it took everything she had not to cross her legs and start dancing like a five-year-old who drank a gallon of lemonade.

"Let's get you something to eat," Cole said.

Lexi nodded, but she was too tired to speak, and she wasn't sure she had the strength to eat anything. She hadn't asked for food or to use the bathroom because Cole and Brokk didn't ask for either thing.

She didn't know if not eating was part of the dark fae mourning process, and she wasn't about to question it. The not peeing thing was probably because they were freaks of nature.

"And a bathroom," she said.

"Why didn't you go?"

"I didn't know if it was allowed."

"Of course it's allowed. Whenever you need anything here, ask for it, and you will have it."

"Okay, great. I know that for next time, but I'd really like to go *now*."

Brokk chuckled as he descended the steps of the dais. "I'll see you both tomorrow."

"Good night," they both replied.

Cole led her across the dais and into the back area where she stood the first time she watched him with the council. She glanced back into the hall to discover Brokk already gone, and helots were slipping inside to take away the crown and coffin.

"Will they bury the coffin?" she asked.

"Yes, but first Brokk and I will add some private mementos from him and all of his children. I've ordered it placed in the same mausoleum as my mother. He'd want to be by her side."

A lump formed in Lexi's throat, and she blinked away her tears. "That would be lovely. How are you doing?"

"Fine."

It was a lie; they both knew it, but he would grieve in his own way, and she understood that. She would be here for him when he needed her.

Cole stopped outside a closed door and waved a hand at it. "A bathroom, my love."

"Oh, thank God," Lexi breathed and rushed inside.

CHAPTER FORTY-SEVEN

COLE STARED out the window as the sun rose on the land he would take control of today. Some of the dark fae were already waking and slipping from their homes. They had fields to tend, children to chase, and a coronation to witness.

A contingent of soldiers was gathering in the bailey. They would be on duty during the coronation. He planned to keep things casual today, but he would be a fool not to have a guard present, and he wasn't about to take any chances with Lexi's life. Most of the soldiers would remain hidden.

Yesterday, nearly *all* the dark fae had come to say goodbye to their king. Cole expected the numbers to be almost as many today. They would all gather to watch while he stood on the stage he'd directed the helots to build outside the palace gates and claimed the crown his father once wore.

When anger started to build inside him, he turned away from the window and focused on Lexi as she sat on the bed. A tray loaded with oatmeal, strawberries, and milk was propped over her lap.

She'd done amazingly well yesterday. He was proud to have her as his mate and that others would see she'd chosen him.

However, he was more proud of the strength and pride she exhibited yesterday, all while keeping her inner turmoil hidden.

All of this was going to be difficult for her, but she would adjust. Of that, he had no doubt. His queen would rule this realm with grace and dignity. And once he had the crown and ruled this realm, he would make her his queen.

He'd tucked his mother's ring securely away in a dresser drawer. He was waiting for the right moment to ask Lexi to marry him. That moment wouldn't be today, but it would happen soon.

Once she was his queen, she would be a target for his enemies, but she would also have him and a fae army to protect her. She wouldn't give up her life in the human realm, but he would make sure she remained safe when she returned.

She buttered her toast and took a bite before looking up at him. "What time is the coronation?"

"It will start at two."

Her gaze went from him to the window as the loud banging of a hammer pierced the day. They were still working on erecting the stage for the event.

"Are you ready?" she asked.

"No, but that doesn't matter."

"I suppose it doesn't."

"I should go down there to oversee things."

She set aside the toast and wiped her hands on a napkin before moving the tray. She tossed aside the blankets and rose to walk over and join him.

When she encircled her arms around his waist, he hugged her close. He savored the love she so easily gave before a shout from below pulled him away.

"The helots will return with your dress before the coronation," he said.

"Do you mind if I explore the palace a little? It's a fascinating place."

"Not at all. You'll be safe inside here, but stay to the areas you know; it's far too easy to get lost in this place, and it could take us days or weeks to find you again."

She chuckled and brushed aside a strand of her hair. "I won't venture too far."

"I'll return for you before the coronation starts."

"I'll be here or roaming around somewhere."

Cole kissed the tip of her nose before turning and leaving. He strode into the sitting room and exited into the hallway. Descending the stairs, he stopped to knock on Brokk's door and waited for his brother to answer.

Yesterday hadn't been a good day for either of them, and today wasn't going to be an easy one either. The previous kings who took the throne probably did so with a thrill of excitement; he would claim it with a knot of dread in his stomach.

Not only did he have the throne because his father was dead, but he had a lot to live up to when it came to his father's legacy.

And he would make sure he succeeded in doing so.

∾

LEXI WAS SHOWERED and dressed in the clothes she brought with her when someone knocked on the outer door. She drank some of the birth control Sahira had given her and tucked it back into her bag.

Cole was also taking a form of birth control, but she was extremely careful about it. She was definitely *not* ready for babies. When a knock sounded again, she left the bedroom behind for the sitting room.

"Come in," she called as she walked.

Amaris opened the door and poked her head inside. She smiled when she spotted Lexi and pushed the door further open to enter. Draped over her arm, the striking blue dress she carried was the same shade as Cole's eyes.

Lexi gaped at the thick, satin-looking material that shone in the sun spilling through the windows. "Is that for *me*?"

"Yes."

Amaris's smile lit her black eyes. Today, she'd pulled her thick black hair into a braid that dangled over her shoulder. The brown dress she wore was slitted to midthigh on both sides.

"Do you like it?" Amaris asked.

"It's beautiful, but it's... it's... too much."

"Of course it's not," Amaris scoffed. "It's a dress fit for a queen."

"I'm not a queen."

"Not yet, but you will be."

Lexi couldn't argue with that. Cole hadn't formally proposed, but he'd made his intentions clear.

Closing her mouth, Lexi stared at the dress as Amaris laid it across one of the chairs. When the sun's rays lit on it, they turned it a more spectacular shade of blue.

"I'll return to help you dress in a couple of hours," Amaris said. "I have some plans for your hair that I think will be lovely. It's such a pretty shade."

Lexi couldn't stop herself from touching her hair. "Thank you," she murmured. "Are you all alone today?"

"Yes. The others are helping to prepare for the coronation and the celebration to follow. We all miss King Tove; he was loved by many, but a coronation is a time of celebration, and after the war and now King Tove, we could all use some celebrating. Many are excited to see Lord Colburn take the throne; he is also loved by many here."

"Even though he's only half dark fae?"

"He led our side to victory during the war. I'm sure you've heard of his reputation in battle?"

"I have."

"The dark fae respect power and might, and Lord Colburn possesses both. If he survived the trials, he is stronger than the many other dark fae who failed before him, and his dark fae side must be the more dominant of the two. That is enough for most."

Lexi wasn't sure she would agree with the dark fae being the more dominant part of Cole, but she wasn't going to say that. Amaris was already saying *many* instead of *all* the dark fae when she talked about Cole and the fae. Lexi didn't need to give the woman gossip to spread that could turn *many* into *some*.

"And what do they think of me?" she asked.

Amaris's eyes darted away. "They don't know much about you."

But that's not stopping them from talking about me.

Lexi didn't ask her for more information. The topic clearly made her uncomfortable, and she doubted Amaris would reveal what the fae were saying about her.

"I was going to explore the palace for a bit; Cole said it would be okay," Lexi said.

"If you'd like, I have some time and can join you for a bit."

Lexi couldn't stop herself from beaming at the offer. "I'd like that very much."

CHAPTER FORTY-EIGHT

AMARIS STAYED with Lexi as she made her way lower through the palace. She opened doors and peered into countless rooms. Many of them were bedrooms, and some were nurseries; there were dens, libraries, art studios, a couple of music rooms, and one trophy room that made her blood run cold before she shut the door.

And those were the doors that opened for her. There were more than a few that simply refused to budge. She stared curiously at those doors and pulled on the knob a little more than she should have before conceding defeat.

"Many of the rooms have never allowed us entrance," Amaris said.

"Have you been through the whole palace?"

"I think so, but I'm not sure. I swear the palace sometimes changes around us. Or maybe I only believe that because those have always been the rumors. But it's so large, and there are so many halls, rooms, secret passages, and stairwells it's impossible to keep track of them all. I could have been through this whole place dozens of times, or maybe I've only ever seen a quarter of it."

"How fascinating," Lexi murmured.

"It is a wondrous place."

"Do you... do you work here willingly?"

"Yes. Though some helots are here because they're being punished or owe a debt, many others are here to serve our king. I am here to serve my king."

"Good."

Lexi would have *hated* it if this beautiful, kind woman was obligated to be here. But then, for all she knew, Amaris was playing with her and she wasn't kind at all. She could be trying to gain her trust to learn secrets about Cole.

An uneasy feeling churned in her stomach. She couldn't trust anyone in this realm, but she hoped time would change that.

When they arrived on the first floor, the unseen clock chimed eleven in the distance.

"I must leave for a bit," Amaris said. "Would you like me to return you to Lord Colburn's rooms?"

"No, thank you. I'd like to find the moon room again."

"It's right down that hall." Amaris pointed to the hall on their right. "You can't miss it. I'll meet you there at twelve, and we can return to get you ready."

"Thank you for staying with me."

"It has been my pleasure."

When Amaris walked away, Lexi strolled down the hall. As she wandered, she opened and closed doors. Her face reddened when she came across the dance studio, but she smiled before shutting the door.

The next few doors wouldn't open to her, and then she was in the moon room. A sense of peace descended over her as she took in the glass walls and gold beams carved to look like branches running across the ceiling.

Countless brown vines and green leaves covered half of the glass walls, but the ceiling remained clear of the plants. One of the four moons was directly overhead, but the sun's glow drowned out its silver radiance.

The multicolored, vibrant blooms of the luna flowers turned toward that moon; they weren't as fully in bloom as the last time she saw them. She suspected the sun's rays had caused this change.

She entered the room, settled onto the bench, and rested her head against the glass to study the flowers. Some of them turned toward her and revealed their beautiful petals before they closed. When they turned back to the moon, their petals unfurled once more.

The vines rustled as they moved across the glass, and then one of them caressed her hand. She almost jerked her fingers away from the exploring vine that wiggled in the air like a caterpillar in search of a more stable perch but stopped herself before she did.

When she left her hand on the bench, the tip of the vine brushed her finger again before encircling it. The vine enclosed her finger and hand before stopping at her wrist. There, it rose a couple of inches in the air and wiggled its tip like it was waving at her.

Lexi giggled and waved back. When she did, it dipped down and curled into itself a little. It was as if it were ducking bashfully before rising to poke her arm. When she held out her palm, it tapped her as if they were exchanging a high five.

She'd never seen anything like these amazing flowers before; she could spend every day in here playing with them. And they *were* playful.

The vine relinquished her hand and slid forward until it rested on her lap. Lexi stroked its leaves as it settled there like a dog looking for love. As she caressed the leaves, more vines slid forward until they covered both her hands and her lap.

One of them brushed against Cole's mark before tapping it as if in recognition. Then it snuggled close against her neck.

There were so many of them, but she didn't feel uneasy around the plants. Instead, she felt safe and protected beneath their growing weight and the patch of green encompassing her lower half. Resting her head against the glass again, she closed her eyes as she tilted her face toward the sun and moon.

Lexi wondered how Orin and Sahira were getting along, but she would find out soon enough. Tonight, after the ceremony, she would tell Cole about Orin. Once she did, he would want to see his brother. She didn't know what would happen afterward.

Until then, she planned to enjoy this room and these plants. When she closed her eyes, the warmth of the room and the comfortable weight of the vines lulled her into a peaceful sleep.

CHAPTER FORTY-NINE

"What are you doing here?"

The question, barked at her in a haughty tone, jerked Lexi from sleep, and her eyes flew open. For a second, she had no idea where she was as the weight in her lap and the green surrounding her was unfamiliar.

When the vines shifted and some of the flowers turned toward the room, she recalled where she was. Blinking against the sleep still clinging to her, she rubbed her eyes and yawned as she studied the sky.

She didn't know how much time she spent asleep, but it couldn't have been long as the sun and moon had barely moved. Lowering her hands, she looked around the room in confusion as she recalled someone had woken her. Her heart sank when she spotted Becca standing in the doorway.

When she sat upright, most of the vines slipped away, but a couple remained to brush the tips of her fingers like they were seeking to give her support as Becca glowered at her. With a sigh, Lexi rose and straightened her red T-shirt before smoothing her jeans.

"I was enjoying some peace," she said.

"You don't belong here," Becca retorted.

"Cole asked me to stay here, so yes, I do."

Fury simmered in Becca's black eyes. "You shouldn't be wandering around the palace. This is *not* a place for you."

"I asked Cole if I could explore it, and he said yes."

"This room is off-limits."

"The luna flowers have welcomed me, so I don't think it is."

Becca's upper lip curved into a sneer as her gaze raked disdainfully over Lexi. "Do you think you're different because you're fucking him? Do you know how many of us he's been inside?"

Unable to stop herself, Lexi recoiled as Becca's words struck her like a blow to the gut. Cole had a past with women, and he was part dark fae, so it was an extensive past, but she hated the stark reminder that there were countless women before her.

It doesn't matter. You'll be the last woman.

That was true, but she couldn't think about Cole being with *this* woman. If she did, she might throw up. Becca was disgusting and hateful and one of the worst beings Lexi ever had the misfortune of encountering.

She was right up there with Malakai, except where he preferred physical assaults, Becca was all about the verbal abuse. And this bitch knew exactly where to strike to hurt her the most.

Although being in this woman's presence made her physically ill, and she'd much prefer to get as far from her as possible, she refused to back down from the malicious creature.

"No, I don't know," she said. "But I do know how many of you he'll be in *after* me. And that is zero."

The harsh bark of laughter Becca released grated on Lexi's nerves. When the vines moved around the room and slid across the floor, Lexi realized they were creating a small barrier between them. She appreciated what the leaves were doing, but the plants couldn't help if Becca decided to attack.

"Oh, honey, you're nothing special," Becca said in a condescending tone that dripped venom. "You're a mousey little thing he's using to keep himself entertained. Sometimes, we all enjoy a little unusual."

"Oh, honey," Lexi drawled. "You just keep deluding yourself."

With that, she turned and strode toward the other doorway. She refused to back down from this woman, but she didn't have to stand here and listen to her either.

When she left the moon room behind, she glanced back to discover the vines had dropped from the ceiling to create more of a barrier between her and Becca.

Keeping her shoulders back and her chin high, Lexi strolled down the hallway as if she didn't have a care in the world. She walked as if everything inside her wasn't clamoring to return to the moon room and beat that bitch into a bloody pulp.

Becca's words were nothing but vitriol and lies; however, they'd rattled her more than Lexi cared to admit. If she was going to be Cole's queen, then she would have to reside here with that woman, who was a member of the council, had power in this realm, and hated her.

And how many other women were out there who would hate her too?

She'd never been hated before, but she was now, and she didn't like it. It would be one thing if she was despised because she was an awful person or did something to deserve it, but all she'd done was fall in love with a man who had questionable taste in women.

And she didn't care that *she* was one of those women.

When she sensed the presence behind her, she glanced over her shoulder and spotted Becca coming after her. Lexi mentally reviewed everything Brokk taught her, but she didn't know how much good her training would do against a dark fae who could control the elements.

She should have brought her dagger with her, but she left it in her bag in Cole's rooms. She hadn't expected a threat in the palace.

"Where do you think you're going?" Becca demanded.

Lexi didn't answer as she casually tried to open one of the doors; it remained locked. Every part of her yearned to bolt away from this malicious woman, but she wouldn't give Becca the satisfaction of seeing her do that. So instead, she tried to pretend the woman didn't exist.

She was reaching for another knob when Becca seized her wrist. Lexi jerked her hand away and spun on her. "*Don't touch me.*"

When Becca smirked at her, Lexi realized she'd given the woman what she wanted by reacting in such a way. Lexi reined in her temper as she tried to assume an air of indifference once more.

It was a lot harder to do so this time as the woman was far too close for her liking. She suspected the woman was trying to get her to lash out. It would give Becca an excuse to come after Lexi with every bit of the power she possessed.

Lexi was far more confident in her ability to run, punch, and kick after her training with Brokk; she wasn't confident in her ability to withstand a fireball to the face. Turning, she compelled herself to walk away when what she really wanted was to launch herself at Becca and claw the eyes out of her pretty little head.

"You shouldn't be here," Becca said as she trailed Lexi.

Lexi didn't bother to respond, and she didn't look back, but Becca's steps continued to trail her down the hall.

"Listen, whore—"

This time when Becca grabbed her, Lexi's temper unraveled, and before she could stop herself, she spun and stomped on the woman's foot.

"Ow!" Becca blurted.

When she lifted her leg in response to the stomping, Lexi delivered a solid blow to her solar plexus. The impact caused the air to erupt out of Becca, and she staggered back.

Her hands flew to her chest as she wheezed for air. Lexi wasn't sure who was more astounded by the punch, her or Becca, but she had to admit it felt *great.*

"I told you *not* to touch me," Lexi snarled.

Becca's breathing started to return to normal, and the flames along the walls sputtered. When Becca lowered her hands, the air crackled as her power seeped out around her.

CHAPTER FIFTY

LEXI BRACED herself as the woman advanced on her. She couldn't fight Becca's powers, but if she could keep the woman from unleashing her abilities, she might have a chance at fending her off.

Lexi was about to rush at her when a door swung open and crashed into Becca's face. The flames stopped dancing, and the friction in the air released. A bubble of laughter rose in Lexi's throat as the door slammed shut again.

Once closed, Lexi could see Becca standing there with her hands covering her face. Blood poured down and dripped onto the ground.

She couldn't see most of Becca's face, but the shock in her eyes was evident. Lexi gawked at the door; she was fairly certain that when she tried that door, it wouldn't open.

"You bitch!" Becca spat in a nasally tone.

Lexi couldn't stop herself from laughing. She probably shouldn't find such amusement in what happened; the palace might smack her for laughing, but she couldn't help it. Even if it delivered a door to her face next, she loved this place.

"I didn't open the door," Lexi said in between her laughter.

"Who's back there?" Becca demanded.

Her blood-coated fingers slipped on the surface of the knob as she tried to yank it open, but the door didn't budge. It *was* one of the sealed rooms.

Lexi was still marveling over that when Becca spun on her. The blood spilling from her nose dripped off her upper lip to splatter the floor.

"You bitch!" Becca spat as she advanced on Lexi.

Refusing to back away, Lexi planted her feet apart as she tried to figure out how to deflect Becca's powers while beating her ugly. When the flames in the torches danced higher, Lexi couldn't stop herself from glancing at them.

Keep your attention on your enemy!

Brokk had drilled that into her head, and she was already screwing up. Refusing to be distracted by Becca's abilities again, she focused on the woman. The hatred oozing from the woman was so thick it crept like insidious, poisonous spiders over her skin.

"I'm going to make you pay," Becca promised.

Lexi suspected she was more interested in making her pay for being with Cole than for punching her. When Becca's hands rose at her side, the flames shot higher. Their heat warmed Lexi's cheeks as a breeze flowed down the hall. The breeze went from gently blowing Lexi's hair back to causing it to whip around her as her clothes plastered to her body.

Standing on her toes, Lexi prepared herself to attack, and as Becca was about to unleash her power, she released a front kick that would have caught Becca in the throat. However, the dark fae was too fast and dodged in time to avoid it.

When Becca recovered, a burst of fire shot at Lexi. Throwing up her arms, she lurched back in time to avoid being charbroiled.

Becca planted her feet and lifted her hands at her sides. Lexi prepared to charge and tackle her when all the doors in the hallway swung open. The blast of air they created caused the flames to waver and distracted Becca. She glanced warily at the doors as they shut before flying open and slamming closed once more.

The cacophony of their closing rebounded down the hallway. The following hush was somehow as unnerving as the simultaneous opening and closing of all the doors.

It was like a poltergeist haunted this place, but Lexi thought that was too easy an explanation for what was happening. It was impossible, but she swore rage vibrated the walls. And apparently the doors in this place opened in *and* out.

Is the palace alive in some strange, inexplicable way? Or if it's not alive, is it aware?

It was completely insane and improbable, but she couldn't shake the notion it might be true. Then Becca's eyes returned to her, and her power swelled once more.

She was beginning to loathe this bitch, but she had to give Becca credit. She was brave, considering it seemed like the palace was trying to kill her or maybe both of them.

When the flames rose higher again, Lexi heard something that made her blood run cold.

CHAPTER FIFTY-ONE

"IF YOU UNLEASH THAT FIRE, I'll rip you to pieces and set each of those pieces ablaze," Cole growled.

When Lexi's gaze darted around the hall and Becca froze before turning to search for him, he realized he'd drawn the shadows around him without any plan to do so. As he stepped forward, he released the shadows, and they returned to where they belonged.

Lexi gasped, and Becca stumbled away when he appeared only a few feet away from her. He made sure Lexi was uninjured before focusing on Becca's blood-streaked face.

"I'd suggest you get out of here," Cole snarled.

Becca nearly collided with Lexi as she reeled backward.

"Don't touch her!" Cole commanded.

Becca came to an abrupt stop and slunk to the side before regaining her composure and throwing her shoulders back. She wiped away the blood trickling from her nose and flung the drops onto the floor. Somehow, she managed to look dignified while doing it.

"I caught your whore going through the rooms," Becca said.

"Watch. What. You. Say," Cole bit out. "I *won't* have you talking about her like that."

Becca seemed not to hear him as she continued like he hadn't spoken. "She was in the moon room."

"I granted her permission to explore."

"Outsiders should *not* have free access to our world and our secrets."

"This palace is perfectly capable of guarding its secrets, and it is *my* home, not yours. Now, get out of here before I throw you in the dungeon."

She gaped at him like he'd sprouted feathers and started quacking like a duck. "You wouldn't dare. I am a member of the council."

"Tell me again that I wouldn't dare."

A vein throbbed in Becca's temple, but she didn't speak.

"Do not return to the palace until I permit you to do so. If I catch you in here again, I'll put you in the dungeon. And if I catch you threatening *her* again, I'll kill you," Cole stated.

As it was, he was barely restraining himself from wrapping his hand around her throat and tearing off her head. However, she was a council member, and he couldn't go around destroying his council members.

He had to earn the trust of the dark fae here, and he couldn't do that by killing another member of the realm's most powerful families. That wouldn't earn him the loyalty of the fae who worked on the lands and in the homes and businesses run by those families.

Aelfdane was an understandable kill; he'd agreed to it when he volunteered for the trials. Becca was something else. He'd warned her, and if she tried to harm Lexi again, he would destroy her.

"Go," he ordered.

Becca turned and hurried down the hall. Though she kept her shoulders back and her step dignified, he sensed she was struggling not to run.

Cole's gaze shifted to Lexi as Becca disappeared down another hall. "Are you okay?"

"I'm fine."

She wasn't fine; he could see that in her eyes.

"Did she hurt you?" he asked.

"No, but she hates me. And she's a *hideous* woman. The things she said...."

Lexi broke off and focused on the door to his right. He glanced at the blood-covered knob before returning his attention to his mate.

"You have some really *bad* taste in women," she muttered.

He chuckled. "You do realize *you're* one of those women."

The glare she sent him ended his amusement. Apparently, she was not in the mood to be teased.

"You won't have to see her again," Cole said.

"But I will if I stay here. She's a powerful dark fae, a member of your council, and has free reign of the palace."

"She does not," Cole said. "She was allowed in today because of all the preparations. The rest of the council is here too. She will *not* be allowed in again unless I say so, and she will only be around if I am there too."

"Great, so I'll stay here and not go into the realm at all then."

The irritation in her voice made Cole realize he was picking his way around the edges of a ticking time bomb and had to proceed carefully. He would not lose Lexi because of *Becca*. He refused to let it happen.

"And after what happened today, she's going to hate me even more, which I wouldn't have believed possible before," she continued.

His claws extended and dug into his palms when he clenched and unclenched his hands. "Do you wish to leave?"

"No. I want to stay with you, but...." She shrugged. "But it will take me some time to get used to this place and all the politics that go with it. I also don't want to be locked up in the palace when I'm here. I know it can't happen this time, but if you expect me to be the queen of this realm, then I have to go out and into it."

She would be queen, but he didn't like the idea of her out in the Gloaming. Maybe when things were more settled, but that could be years. He kept his concerns to himself; it was an issue they could deal with later, and she was already annoyed enough without him aggravating her more.

"Becca won't harm you," he said.

"I'm not so sure of that."

"I am. She won't be allowed in this palace again without supervision, and once you're my queen, if she does anything to you, it is an act of treason, and she will pay dearly for it."

"I don't think she cares about that. She loves you, Cole."

"No, she doesn't. She loves the power I represent, and she craves it. Power and a better position in this realm are all she's ever wanted from me."

"You're wrong. No one is that angry and spiteful about something because of power. She loves you."

"Lexi, I know the dark fae well, and what Becca loves is power and that I could offer her so much of it. She does *not* love me."

Lexi bit her lip as she studied the blood-splattered, gray stone floor. She looked so defeated he couldn't resist pulling her into his arms. He nestled her against his chest as he rested his chin on her head.

"I'm sorry you had to deal with her today," Cole said.

"I guess that's life when you're dating a guy who has a *lot* of exes. How did you know we were here?"

"I followed your scent, but I sensed something was wrong because of the palace."

She leaned back to look up at him. "Huh?"

Cole grinned at her. "Ever since the trials, I've had a strange connection to this place. It's almost as if it's alive."

Lexi blinked at him before laughing. "I had that same thought when it bashed Becca's face with a door."

"It did?"

"It was *awesome*."

Keeping his arms around her, he started leading her down the hall. "You're going to have to tell me all about it."

CHAPTER FIFTY-TWO

LEXI STOOD at the bottom of the stairs leading up to the large, wooden stage the dark fae erected for the coronation ceremony. Cole had said he wanted her by his side, but the ceremony centered on him and the man crowning him, Elvin.

She and Brokk remained at the bottom of the stairs Cole had ascended to stand twenty feet above the crowd. And what a crowd it was. Thousands of dark fae gathered in the large, rolling green fields outside the palace. There were so many they vanished into the hollows of the hills before reappearing again on the next rise.

They crammed every inch of the lawn and watched with rapt attention as Elvin lifted the crown high. Sunlight flashed off the three black oplyx stones set into the large crown. It was larger than the crown she first saw Cole wearing in the Gloaming, and she recognized it as the one his father wore.

Though he showed no reaction, Lexi winced for him when the crown settled on his head. She couldn't imagine what the weight of it must feel like to him.

Lexi glanced at Brokk as he watched his brother. His face revealed no emotion, but she saw the sorrow in his eyes. Neither of them wanted this, and they would have to fight to keep it as, despite the air of excitement from the crowd, she also sensed their turmoil and unease. They whispered and shifted behind her and the guards who surrounded her.

She hated having those guards there, but Cole insisted. Their faces were stony, and they looked as approachable as an irate porcupine. However, they were armed and loyal to their king. If something went wrong today, they would defend him.

The whispers continued as Cole lifted his head to take in the crowd. Despite her pride over everything he'd been through to claim that crown, she was also scared.

What if the dark fae never accepted him as their king? She could live with it if they never accepted *her*, but would Cole have to spend the rest of his life fighting to control them?

He was already scarred from the last war he fought; what would it do to him if he constantly had to fight his kingdom all while trying to fend off the Lord?

Lexi gulped and resisted tugging at the collar of her dress as sweat trickled down her neck. She loved the gown; it made her feel beautiful and special, but it suddenly felt as if it weighed a hundred pounds and was choking her.

"I now present to you, King Colburn of the dark fae!" Elvin declared in a voice that boomed across the crowd.

Despite the whispers and unease of the crowd, they erupted into applause and cheers. Loud whistles pierced the day, and they stomped their feet until the ground shook. Their exuberant response to Elvin's words doused some of her unease.

Tears burned her eyes, but she didn't shed them as she clapped loudly and cheered with them. When she caught Brokk's eye, he grinned at her, and she beamed back at him.

Maybe things weren't going to be so bad after all.

～

IN THE GLOW of the candles, Cole studied Lexi sitting beside him at the table. He had decided against the normal, lavish ceremony typically following a coronation. It was too close to his father's death and memorial ceremony for a party that extravagant.

Instead, he'd opted for a more subdued feast for all who attended. The minstrels played their lutes, but there was no dancing.

Tables of food were set up outside the gates for all those who attended. He'd made sure to have his table placed so the dragon head was directly behind him. No one could miss it or the remains of Sindri's body.

He wanted the fae to consider him a benevolent and fair king, but he would drill it into their heads that he destroyed the dragon. They needed to be wary of pissing him off.

Cole had insisted on making it so all those who came by would have the opportunity to speak with him. And so far, there were no problems. The fae came, they feasted, they talked, and they celebrated as Cole looked on with Lexi and Brokk.

Many of them came to the table to speak with him and to give their condolences and congratulations. Few of them did anything to hide their curiosity about Lexi, but she handled it well as she smiled at them and spoke with the ones who talked to her.

With him by her side, none of them were outright rude to her, but he didn't kid himself into believing it would be that way if he wasn't here. The dark fae weren't known to be welcoming toward outsiders.

Many of the fae moved on to speak with the council after talking with them. Their table sat to the left of his. Ten feet separated them, but Becca sat closest to him.

He wasn't sure if she would show up, but she'd sauntered up to the table as if nothing occurred earlier, and it looked as if nothing had as her face was already healed. She'd flashed him a smile and given her congratulations before settling into her chair, where she openly flirted with all those who stopped to speak with her.

The candle's flames turned Lexi's hair to fire as it caused the deep red highlights to shine. In the blue dress, she was an unrivaled beauty. Someone had taken her hair and created two small braids at her temples, and combined them behind her head.

She looked queenly as she sat there, smiling while she sipped her wine and talked with a fae woman who had stopped to meet him before introducing herself to Lexi. Soon, she would wear his mother's ring and crown.

As the night wore on, he found himself watching her more and more. All four of the moons were high overhead, and all of them full. Their rays beating down on him, combined with the alcohol and Lexi's sweet scent, had awakened the lycan.

However, he remained at the table until well after midnight when the last of his followers trickled away. The council remained at the table, but he told them they could go home as he rose.

"We will see you tomorrow," he said to Brokk, who had walked over to talk with some soldiers.

Brokk bowed his head. "Good night, brother."

Cole held his hand out to Lexi, and when her fingers connected with his, a thrill of excitement rippled through him. He didn't look back to see if the council left before leading her through the gates.

He hungered for her, but unlike last night, he was able to take her back to his rooms before giving in to his desire. There, they stepped inside together, and he closed the door behind her.

At some point, the helots had come in to light some of the torches. Their flames cast shadows around the room. The silvery rays of the moon spilled through the windows, across the floor, and ended at the edge of Lexi's feet.

He set the crown on the table near the door before tenderly turning her, so her back was to him. Lifting her hair, he draped it across her shoulder as he undid the numerous buttons running down her back. He was eager to have her naked and beneath him, but he savored undoing the buttons and gradually exposing more and more of her creamy skin.

When her dress fell open to reveal her silken flesh and the strap of the blue bra beneath, he ran his fingers up her spine.

"Cole, there's something I have to talk to you about," she whispered.

"Later," he murmured as he kissed her nape.

He pushed the sleeves of her dress forward until they fell off her arms and the top half of the dress rested against the skirt. Last night, he was desperate to be inside her, and though that fiery hunger still burned in him, he would take his time with her tonight.

"Cole...."

Her words trailed off when he slid his hand down her belly toward the waistline of the dress. He pulled her back, so she was nestled securely against him and dipped his hand beneath the dress. Stroking her thighs, he pulled them further apart as his mouth discovered her nape again.

When his lips found his mark on her, he ran his tongue over his bite. The marks were still clearly evident on her, but he would mark her again when they healed. From now on, she would bear his mark.

Leaning over her, he pushed the dress lower. The material made a whispering sound as it fell to the floor. Turning her, he brushed the hair back over her shoulder as he drank in her slender, hourglass figure.

"Cole—"

"Tomorrow, Lexi. Tonight, I just want you."

He lifted her into his arms and carried her into the bedroom to set her on the bed. Kicking off his boots, he undid his pants and tugged them off before tossing them aside. He unbuttoned his shirt and shrugged it off before joining her on the bed.

Tonight, he intended to explore every inch of her body. Starting with her lips, he kissed her from there to the tips of her toes. Once there, he turned her over and worked his way back up before turning her over again.

She was begging for release when he finally entered her. She wrapped her arms around his back and clung to him as her legs encircled his waist. Rolling with her, he gripped her hips as he positioned her on top of him.

His fangs lengthened as her head fell back and her hair cascaded down to brush against his thighs. When the moonlight caught her marking, it glowed silver.

She was magnificent and *his*.

When she came with a loud cry, he followed her over the edge. She shuddered before collapsing onto his chest and nestling closer.

Cole cradled her against him as her breathing slowed and she slipped into sleep. The moons shifted as the night deepened, but he couldn't bring himself to release her. With her in his arms, he held a piece of heaven, and he was never going to let it go.

CHAPTER FIFTY-THREE

LEXI WOKE the next morning to discover Cole sleeping in the chair next to the window. Pushing herself up on the bed, she leaned against the headboard as she sat and studied him. She loved him so much it was a physical ache in her chest, and once he woke, she was going to tell him something that could destroy everything they'd built between them.

Her heart raced at the possibility, and everything in her screamed not to tell him. She could order Orin to leave and never come back. Cole would never have to know he was ever there.

But there would still be the refugees, and she couldn't kick them out. Orin could fend for himself, but many of them had nowhere else to go, and there was no way she could be responsible for Jayden and Nessie's deaths.

And she'd never be able to live with herself if she decided to keep this secret from Cole the rest of their days. Since her dad's death, she'd learned she was capable of doing a lot more than she ever believed possible, but this secret would eat at her until it became a poison that either spilled free or destroyed their love.

She didn't know how much time passed, but eventually, she had to rise to use the bathroom. When she returned, Cole was awake and sitting on the bed. He watched her from hooded, voracious eyes.

Lexi's step faltered when she saw that look. She allowed him to silence her last night, but she couldn't let him do it again.

"Cole, we have to talk," she said.

"We can talk when you're in bed."

Lexi sat on the edge of the mattress but didn't go any closer. He rolled toward her, slipped his arm around her waist, and pulled her back against him. She squirmed against his embrace, but his arm remained firm around her.

"Cole...."

She stopped speaking when his eyes traveled over his bite mark on her. A shiver ran down her spine. No matter how much she tried to withstand the magic of his touch, she couldn't stop her body from reacting to his.

No! You're using this as another excuse to keep putting it off. Tell him now!

Lexi wiggled around to face him and planted her hands against his chest. "Stop it," she said. "This is important."

The sexy smile curving his far-too-kissable mouth faded, and the sparkle in his eyes vanished. She'd finally broken through his playful demeanor, and now he looked like he was waiting for her to hit him.

Her heart raced, and unexpected tears burned her eyes as a lump formed in her throat. She couldn't lose him.

"The time I've spent with you has been the best time in my life," she said.

He abruptly released her and sat up to settle his back against the headboard. She could already feel him withdrawing from her, and he didn't know what she was about to say.

~

COLE DIDN'T SPEAK as he studied Lexi. The look in her eyes and the broken tone of her voice would have had him drawing her into his arms at any other point in time, but her words kept him away.

It sounded like she was saying goodbye.

"What is it?" he demanded.

His tone came out rougher than he expected, but if she was about to leave here and never look back, he wasn't going to be nice about it. Had she decided she didn't want to be a queen? Was the duty she would face in the position too overwhelming for her? Or had Becca managed to chase her away?

"You have to let me tell you *everything* before you react," she said.

"I will."

"I mean it, Cole. You *have* to let me finish speaking before you get mad at me."

"I won't be mad at you."

No, if she had decided to leave him, he would be *infuriated*. If she walked away, he would let her go because he would have no other choice; he couldn't imprison her here, even if a part of him considered doing exactly that.

However, he wouldn't let her go without a fight.

"Yes, you will," Lexi said.

"Tell me."

Lexi gulped before blurting, "I know where Orin is."

He'd been so certain she was about to tell him she was leaving and never coming back, that it took his brain a couple of seconds to figure out what she said. When it did, everything in him came screeching to a halt.

Her gaze darted around the room before settling on him again. She fiddled with the blanket as she edged away from him. What was going on here?

"Where?" he demanded.

"Promise me you'll let me tell you everything before you react."

"*Where?*"

"Promise me, Cole."

"I promise."

She frowned at him as she seemed to debate whether or not to continue. Finally, she took a deep breath and plunged in. Cole didn't react as she spoke, but as her revelations continued, his fury mounted until it became a cacophony reverberating throughout his entire being.

In the corners of the room, the shadows swayed as they slithered forth before retreating again. Lexi's hands stilled on the blanket when she noticed them, but she didn't stop talking.

Cole's blood thundered in his ears as the depth of her revelation sank in. His brother had been beneath her manor this *entire time*; she'd kept this secret from him this *whole time*.

His hands fisted, and his claws dug into his palms. The blood welling in his hands dripped onto the bedspread.

"Don't," she whispered, but when she reached for him, he pulled away from her.

Her hands hung in the air between them before falling to the bed. She stared at the blanket as she told him the rest. When she finished, the seconds ticked away as he tried to process everything she revealed.

"Why didn't you tell me this sooner?" he demanded.

"The time was never right. When you and Brokk first came to the manor, I didn't know if I could trust you not to turn me in to the Lord for hiding him. And after things changed between us, I didn't want you to hate me. After you left with Brokk, I got him out of the tunnels. But then, when you didn't come back and he did, I decided it was time to choose a side."

"And you decided to choose the side against me."

"That's not why I decided to help Orin again. You haven't seen those people and immortals living in those tunnels, and believe me, they do *not* have much of a life. They're battered, hungry, scared, and being ruthlessly hunted by a monster. My father died fighting for the Lord, but I couldn't turn those people and immortals away. I was handing them a death sentence if I did, and I could *never* live with that.

"And then you returned with news of your father's death and the revelation you were going to face the trials. I couldn't tell you about Orin then. You were already nervous about leaving me behind because of Malakai. It would have broken me if you died during the trials, and I would have always questioned if it was because you were distracted by me."

"So, you continued to lie to me."

She winced, and her head fell forward so that her hair shielded her beautiful features. He'd trusted her more than any other woman in his life, and she'd kept this *massive* secret from him. He'd always known women could be treacherous; he just hadn't expected it from *her*.

Then she lifted her head, and her chin rose defiantly. "I did what I believed was best, and I won't apologize for that. When you returned from the trials, I decided to tell you everything, but then there was your father's memorial and your coronation to deal with first. I couldn't dump Orin on you before all of that.

"However, I can't keep it from you any longer. You have to know everything, and after what happened to your dad, I didn't think you'd turn me in to the Lord, or maybe you will. I'm not sure of anything anymore, but this has been eating me up inside, and I can't keep it from you anymore."

"Eating you up inside? You're a very good actress then."

And that was what incensed him the most. He'd never suspected she was *capable* of keeping something this big from him.

"I'm sorry I didn't tell you sooner," she said. "I didn't know how to do it, and I never saw a good time to do so."

A niggling doubt wormed its way insidiously through his mind. She'd spent a lot of time with Orin while he'd been gone. Had something more developed between them? Would she tell him if it had?

"Are you fucking my brother?" he asked.

She recoiled as if he'd slapped her. The distress she radiated almost made him regret the question, but then he recalled that she was a *great* actress.

"No!" she cried. "He's an asshole."

Cole couldn't argue with that. "Some women like that in a man, and he is a dark fae. We are known for our ability to seduce."

"I deserve your anger and distrust, but I would never do that to you. I love you."

Those three words managed to work through some of his fury, but was she telling him the truth, or was it some sort of manipulation?

He'd never doubted her before, never would have put her in the same category as Becca, but now he wasn't sure what to believe.

Had she been using him for power? Did she intend to play him and Orin against each other?

The rational dark fae part of him understood why she'd kept this from him. He hadn't told her everything about himself either. Still, the lycan part was furious, jealous, and determined to see her and Orin together so he could judge their relationship for himself.

The more emotional lycan was winning.

He took a couple of steadying breaths, and for a second, it helped to calm him. Then he pictured Orin beneath her manor and near her when he couldn't be, and his blood pressure skyrocketed.

Swinging his legs out of bed, he rose and stalked over to his armoire. He tore the door from the hinges when he yanked it open. He almost smashed it against the wall, but he retained enough control to set it beside the armoire.

"Is Orin still there?" he demanded.

"I think so, but he comes and goes. He finds more refugees and brings them back before going back out to find food for them. Sometimes he's gone for a few days."

"Get dressed. We're going to see him."

"Cole...."

He didn't look back at her as he pulled on a pair of pants and a tunic.

"Cole...."

Steeling himself for the wave of anger he knew was about to follow, he glanced at her over his shoulder. Cole gritted his teeth and tried not to picture Orin touching her and knowing her in the same intimate way he did.

"I am sorry I kept this from you, but I didn't lie to you. I just didn't tell you," she said.

"Semantics."

"Maybe, but I do believe I'm doing the right thing by helping those refugees. No matter what, I love you and would never betray you with anyone else."

He wished he could believe her.

CHAPTER FIFTY-FOUR

LEXI TRIED to keep up with Cole as he stalked through the palace. When he stopped outside a door, she stood to the side and waited while he banged on it.

She had no idea what to say or do to get through to him, and she wasn't sure she could. Ever since she'd told him about Orin, his eyes had burned silver fire. The lycan part of him was in control now, and a pissed-off lycan was far from reasonable.

She'd expected him to react badly to her revelation, but she hadn't expected this distance or for him to think she'd slept with Orin. She winced as she recalled that accusation and the way his silver eyes shuttered over when he asked if she was sleeping with his brother. It was as if she ceased to exist to him.

She'd never imagined he would jump to that conclusion, but she'd also never seen him this livid. She ached to hug him and tell him that she'd never considered sleeping with Orin, but he wouldn't welcome her touch. He'd probably push her away, and she couldn't handle that.

And truth be told, she was angry too. She was working to keep it under control, but he'd accused her of being unfaithful when she'd *never* given him any reason to doubt her.

You kept the brother he's been hunting hidden from him. A brother who is a good part of the reason his father is dead. That could be why he doubts you.

And that was the only reason she hadn't told him to fuck off when he accused her of cheating on him. If he continued not to believe her, she'd tell him exactly where to go and how to get there.

She loved him, but she wouldn't put up with that.

When Cole banged on the door again, it rattled in its frame. A muffled shout came from the other side, and a few seconds later, the door swung open to reveal Brokk. His pants hung low on his hips, and his blond hair stuck up around his handsome face as he glowered at Cole.

"Do you know what time it is?" he demanded.

"Get dressed and meet me outside in five minutes. We're leaving," Cole said.

The sleepy look left Brokk's face, and his shoulders went back as he glanced between them. "What is it?"

"Not now. Meet me in five minutes."

Cole didn't wait to hear Brokk's reply before he turned and stormed away. Lexi glanced at Brokk, who stared after Cole in confusion. Once Brokk learned the truth, he'd be pissed at her too. She was also going to have to face Sahira's wrath.

This was not going to be a good day.

∾

"WHAT CRAWLED UP HIS ASS?" Brokk asked as he nodded toward Cole, who rode his black stallion fifty feet ahead of them.

Cole's shoulders were back and his head high. On his back, he wore the fae sword he'd retrieved from a weapon room almost the size of her manor. The metal handle of the sword glinted in the sun spilling down on it.

Lexi shifted on her horse as she tried to think of how to answer him. It hadn't helped Cole's mood when she insisted on bringing her horses back with them. He hadn't wanted to wait while they were saddled and brought to them, but she wouldn't leave them behind. He might decide she wasn't welcome in the Gloaming, and these horses were her friends.

"I did something I shouldn't have," she said. "No, that's not true," she corrected. "I *should* have done it. I don't regret it, but I should have told him about it sooner."

"Can I ask what that something is?"

"You're about to find out," Lexi said as her manor came into view.

Brokk didn't question her further as they rode around the lake and toward her home. Normally, the sight of her manor brought a rush of joy. This was her home; it was where she grew up surrounded by love and laughter, but now it seemed ominous and menacing.

What was Cole going to do when he saw Orin? What was Orin going to do when he saw Cole? She glanced at Brokk and bit her lip. He was far more easygoing than either of his older brothers, but how was he going to react to this revelation?

And then there was Sahira. She didn't want to see the hurt on her aunt's face, but there was no avoiding it.

Cole dismounted, removed his horse's bridle, dropped it on the ground, and left the animal standing where it was before striding up the steps to the front door. The animal didn't wear a saddle. When Lexi and Brokk rode their horses toward the barn, George hurried out.

When Lexi dismounted, he took her reins. "Do you want me to take them inside?" he asked.

"Yes, please," she said. "Thank you, George."

"My pleasure, miss."

When she turned back to the manor, Cole remained standing by the front door, and his horse was happily munching grass. She suspected it wouldn't go anywhere without him.

Lexi jogged up the stairs, and when she approached him, he turned away to make sure she didn't accidentally touch him. The subtle rejection stung.

"What is going on?" Brokk muttered from behind her as she opened the door and entered the shadowed hallway.

"Where is he?" Cole demanded.

"I should get Sahira; she should know about this too," Lexi said as Brokk closed the door behind them.

"She doesn't already know?" Cole asked.

"Nobody else knows."

"What don't I know?" Sahira asked as she emerged from the shadows of the hallway leading to the kitchen. She dried her hands on a dishtowel as she stopped near the stairs. Her eyes shifted questioningly between Lexi and Cole before settling on Lexi; she smiled. "You're home."

Lexi managed a tremulous smile in return. "I'm home."

"How did it go?" Sahira asked as she crossed the hall to embrace Lexi.

Lexi clung to her aunt. The familiar comfort of Sahira's warm embrace almost made her burst into tears. Sahira was about to be as angry at her as Cole.

"It went," Lexi said.

When she pulled away from her aunt, Sahira smoothed her hair back and tucked it behind Lexi's ear. The familiar, comforting gesture was one she often experienced as a child, and it only made all of this worse.

"So, what is it that I don't know?" Sahira asked.

Lexi closed her eyes, took a deep breath, and turned toward the library. Her gaze settled on the gray stone fireplace across the room.

"I did something," she whispered. "And now it's time to face the consequences."

She walked over to the fireplace, found the stone to open the passageway, and pressed it.

"Lexi," Sahira hissed.

No one was supposed to know about the tunnels, but it was far too late for that secret to remain hidden.

"It's okay," Lexi said. "This is only the beginning." She looked back at her aunt. "I'm sorry; I should have told you sooner, but it's time for you to see what's below."

Lexi didn't look back as she entered the passage. She removed the flashlight hanging from the hook near the entrance and clicked it on. She had no idea how Orin would react to their arrival, and she didn't care.

As horrible as everything was between her and Cole right now, she felt more carefree than she had in weeks as she led the way through the tunnels. She was glad everything was finally out in the open.

She just hoped no one died today.

CHAPTER FIFTY-FIVE

COLE FOLLOWED Lexi into the passage. The damp earth aroma hung heavily in the air as the shadows danced away from her beam. They coalesced behind her to glide over his skin.

Their presence fueled his power, and his fingers flexed as he prepared to use the air against his brother if it became necessary.

"What is this place?" Brokk inquired.

"It's supposed to be a secret," Sahira said.

Lexi didn't respond as she turned a corner. When she did, her beam caught and reflected in Orin's black eyes. However, she didn't see him. Cole did, though.

Orin smiled at him. "Hello, Cole. Brokk."

Lexi and Sahira jumped as Brokk stopped walking.

"Holy shit," Brokk blurted. "Holy *shit!*"

When Orin emerged from the shadows, Cole's gaze raked over him. He'd caught glimpses of his brother on the battlefield during the war, but this was the closest they'd been in a few years.

The last time Cole saw Orin this close, his brother told their father that he wasn't doing enough to take down the Lord, and he was joining the rebellion. Cole tried to follow him out the door to tell him he was making a mistake, or to beat some sense into him, if that was what it took.

His father stopped him and told Cole to let him go. His father believed Orin needed to follow his own path, even if it went against his. Tove had set him free, knowing full well he might never see his son again, and he never did.

And now, their father was dead. A big part of why stood across from him looking as arrogant as always. His father had sought to keep Orin alive, and Cole would try to respect that, but he'd kill Orin if it became necessary to save the Gloaming.

Brother or not, he was only one life compared to thousands.

At one time, he and Orin were extremely close. With only thirty-five years separating them, Orin was closest to him in age. They'd butted heads numerous times, but they worked it out by punching each other or laughing it off before going out to share drinks and prowl for women.

They would not get over their differences so easily this time.

Lexi edged away from Orin and closer to him, but she didn't get too close. Cole studied Orin and Lexi as he tried to gauge their reaction to each other.

Sahira stared at Orin with an expression of utter confusion. She looked to Lexi and then to Cole; whatever she saw on his face made her eyes widen, and she stepped away.

"What's going on here?" Sahira asked. "And who are you?"

"This is Cole's brother, Orin," Lexi said when no one else answered her.

Sahira gawked at her. "*What* did you do?"

Lexi's chin rose, and pride burned in her eyes when they met Cole's. She stared at him as she answered her aunt. "The right thing."

Her defiance caused his fingers to twitch. He wasn't used to anyone being so openly defiant of him, and while he admired her for it, it also pissed him off.

"I was wondering when she would bring you here," Orin said.

Lexi frowned at him. "Why did you think I'd bring him here?"

"You've got a rebellious side, Kitten, but you're not one for secrets. It was only a matter of time before you spilled to big bro."

"*Don't* call me that!"

The nickname caused the hair on Cole's nape to rise. His muscles swelled as the lycan tried to assert its dominance. "If you knew I was coming, then why didn't you run?"

"Because the Lord killed our father, and I knew you would seek revenge for that."

"And you're going to help me get it?"

"Yes."

"Are you gathering forces to start another rebellion?" Cole demanded as he stepped toward his brother. For once, Orin had the sense to look a little wary as he edged away. "The Lord believes you are. *That's* why he killed Father."

Orin's eyes shifted to the shadows behind him. His Adam's apple worked as he swallowed before speaking again. "The rebellion never ended just because the war did."

"How many fighters do you have?"

"Not enough."

"How. Many?" Cole bit out.

"A couple hundred at most, and that's being generous."

"Not enough," Brokk murmured.

Nowhere near enough, Cole thought. Their father died for the rumors of a rebellion that could do *nothing* to the Lord. He would change that.

"You look familiar," Orin said as he prowled toward Sahira. "Do we know each other?"

"I've never seen you before," Sahira said.

Orin stopped circling to stand in front of her as he rubbed his chin. "Are you sure we don't know each other?"

Lexi's brow furrowed as she watched them; Cole absorbed her reactions as he tried to ascertain if they were real or not.

The witch frowned when his brother grasped a strand of her mahogany-colored hair. She yanked it away and glared at Orin.

"I'm positive I don't know you," she spat.

"I swear I've seen you before, or maybe I've been inside you. There's been so many over the years, and they all blend together."

Sahira looked like a tiger tossed into a bubble bath. "I'd *never* fuck a dark fae."

"Never say never, beautiful lady. We are quite… intriguing."

"That's enough," Cole growled.

Watching the interaction between them was enough to convince him that Sahira did not know of Orin's presence down here. Orin's black eyes gleamed when they shifted back to him.

"Have you claimed the throne yet?"

"I have."

"Did the throne or the trials infuse you with so much more power?"

"The trials."

"Interesting," Orin murmured as he studied him. "You feel stronger than Father; is that because you recently completed the trials, or is it permanent?"

"Time will tell," Cole said. "Where's Varo?"

"Elsewhere."

"Is he well?"

Orin shrugged. "Are any of us? Well… I guess *you're* well. You are the king of the dark fae now. Father would be so proud."

"I had no choice. Unlike you, I can't throw my duties and family aside for the sake of my pride and a chance at glory."

Orin's jaw clenched, but Cole continued before his brother could speak.

"When the Lord killed our father, he made it clear I either took the throne or he would destroy the Gloaming."

"And if you died during the trials?"

"I'm sure part of him wishes I did."

"And I'm sure part of *you* is thrilled to have so much power and all the glory that will come with it."

CHAPTER FIFTY-SIX

LEXI NEVER SAW Cole move before he seized Orin by the throat, lifted him off the ground, and bashed him into the wall. She gasped, and her hand flew to her mouth as Cole leaned forward until their noses almost touched.

Orin's feet dangled above the ground. He was about four inches shorter than Cole, and those inches separated him from the ground. Lexi wanted to tell them to stop, but this was between them.

Still, she wouldn't mind slugging Orin over that last statement. Cole would gladly give up every bit of his newfound power to have his father back. Orin knew it, too; he was just being an asshole.

"Do *not* fuck with me," Cole snarled in a tone that raised the hair on her arms.

Somehow, even with his toes dangling above the ground, Orin managed to retain an air of dignity.

"I never wanted this," Cole said. "*Father* never wanted this."

"Maybe if all of you had taken a stand against the Lord, instead of playing along with him while secretly plotting behind his back, none of this would have happened," Orin retorted.

Lexi's eyes flew to Cole. She would have been less shocked to learn aliens were playing hopscotch in her yard than she was by that revelation.

"*What?*" she blurted.

Cole didn't acknowledge her question as he rested his other hand beside Orin's head on the wall. His claws clicked against the concrete.

"Or maybe, if you hadn't been a stubborn asshole who ran off to play little war hero... No, *failed* war hero, we could have kept all our forces together and brought the Lord down. Instead, you got it in your head that you were right and Father was wrong, and you were going to prove it.

"But all you succeeded in doing was becoming one of the hunted. And now, you're living beneath the earth and manipulating others to do your bidding. I never wanted this, but I did what was right; you turned against your family and have nothing to show for it."

"I have my dignity; what do you have?"

"My dignity, my duty, my family, and a throne."

Orin's eyes flicked to Lexi, and a smile tugged at the corner of his mouth before he spoke. "What about a queen? Or have you decided she's not worth it? You were always quick to throw aside those who didn't fall into line with you, and Kitten has been keeping a *big* secret."

Lexi contemplated giving him to the Lord herself. She didn't care if he killed her too, as long as she got to watch one of those dragons eat Orin first.

"I never threw you aside," Cole said. "*You* walked away. You made your choice, and now you're facing the consequences of that choice. That is not my fault, Father's fault, or Brokk's."

"So, are you going to turn me and *her* in to the Lord so you can keep your throne? And be the good little lapdog he expects you to be?"

Blood trickled from Orin's neck when Cole's claws pierced his flesh. "You're a fool. Brokk and I have been hunting for you because Father wanted to make sure you were safe. You turned your back on him, but he still worried about you. He's dead because the Lord knew he would protect you even though you abandoned him."

"And the Lord put you in his place because he knew you would end me."

The sound Cole released caused Lexi and Sahira to step away. Pulling his hand back, Cole drove his fist into the wall centimeters from Orin's head. Orin flinched and turned away as broken concrete sprayed his face.

"Fuck you!" Cole spat and shoved Orin away.

Orin staggered forward as his feet hit the ground, and his hand flew to his throat. His eyes glinted with fury as he looked up at Cole, but he was smart enough not to attack. Lexi suspected Cole would kill him if he did.

Then Cole's silver eyes found hers. They stared at each other for a minute before he turned and paced away.

"I think we should all calm down and figure things out," Brokk said.

"Well, look at you, little brother. Still playing peacekeeper, I see," Orin drawled.

"Honestly, if I were you, I'd keep my mouth shut. Right now, I'm more likely to turn you in to the Lord than Cole."

Cole stopped pacing and looked at Brokk over his shoulder while Orin quirked an eyebrow.

"Is that so?" Orin asked.

"You're the reason our father is dead. I can barely stand to look at you right now."

Orin placed his hands over his heart. "Right through the heart."

"You'd need a heart for that."

Orin chuckled. "Touché, little brother. So, what do we do now? Are you going to bind me to take me to the Lord, or can I walk freely to my death?"

CHAPTER FIFTY-SEVEN

"I'M NOT TAKING you to the Lord," Cole said.

He badly wanted to as he'd love to watch a dragon devour him as it had their father, but he couldn't do it.

"It got him killed, but Father wanted you alive," Cole continued. "I have no idea why."

"There was a time when you did," Orin said.

"That was years ago. However, I'm going to try to abide by his wishes."

"So, what do we do now then?"

"I don't know," Cole admitted. "I have to give the Lord something, and if we don't figure out a way for it to be *you*, he's going to destroy the Gloaming. I can't let that happen. If it comes between you and the thousands of fae who live there, there is no choice. I have to protect them."

"So, let's give the Lord a body," Sahira said.

Brokk chuckled, and Cole's eyebrow rose. Sahira had never struck him as cold-blooded; she was tough and protective of Lexi, but she wasn't callous. Orin shot her a disgruntled look.

"I'm sorry I screwed you and forgot you, but do you have to

throw me under the bus they just decided *not* to run me over with?" Orin inquired.

Sahira folded her arms over her chest. "I've never met you before in my life, and you know it. Now, you can continue to be a giant prick, or you can listen to my suggestion."

"Your suggestion has me dead."

"No, it doesn't. I'd much prefer it that way, and I'm sure most everyone who knows you would too, but there is another option."

"And that is?" Brokk inquired.

"The harrow stone," Sahira said.

"What's that?" Lexi asked.

"Isn't it cursed?" Cole asked.

"Sort of," Sahira hedged.

"What is the harrow stone?" Lexi demanded.

"It's a stone that can duplicate another, and whoever creates the duplicate can do anything with it. It doesn't create a real being, but in a way, it does. But, if we want to duplicate Orin as a dead man, we can do that," Sahira said.

"Where is it?" Brokk asked.

"It's located in an outer realm and guarded by a crone witch. I would have to convince her to let me use it, and I have to return it, but it could be the answer to saving this jackass and the Gloaming. If that's what you want to do?"

When Brokk and Cole exchanged a look instead of responding, Orin scowled.

"Of course it is!" Orin insisted.

"Eh," Brokk said, and Sahira laughed.

"What do you mean it's *sort of* cursed?" Lexi asked.

"There are rules that must be obeyed if you're granted use of it," Sahira said. "If one doesn't abide by those rules, then the harrow stone makes them pay."

"No," Lexi said. "I'm not going to let you risk your life for him."

Orin rolled his eyes. Cole studied Orin and Lexi as they stared at each other. If there was something between them, it wasn't love.

"Thanks, Kitten," Orin said.

"She's the only family I have left. And I'm not risking her for *you*," Lexi retorted.

"But you risked *yourself* for him," Sahira said.

Lexi cringed before sighing. "He was injured, and I couldn't leave him out there to be hunted and killed. And then, when he came back, he brought the refugees with him, and I couldn't turn them away. He's not here because I trust him or think he's a great guy; he's here because we have the same goal."

"And that is?" Brokk asked.

"To save others."

"That may be *your* goal, but it's not Orin's. I haven't talked to my brother in years, but I can assure you that he doesn't put anyone else ahead of himself."

"It's good to know how highly you think of me, little brother," Orin said.

"My opinion changed when you decided to become the enemy, and over the years, you've done nothing to change it."

Cole swore a flicker of distress crossed Orin's face before he hid it. "It's okay, little brother. I've always known you were going to follow blindly behind Cole, no matter what. You're a good little puppy that way."

"And you're a gigantic piece of shit."

"Then why keep me alive?"

"Because you could prove useful against the Lord, and we need all the help we can get to bring him down," Cole said. "And it's what Father would have wanted us to do."

"Father wasn't always right," Brokk muttered.

"Do you think you can get the harrow stone?" Cole asked Sahira.

"I'm not sure if the crone will give it to me, but it's worth a shot," she said.

"It might be the only one we have," Brokk said.

"The Lord is a warlock; won't he see that the harrow stone has created another Orin? We'll also need to duplicate Varo," Cole said.

"That's the beauty of the harrow stone; *no* one can see through its magic. And I can do that, but he'll have to be present for it to happen."

Orin clapped his hands together. "Well then, it sounds like we have a plan. Let's do this!"

"I hate him," Brokk said.

Cole couldn't help but agree. But then, Orin had always been an asshole. Cole enjoyed that assholishness a lot more when it amused instead of irritated him. And when he was sure his brother wasn't screwing the woman he loved.

However, as he continued to watch their interaction, he began to doubt they were sleeping together. That didn't eliminate the jealousy burrowing into his gut or completely appease the irritated lycan.

Orin clearly irritated Lexi, and he suspected she didn't like him very much, but they'd shared something down here, and she'd still kept this from him. He paced over to stare down one of the tunnels as the lycan demanded his brother's blood.

"No," Lexi said. "The harrow stone isn't an option if it's going to be dangerous for her. I'm sorry, but it's not."

"Oh, come now, Kitten. What fun is life if it doesn't have at least a little danger?" Orin asked.

"*Stop* calling me that!" Lexi snapped.

Orin chuckled, but Cole's words ended his laughter. "If you'd like to keep your tongue, I'd suggest not using your little nickname for her."

"When did you stop being fun?" Orin asked.

"Around the time I watched a dragon eat our father."

All Orin's amusement vanished. His eyes darted away from Cole as a muscle in his jaw twitched.

"That never should have happened," he muttered.

"But it did, and now we have to destroy the man who made it happen."

"I will try to get the stone," Sahira said. She held up her hand to silence Lexi before she could protest further. "Going to get the stone shouldn't be dangerous. If I can convince the crone to give it to me, I'll have to follow the rules afterward. As long as I do that, everything will be fine."

"I don't like it," Lexi said.

"I don't like what I discovered down here, but we're both going to get over it."

Lexi bit her lip before closing her eyes and nodding.

"I'll go with you to help ensure you get there safely," Brokk offered.

"I don't know how the crones are going to feel about *two* half vampires showing up in their land," Sahira said.

"Can you send someone else?" Cole asked.

"No, that would guarantee my death the second the stone fell into my hands. The crone has to deem the holder worthy; *she* has to give it to me."

"So would it be better if Brokk stayed behind?"

Sahira studied Brokk before shaking her head. "She's going to hate seeing me as it is; maybe if there's two of us pleading our case, she'll be more swayed toward our cause. Besides, it's *me* she'll be judging. Since I'm the one who will use it, *I'm* the one who has to be worthy of the stone."

"Then I'll go with you," Brokk said.

"Okay," Sahira agreed.

"Now," Cole said and turned to Orin, "where is this army of rebels you're building?"

"Some of them are down here," Orin said.

"They're not an army," Lexi protested. "Half of them are human, and the rest are so beaten down they couldn't fight off anyone right now."

"This isn't his army," Cole said. "Or at least not all of it. He's gathering some down here, but the others are elsewhere, aren't they?"

"Yes," Orin admitted. "How many do you have that will fight against him?"

"Nowhere near enough. I want to see the fighters you have here."

"They're not fighters," Lexi insisted. "They're refugees. They're broken and lost and need time to heal."

"I still want to see them."

Lexi stared at him before her shoulders slumped a little, and she whispered, "This way."

CHAPTER FIFTY-EIGHT

COLE KEPT Orin beside him as they followed Lexi deeper into the earth. After a few minutes, a flickering light emerged from the gloom ahead of them. They stepped into a section closed off by a gate.

Lexi unlocked the gate and held it open for them to follow her through. A group of thirty or so refugees sat huddled together around a small, magical fire that created no smoke but threw off a lot of warmth.

They held their hands over the flame as they watched them with open curiosity and distrust. Dirt streaked their features, and the odor of unwashed bodies tinted the air but wasn't overwhelming. One of the women cradled a baby against her chest as she retreated down the hall.

Boxes of food and water lined the walls. Blankets were spread across the floor and down the passageway; each of them created a small bed. Sleeping immortals occupied some of them.

"Andi!" a young boy exclaimed.

The child leapt to his feet and ran to throw his arms around her waist. Lexi's face lit with joy as she embraced the boy.

"Hey, J, how's it going?" she greeted.

"I've been pretty bored. Do you want to play checkers?"

"Maybe later. I brought some of my friends to meet you." She kept her arms around the boy's thin shoulders as she turned him to face Cole. "Jayden, this is Cole. Cole, this is Jayden."

Cole extended his hand, and when the boy smiled at him, he saw the small fangs marking him as at least part vampire.

"It's nice to meet you, Jayden," Cole said as the boy shook his hand.

Some of the others smiled as they rose and came over to greet Lexi. She introduced each of them to him, Brokk, and Sahira before they retreated again. When the introductions ended, Jayden tugged on her hand and drew her further down the tunnel.

"This way, Andi," he coaxed. "I've been practicing. Aunt Nessie isn't very good, so I need a challenge."

Lexi laughed as she sat near the fire and the boy broke out an old checkerboard. He laid it on the ground between them before setting the checkers on it. Watching her with the child and the rest of the refugees, Cole understood why she hadn't turned Orin away when he returned to her.

His brother had used and manipulated her to get what he wanted. And he'd put her at risk by doing so.

Orin had pissed him off multiple times over the years, but none so much as now. He'd love to smash his brother's head into the wall until only bloody mush remained.

Killing him wouldn't do any of them any good and would probably send the refugees into a panic. Instead, he contented himself with his musings of battering Orin into pieces.

"Why do they call her Andi?" Brokk asked.

"It's what she told them to call her," Orin replied. "They've all taken a potion to make them forget how they got here, and none of them ever leave, but I guess she assumed it added protection."

"Del used to call her Andi sometimes," Sahira said. "When she was a little girl."

Sorrow for her tugged at his heart while he watched Lexi and the boy lean over the board. They laughed and talked while moving their pieces around.

She'd loved her father dearly and probably given them that nickname for added protection as well as to have a little reminder of him. Her love for the child was evident, as was the refugees' love for her.

The refugees gathered closer to watch as the game progressed. They smiled when she smiled, groaned when she did, and cheered when she or the boy took a piece.

"They love her," Sahira stated.

"They do," Orin said.

"And you used them to manipulate her," Cole said.

"I did what I had to do," Orin replied. "She doesn't see them as fighters, but at least half of them are. They are lycan, vampires, and witches as well as humans, and they fought against the Lord. And for the protection I've given them, they'll fight again."

"You should have stayed away from her," Cole bit out. "She's not like you or me; losing just one of them will break her heart."

"She should get used to that; the first war was nothing compared to what the second will bring."

Cole hated to agree with him on anything, but he couldn't argue that. Things were about to get a lot worse, and considering the condition of the human realm, that was saying a lot.

"Where do they go to the bathroom?" Brokk asked.

"There are toilets down here," Orin answered.

"Del designed the tunnels so they could be lived in if necessary," Sahira said.

"Why did he design them?" Brokk asked.

"You don't have any secret exits and hiding places in your palace?" When none of them replied, Sahira continued. "Every smart immortal has numerous escape plans, especially with that madman on the throne."

Cole couldn't argue with that. Plus, he'd fought beside Del; the man was a methodical, military genius. He would never allow himself and his family to be trapped and killed inside their home.

"Come with me," Cole said and nodded toward the tunnel they'd entered through.

They slipped far enough away so no one could overhear them but remained close enough to watch Lexi. The joy on her face made his heart ache. There was nothing between her and Orin; she'd done this for *them* and would continue to do so.

He wished he could protect her from the unhappiness her decisions would cause when some of these refugees inevitably died.

"Can you put a tracking spell on him?" Cole asked Sahira as he waved a hand at Orin.

"I can," she said.

"I'm not going to let that happen," Orin said.

Cole grinned at him. "It's cute you think you have a choice. You either allow this to happen, or I'll take you to the Lord. I will *not* take the chance of you running away when the Lord is threatening the Gloaming."

When Orin glared at him, Cole smiled in return. "The choice is up to you, *little brother*."

Brokk released a snort of laughter, and Orin scowled at the wall.

Cole turned to Sahira. "What do you need to make it work?"

"A spell and my blood," she replied.

Cole pulled the sword from his back and rested the tip on the ground. "We can use this for the blood."

"That works for me," Sahira said.

When they all turned to Orin, he stepped away from them but didn't try to flee.

"Wise choice, little brother," Cole said.

"I won't give you Varo," Orin said. "If the mission for the harrow stone fails, I won't tell you where he is."

"I didn't expect you to," Cole said.

Orin was a heartless prick most of the time, but they were all still brothers, and he wouldn't give Varo up, even if it might save him, which it wouldn't.

"Go ahead," Cole said, and Sahira stepped toward Orin.

Her hands started moving through the air in a graceful dance as sensual as it was eerie. It had always unsettled him how the witches could weave their magic so intricately through the air.

He wasn't the only one it unsettled as Orin shifted uneasily beside him and Brokk shivered. Goose bumps broke out on Cole's arms when the damp chill in the air intensified and the flow of it increased around them until it plastered his shirt against his chest and ruffled his hair.

As the breeze escalated, Sahira spoke. "What wanders free will never truly be free as long as they are bound to me."

Without any warning, she seized his blade. He scented her blood on the air before the red liquid slid down the silver metal to stain the ground.

When she stepped toward Orin, he backed away, but Cole grabbed his arm and jerked him back. Orin fisted his hands but didn't try to hit him. They both knew it would be a colossal mistake if he did.

They were once nearly equal power-wise, but that time had come and gone. He was a lycan who had found his mate and a dark fae who'd survived the trials to become king. Orin didn't stand a chance against him, and he knew it.

When Sahira grasped Orin's arm, the air crackled with her power before a loud snap echoed throughout the tunnel. Lexi and the others looked around, but no one rose to come to explore. They were probably all too tired to bother.

Cole released his brother when Sahira started speaking again.

"What wanders free will never truly be free as long as they are bound to me," she repeated.

Smoke wafted from Orin's skin as the smell of burnt hair and flesh filled the air. Orin's teeth skimmed back, but he kept himself restrained.

The power suddenly sucked out of the air and retreated into Sahira. When she removed her hand from Orin's arm, the bloody handprint she left behind burned brightly before vanishing.

Sahira smiled sweetly at Orin. "Now, you'll always remember that you've met me."

Orin glowered at her as Cole and Brokk smiled.

CHAPTER FIFTY-NINE

LEXI LEANED against the doorway as she watched Cole standing by the lake. He stood with his shoulders back, but she sensed a sadness to him that she yearned to ease. However, she didn't think he wanted her anywhere near him.

He hadn't spoken to her after they left the tunnels. Instead, he'd walked out the door and gone to stand by the lake.

Sahira came to stand beside her. "How could you not tell me about what was going on below?"

Lexi had known this was coming, but she still wasn't ready to deal with it. "I was trying to protect you."

"*I'm* the one who is supposed to be protecting *you*."

"I'm not a child anymore. I don't need protecting."

"And neither do I. We're in this together, Lexi. We're all we have left of our family, and I can't lose that."

She braced herself to look at her aunt, who stared back at her with a desperation that tore at Lexi's heart. "I'm sorry. I never meant to hurt you or anyone else; I just... I... I couldn't turn them away."

"I understand, but you still should have told me."

"How mad are you?"

"I'm not mad; I'm sad you didn't think you could trust me."

Those words were a knife to her heart. "I trust you, but I was trying to keep you safe."

"I understand. From now on, no more secrets."

"No more secrets," Lexi promised.

Sahira squeezed Lexi's hand before kissing her cheek. "I have to go pack."

"Are you sure about this?" Lexi asked.

"Yes."

"I don't want you to get hurt."

"I'll be fine."

When Sahira walked away, Lexi focused her attention on Cole again. It was a few minutes before Brokk came to stand beside her.

"Do you hate me too?" she asked.

"Not at all," Brokk replied. "I consider you a friend, but I wouldn't have trusted you with the secret of those tunnels either."

Lexi tore her attention away from Cole to focus on Brokk as he leaned against the doorframe with his arms crossed over his chest.

"You helped save my life, Lexi, and you saved Orin's," Brokk continued. "And as much as I hate him, I also love him."

"I get that."

"You did what you felt was right, and my brother has a way of bending others to his will."

"I'm not completely naïve. I know he was trying to manipulate me when he brought the refugees here, but I decided to help because *I* wanted to."

"I understand." He shifted his attention to Cole and nodded his chin at him. "Are you going out there?"

"I don't think he wants to talk to me."

"He does."

"He accused me of sleeping with Orin."

"Ouch," Brokk muttered.

"Yeah, ouch. I would *never* do that."

"You have to remember that we're from completely different worlds. To the dark fae, that would be a normal thing to have happen. We're not faithful to anyone who's not our spouse, and we expect everyone else to be the same way, even if it's not true. Plus, the lycan aren't exactly known for being logical, and when it comes to you, the lycan is the more dominant part of him."

"I know," she murmured. "I'd still like to punch him."

"Then do it." When she shot him a dubious look, he chuckled. "He's not going to punch you back."

"True." And it was extremely tempting.

She focused on Cole again as she tried to decide what to do.

"Go," Brokk urged.

Taking a deep breath, Lexi steeled herself for the possible rejection to come before descending the stairs. She crossed the open expanse of lawn and stopped beside him. Memories flitted across her mind as she stared at the serene, glassy surface.

"My dad and I spent a lot of time out here. We'd read by the water, feed the ducks, and over there"—she pointed to a rowboat now covered in vines—"is the boat we'd take out to fish. As you can see, I didn't use it much after the war started. And once he died...."

She turned away from the boat that was once a favorite place to spend time with her dad.

"Things changed," she finished.

"They always do," Cole said, but he still didn't look at her.

"If you decide to turn Orin in to protect the Gloaming, I'll understand, but I'll fight you on the refugees. I *will* do whatever I can to keep them safe."

"Will you fight the Lord for them?"

She lifted her chin. "I will. When Orin turns me in—"

"He won't do that."

"What do you mean?"

"If I turned Orin over to the Lord, he wouldn't turn you in too. He's a bastard, but he doesn't turn on his family."

"He already turned against you and his father."

"Not in the same way. He disagreed with my father and went against him, but he wouldn't have tried to take over the Gloaming. I know it doesn't make any sense, but there are lines Orin wouldn't cross, and purposely taking down another member of his family by ratting them out to the Lord is one of those lines."

"I'm not family."

"He knows you're important to me; that makes you family."

"And you don't think he'd turn us both in for knowing about where he's been if you handed him over to the Lord?"

"No. He would understand I was doing what was necessary to save the dark fae in the Gloaming. He doesn't have many standards, but he does have some."

"I never had sex with Orin."

"I know. I shouldn't have accused you of that."

Relief flooded her at his words, and she almost grasped his arm but stopped herself. Despite his words, a gulf remained between them.

"I would *never* do that. I'm not a dark fae; I'm not *you*. I know I shocked you with my revelation, and I'm sorry I didn't tell you sooner, but I'm with you because I want to be and because you're special to me. I had sex with you for the same reason. If things ended between us tomorrow, I wouldn't jump right into someone else's bed, and I certainly wouldn't screw one of your *brothers*."

"I never should have said it. I'm sorry."

He didn't say those last two words often, and she knew they meant something, but she wasn't done.

"I'll *never* cheat on you, and I love you, but if you *ever* accuse me of that again, I'll leave you."

His jaw clenched, and silver flashed through the vibrant blue of his eyes. "It will never happen again."

"Good."

He smiled at her, but that gulf didn't close as neither of them moved toward the other.

"My father and I would go fishing too," he said as he turned back to the water. "There's a lake behind the palace. It has water the color of the sky on a sunny day. It's so clear you can almost see the bottom. We would watch the fish swimming beneath us, but we never caught them."

"Why not?"

A sad smile curved his mouth. "I guess they were smarter than us."

"But you kept trying?"

"Many times over the years."

"It's more about being in the boat, isn't it?"

"It is."

"What did Orin mean when he said you were playing along with the Lord while plotting behind his back?" she asked.

Cole finally looked at her again. The vivid blue of his eyes stole her breath and caused her heart to stutter. He was gorgeous, and though things were strained between them, he was *hers*. He'd claimed her as his mate, and she wasn't going to let him go.

"I was never on the Lord's side. Neither was your father," he said.

Her eyebrows shot up at this unexpected revelation. "It seems we've both been keeping secrets."

A breeze stirred the air and blew her hair forward. His eyes fell to the strands tickling her face, but he didn't brush them away as he would have before.

"We have," he said.

"Should I be as mad at you as you were with me?" And though she tried to keep that anger under control, it bubbled toward the surface. "You accused me of sleeping with your brother and believed I betrayed you.

"I kept Orin's presence here a secret, but I didn't do it out of spite or because I was plotting against you. I didn't do it for the power you possess or a throne. I'm not Becca or the other women you've dealt with in your past.

"This is my life and my home. I miss my dad, but I'm happy here. I don't want to be a queen, but I'd be one for *you*. Yet, you're mad at me for keeping secrets when you were doing the *same* thing."

CHAPTER SIXTY

DURING HIS MANY YEARS, there were countless times when he was a complete asshole and treated others with little to no respect. Not once had he felt bad about it.

He'd broken hearts, shattered prides, and destroyed lives without so much as a twinge of regret. Now, self-loathing burned like water from the acid lake in his throat and chest.

"The coalition is a secret from everyone who isn't a member," he said.

"And the existence of everyone in those tunnels is the same thing. If I'm going to be a part of your world, then you have to tell me everything I could be facing in it."

"I was trying to protect you."

"I'm *tired* of others always trying to protect me. My father and Sahira sought to protect me from the world, but it was impossible. And now you're trying to protect me from everything too. I don't want to be protected anymore. I should know it all if I'm going to be your queen."

"I'll tell you all of it then."

When the wind blew a strand of her hair toward him, he caught it. He admired the different shades of red in it as he let the silken strand slide through his fingers.

"So, are you going to tell me how you and my father plotted to take down the Lord?" she asked.

"Yes, but why don't we talk in a boat?"

Lexi looked at the vine-covered boat and smiled. "I'd like that."

～

DESPITE HAVING NOT BEEN USED in a few years, the boat remained in good condition. It had taken some time to free it from the vines and clear it of debris. Once freed, she discovered the wood was still in good shape, though it required a paint job and one of the boards near the top was rotting.

Cole slipped the boat into the water and held it as she climbed into the vessel. He followed her and used one of the oars to push them off the shore. While he rowed, she admired the bulge and flex of the muscles in his arms as, beneath the sun's rays, his ciphers stood out starkly.

When they floated into the middle of the lake, he set the oars in place and let them drift as he told her about the coalition, his role in it, and her father's role.

She stared at the manor while he spoke. She'd never suspected a thing, but the more he revealed, the more sense it made. Her father never fit in on the Lord's side.

She'd understood why he fought for that monster, but it never seemed like the right side for him. He wasn't an oppressor who wanted more from the human realm; like her, he was a man who was happy with the life he led.

"So many secrets," she murmured when Cole finished speaking.

"*No* more secrets," he said. "This is it; it's all out in the open."

She shifted her attention from the manor to him. His Persian blue eyes shone as he stretched his legs out before him in the boat.

"Is it?" she asked. "You move in completely different circles than me and have a lot more years on me. I'm sure there are many more skeletons in your closet."

"There are many skeletons, and if you ask me about them, I'll tell you, but I'm not going to sit down and reveal all the details of my past unless you insist on hearing them, and then we will need a lot of time."

"I don't want to know all the details of your past, but I do want to know the *really* important things like what you just revealed about the coalition and Orin. And from now on, I want to know it all."

"Then you will, but I expect the same from you."

"You'll have it."

"Good," he said. "There is one more thing I have to tell you, but it's something that will be easier to show you."

She frowned at him.

"I'll show you later, I promise. Now, come here."

When he opened his arms to her, she braced her feet apart on the boat, rose, and slipped across the space separating them to crawl into his embrace. He kissed the top of her head as he held her in his lap.

"I am sorry," he said as he smoothed back her hair.

"So am I," she whispered. "But you have to know I'd never be with someone else; you're it for me."

His arms tightened around her. "You're *everything* for me."

Lexi relaxed into his arms and closed her eyes. A sense of peace descended as his strength enveloped her and the bird's song filled the air. The sun's rays warmed her, and when she opened her eyes, it was to a sky free of clouds.

Her tranquility didn't last as the manor door opened and Sahira and Brokk emerged. Her aunt carried a bag on her shoulder as they approached the lake.

"I don't like this," she whispered.

"Neither do I," he admitted.

CHAPTER SIXTY-ONE

LEXI BATTLED BACK her trepidation as she embraced her aunt.

"I left an extra bottle of your birth control potion on the kitchen counter, just in case you run out before I return," Sahira said.

"You don't have to do this," Lexi said.

"Yes, I do. The Lord has to be taken down, and Orin can help with that. And Cole needs to get the Lord off his back."

"If, at any point, you think it's too risky to continue, promise me that you'll return."

"I will, but there's no danger in the travel."

Lexi wasn't so sure she believed her. Sahira would never tell her the truth if she thought she was protecting Lexi. *More protection and more secrets.*

Though, with Sahira, she doubted it would change. The woman had helped raise her; she would always see Lexi as a child whose scrapes and bruises she kissed to make better. Lexi could never change that.

Her aunt kissed her cheek before releasing her. Lexi stepped back to stand beside Cole as Sahira and Brokk disappeared into the portal Sahira had opened to the outer realm they were traveling to. Once they were out of view, the portal closed behind them.

"Now what?" she asked.

"I have to return to the Gloaming soon," he said as he took her hand. "I have duties I must attend to, but I can't leave you here alone."

Lexi stared at the barn as they approached the manor. "I can ask George to stay on to help. I have to make sure Orin knows he'll be here for a while."

She'd have to figure out how to pay George. For now, she had enough to keep him on for another week, and by then, Sahira should be back. They could figure it out together as she suspected George might have to become a permanent fixture here.

"I can't stay away long," she said. "With Sahira gone, this place will be vulnerable without at least one of us here."

"I'll send men to watch over it."

"Aren't you concerned about them possibly encountering Orin?"

"As long as he's not a fucking moron, he'll be okay."

"So… yes."

Cole chuckled. "We'll make sure he knows George and my men are here. He's gone undetected this long; I'm sure he can figure out how to keep doing it."

"I'll go speak with George now then."

She squeezed his hand and released it before hurrying away to the barn. Cole's horse lifted his head to watch her before returning to grazing. He hadn't traveled far.

When she reached the barn door, she pushed it open and entered the shadowed interior. George was in the tack room, cleaning the saddles she and Brokk used.

He looked up at her, and his weathered face broke into a grin. "Good afternoon, miss," he greeted.

"Good afternoon, George."

"The horses are eating their dinner, and I'm about to head home to have mine. Is there anything else I can help you with today?"

"No, we're all set for today, but I'd like it if you would stay working for us for a little while. I won't be able to pay you much, but we have some extra food you and your family can have."

He put down the sponge coated with leather soap and wiped his hands on a towel. "I'd like that, miss. As you know, times are tough, and any money and food we can get is always helpful."

And she would do her best to help him as much as possible. "Thank you, George."

"Anytime, miss."

She left the tack room and was almost to the door when the jingle of saddles drifted to her. The hair on her nape rose, and her step faltered. The last time she heard that many riders approaching, they were the Lord's men.

She practically ran the rest of the way to the door. With her heart hammering, Lexi stepped outside and shaded her eyes against the fading sun. A knot formed in her stomach when she spotted the riders.

The Lord's white flag with the fire-breathing dragon on it flew from one of the mounts. The horses' hooves dug into the earth as they kicked up dirt while circling Cole. He stood in the center of the riders as the horses pranced around him.

"King Colburn of the house of the dark fae?" the rider closest to Cole asked.

She recognized him as the lycan in charge when they came to search her manor. He hadn't seemed like a bad man before, but his loyalty to the Lord made him treacherous.

Cole's eyes met hers as she approached, but she couldn't get too close with all the horses dancing around him. He held her gaze as he gave a subtle shake of his head, and she stopped walking.

"That's me," Cole said as his attention shifted back to the head lycan. "What's the meaning of this?"

"The Lord wants to see you immediately," the lycan replied.

"Tell him that I'll join him soon," Cole replied.

No!

The word screamed through Lexi's head, but she bit her tongue to suppress it. Cole wasn't one to be summoned anywhere, and the Lord was *not* someone to be disobeyed. He'd killed the last dark fae king, and he would kill Cole.

"My orders are to take you now," the lycan said.

"I don't care what your orders are," Cole replied.

"Cole, don't," Lexi whispered.

When he smiled at her, the head lycan turned in his saddle to look at her. Some of his men followed suit; Lexi didn't move as they all stared at her.

Ignoring the horses prancing around him, Cole strode toward her. He didn't have to push his way through the beasts as the horses fell back to get out of his way.

His eyes were a brilliant silver, and the power he emanated crackled the air around him. The horses all knew a predator when they sensed one, and he was most certainly a predator. He stopped before her and clasped her hands.

"Go," she whispered. "And do whatever the Lord wants. I need you to come back to me."

"Nothing can keep me from you."

She strained to keep her terror repressed. "Do whatever he says, please."

A flash of black crossed his eyes. The effect was so startling and fast she assumed she'd imagined it, but it was almost as if a shadow passed across his eyes.

"I'll be back as soon as possible," he said. "I'm going to call forth a crow so you can send a letter to the Gloaming."

"I'll be fine; just take care of yourself."

Cole kissed her forehead before claiming her mouth. When he released her, he stepped back and raised a hand. A crow flew down from one of the branches and landed on his shoulder.

Cole whispered something in its ear, and when he finished, it hopped over to her shoulder. It ruffled its feathers before settling its wings into place.

"Send the letter to Niall. Tell him that I have requested he come to the human realm to stay with you until I return," Cole said.

"Who is Niall?" she asked.

"A friend. I trust him. Send the letter immediately."

"I will," she vowed.

He kissed her again before turning to face the Lord's men. "Let's go then," he commanded as if this was his idea.

Some of the men exchanged agitated looks, but none of them dared to say anything. Cole agreed to go with them, but if he chose to make their lives difficult, he would succeed.

When Cole let out a low whistle, his horse lifted its head and its ears flicked toward him. It hesitated only a second before trotting over to him.

Cole grasped its mane and swung himself onto the animal's back. When he looked back at Lexi, he smiled before turning his horse away and nudging him in the sides.

When the riders fell in around him, the certainty she'd never see him again hit her.

CHAPTER SIXTY-TWO

ONCE BACK IN DRAGONIA, a warlock led Cole to a room outside the great hall of the Lord. The warlock who led him into the room didn't say a word as he closed and locked the door behind him.

Cole studied the small room with its gray, unadorned stone walls, single bench, and window slit high up in the wall. The fading sun cast shadows across the concrete floor. The room was the definition of sparse, but at least he wasn't locked up in a tower again.

He didn't know if this was better or worse, and he suspected he'd have some time to ponder it. Would he be stuck here as long this time as he was the last time?

As day gave way to night and the moon's rays filled the room, the door opened. The warlock there gestured for him to exit.

"The Lord will see you now," the man said.

Cole didn't reply as he left the room and followed the man down the hall to the double doors there. Each door had a carving of a dragon in mid-flight on it. The warlock opened one of the doors and stepped back to let Cole enter the main hall.

Overhead, the opening in the dome ceiling a thousand feet above him revealed the clear night sky and the thousands of stars piercing the darkness. Dragons lounged sleepily in the room, but when he descended the five steps to the great hall, many of them lifted their heads and turned in his direction.

Their reptilian eyes followed his every step, and he sensed their barely leashed rage. They hadn't forgiven him for killing one of them, and he certainly hadn't forgotten that one of them ate his father.

He ignored them as he walked down the center of the room toward where the Lord sat on his golden throne. The throne sat on top of a dais and was situated fifteen feet above the rest of the room.

Hatred burned like fire in his throat as he kept his attention riveted on the man he'd see dead soon. He was almost to the Lord when one of the dragons shifted to reveal a man standing at the bottom of the dais's steps.

Cole's step slowed, and his claws lengthened as bloodlust burst hotly through him. Behind him, the dragons' tails rasped against the ground, and their claws clicked against the stones.

If he looked back, he was sure he'd see them closing in on him. Still, he didn't take his gaze off Malakai as the vampire smiled at him. It was the smugness of his smile that set off warning bells in Cole's head.

Still, he managed to keep himself under control as he smiled back, baring his fangs. The sight of those fangs caused Malakai to shift uneasily, and Cole knew he recalled what it was like for those fangs to impale him.

Had he run straight to the Lord's hall after their last encounter? That would explain why he wasn't at home, but how close were these two if Malakai felt safe enough to hide from him here?

His gaze fell to the sun medallion hanging from Malakai's neck. He'd done something to earn that amulet from the Lord, and it hadn't been anything good.

Malakai being this close to the Lord did not bode well for him.

"Ah, Colburn, how good of you to join us," the Lord greeted. "Though my men tell me you were in no rush to do so."

It took everything Cole had to tear his gaze away from Malakai and focus on the madman sitting over them. "I was busy, milord. But I came as soon as I could."

"Yes, yes, I heard you were in the human realm. What a strange place to be for a man crowned king of the Gloaming yesterday."

"I had some things to take care of, milord."

The Lord steepled his fingers together and rested them against his chin as he peered down at Cole. "So I've heard."

Cole's eyes flicked to Malakai. What had that prick told the Lord about him and Lexi?

"How does it feel to be king?" the Lord asked.

"It is a great honor."

It was many things, but he wouldn't explain any of them to this man. Cole shifted his attention back to Malakai. The vampire remained standing there, with his hands clasped behind his back. If he started whistling, Cole wouldn't be surprised.

Cole would give anything to finish what he'd started in the barn, and this coward couldn't transport out of this palace. However, he doubted the Lord would let him attack a man he'd brought here without severe repercussion. He'd killed one dragon, but he couldn't fend them all off.

"How were the trials?" the Lord asked.

"They were a tribulation," Cole replied.

The Lord chuckled. "I'm sure they were, but you seem well."

"I am."

"Good, good. And have you heard anything about your brothers?"

"That was one of the reasons I was in the human realm," Cole said. "I'm going to search for them myself."

"And you planned to do this at your lover's manor?"

His knowledge of Lexi and what she was to him didn't come as a surprise. He'd hoped to keep her hidden from this monster longer, but the Lord had probably known about her since Malakai came to hide here.

"Everyone requires a break now and then," Cole replied.

"Of course we do. And who is this woman you're taking a break with?"

Cole glanced at Malakai again; how much had he revealed to the Lord about her? Cole suspected it was everything.

"She is the daughter of a friend who died fighting for *you* during the war, milord," Cole replied.

The Lord's red eyes gleamed with malice, and his lank brown hair fell forward when he leaned toward Cole. "But who is she to *you*?"

When Cole's jaw clenched, a blast of hot air warmed his neck. Glancing over his shoulder, he glowered at the dragon only a couple of feet behind him.

"Back the fuck off," he growled.

The creature's eyes narrowed, and its head lowered until only inches separated them. Its orange eyes glistened in the moonlight, and he sensed its barely controlled desire to destroy him. Cole smiled at it.

"That's enough," the Lord said. "I will not have any fighting in my hall. Go lie down."

Another snort of hot air blew Cole's hair back from his face before the dragon retreated a few feet and settled down. Resting its head on its front legs, the beast watched him with the intensity of a tiger about to pounce. Cole turned his back on it.

"So, Cole, who is this woman to you?" the Lord asked.

Cole shifted his attention back to the snake on the throne. He'd rather face the dragons than this twisted monster; at least he knew what to expect from the dragons.

Cole considered which answer would be best for Lexi. If he confirmed she was his mate, the Lord would use her against him. If he simply said she was his lover, and the Lord discovered she was his mate, it might infuriate him.

No matter what he said, he was trapped, and they all knew it.

"You know what, let me find out the answer for myself," the Lord said.

The Lord lifted his hand and crooked his finger toward the door at the other end. With that finger, he beckoned to someone. Cole turned as the warlock who had escorted him into the room opened the door again.

Cole's heart sank when two lycans entered the room. Each of them held one of Lexi's arms. She struggled in their grasp as she tried to tear her arms free but stopped when she spotted the dragons.

Her face visibly paled as a couple of the dragons lifted their heads and turned toward her. She stumbled back but didn't go far as the lycans kept a firm hold on her.

Then her eyes met his over the heads of the dozen or so dragons, and she lurched forward before the lycans pulled her back. Somehow, Cole managed to suppress the lycan seeking to break free and run to her.

He had no idea how the dragons would react if he set the lycan free in this hall, and he couldn't risk them attacking her.

"Let her go," he said in a low, gravelly voice distorted by the change trying to take him over.

"Why would I do that?" the Lord inquired.

"She has nothing to do with any of this."

"Now that's where you're wrong. She's the daughter of a man who fought for me, the lover of the king of the dark fae, and my very loyal vampire friend here has asked for her hand in marriage."

Cole's pulse thundered in his ears at this announcement. When his gaze swung toward Malakai, the vampire took a step back. His eyes darted around like he was about to run again, but there was nowhere for him to go.

"Not in my hall," the Lord hissed. "If you fight in here, I'll kill you."

Cole's breathing came faster as his attention returned to the

Lord. The man's eyes were shrewd as he assessed Cole. Then the lunatic shifted his attention to Lexi.

Lifting his hand again, he waved at her. "Come here, dear," he called out.

When Lexi jerked on her arms again, the lycans released her. She lifted her chin, but he sensed her fear as she descended the stairs. With cautious steps, she made her way down the hall toward them.

She had to weave her way through the dragons as they remained closed in behind Cole. And the monsters were not going to get out of her way. Half of them remained asleep, a few of them kept their attention on Cole, but a couple lifted their heads to watch her through slitted eyes.

When Cole started toward her, the Lord's words froze him. "Stay where you are."

Cole's shoulders heaved as the lycan tried to take control. His body started to contort, but somehow, he subdued his compulsion to change.

"Do not move, Colburn," the Lord commanded.

When Cole's head swiveled toward him, alarm flashed through the man's eyes. Their gazes held until a dragon shifted behind him and Cole's attention returned to Lexi.

CHAPTER SIXTY-THREE

LEXI COULD BARELY BREATHE AS she picked her way carefully through the sea of huge, man-eating creatures lounging on the floor of the massive hall. She didn't have the time to take in the beauty of the place as her attention remained focused on the dragons.

Don't step on their tails. DO NOT step on one of them.

But that was all she could picture herself doing. And the second she did, it would swallow her like a bird with a worm. She'd probably wiggle a lot less on the way down its gullet.

Lexi tugged on the collar of her shirt as a cold sweat coated her body. When one of the sleeping dragons opened one eye to peer at her, she nearly yelped as her bladder threatened to let loose.

The damn thing yawned as she passed before closing its eye and going back to sleep. She was going to die, its friends were going to eat her, and it was taking a *nap*.

Apparently, it had filled up on something else today, and she was not on the menu. She should be grateful; instead, she was even tenser. If this one didn't eat her, the next one might.

The worst was she couldn't see Cole anymore. Once she descended those steps and became surrounded by the dragons, she lost sight of him. She'd give anything to see him one more time, especially if she was going to die in this place.

One of the dragons shifted, and its tail fell in her way. Lexi froze as it twitched on the ground before settling into place.

Then one of them released a snore. They were *snoring!*

It took her a couple of seconds to start moving again, and once she did, she felt twitchier than a rabbit on cocaine as she crept around that tail.

From a distance, the dragons awed and frightened her, but up close...

Up close, they were *terrifying*. They smelled of fire and the musk of a wild animal. And these things were about as untamed as it got.

In the moonlight, their scales shone as the beasts' large breaths expanded their enormous rib cages. They were a variety of colors from red to green, brown, black, blue, and some were a mix of multiple colors.

When another one of their tails fell into her path, she lurched to the side to avoid it. She wasn't fast enough.

Her foot caught the end of it, and her knee twisted before giving out. She nearly fell but somehow managed to catch her balance before she toppled onto the beast.

As its head swung toward her, she realized it didn't matter that she hadn't fallen on it. Lexi stopped breathing when the tip of its nose collided with her hand.

She didn't dare move, but she wasn't sure if standing here or running was the better option. It couldn't be running. Hunters loved it when their prey ran, but standing here and doing nothing about her imminent gobbling seemed wrong.

Its hot breath heated the back of her hand, and eyes, the pure blue of the center of a flame, met hers. Would it roast her like a marshmallow before eating her?

She didn't know which would be worse, being burned or eaten

alive, and she wasn't eager to find out. They stared at each other before it bared razor-sharp teeth half the size of her.

Shit. Shit. Shit. SHIT!

It took everything she had not to bolt out of the room, but these creatures, and the Lord, would never let her escape. And she couldn't let the Lord or Malakai see her fleeing like a coward. Still, her knees knocked together, and her heart bruised her ribs with its incessant pounding.

"Easy," the Lord soothed.

Lexi's gaze lifted to him. She couldn't see Malakai or Cole, but from his position on the dais, she could see the Lord smiling down at her.

She hated him.

"Come, dear," the Lord continued and beckoned her forward. "They won't harm you."

She didn't find his words reassuring. She knew what the Lord and his dragons had done to Tove and countless other victims. The human realm would never be the same after the destruction they unleashed on it.

However, she couldn't continue to stand here, staring into the eyes of a displeased dragon. Lexi started forward but stopped when the dragon's head inched closer.

She braced herself for those monstrous teeth to chomp her. It was all she could do as she certainly couldn't stop it from happening.

She wasn't ready to die, and she couldn't stand the idea of Cole watching it happen, but she didn't have a choice.

"Stand down," the Lord commanded.

The dragon's head swung toward him before coming back to her. Its sigh caused its hot breath to wash over her again; it settled its head on the ground.

She'd expected its breath to smell like rotten meat; instead, it smelled like the fires her dad would have when she was a kid. She used to sit around those fires with her dad and Sahira. They would tell ghost stories and make smores.

That seemed like a lifetime ago, but it was only three short years. And now, she was standing in a field of dragons who smelled of those fires, and they *were* the stories they told to scare each other.

"Stay where you are," the Lord said.

Lexi didn't move.

"I told you to stay where you were!" the Lord shouted.

For a few seconds, Lexi was confused as she hadn't moved a muscle. Then Cole emerged around the back of the dragon. Nearly as monstrous as the creatures surrounding her, she almost didn't recognize him.

Caught somewhere between lycan and man, he half transformed as he walked. The bright silver of his eyes glowed. His face extended into a muzzle before retracting again. Hair spread across the backs of his hands and retreated.

The changes happened so fast she could barely register them before they faded again. Despite the wrath emanating from him and his obvious lack of control, Lexi didn't have any fear of him.

She only feared *for* him.

A few of the dragons turned toward him, and smoke spiraled from their nostrils. By disobeying a direct order from the Lord, he put himself in the middle of these monsters.

He was in a pit of snakes, and those snakes *despised* him. Not only had one of them killed his father, but he'd killed one of them in return. The dragons edged closer as they prepared to devour him.

"No," Lexi whispered.

Her paralysis broke, and she staggered toward him as one of the dragons lowered its head until it nearly touched Cole's back. He didn't acknowledge its presence as his focus remained on her.

When Cole's hand clasped her elbow, a strangled sound passed her lips before she compressed them. No matter what happened, she would *not* cry in this place.

"The lycans came back for me," she whispered. "You were barely gone before they returned. I wasn't expecting it."

"It's okay," he said in a guttural voice she barely recognized as it was more animal than man.

Despite the horribleness of this situation, a sense of calm descended as she grasped his hand on her arm. At least if they were going to die, it would be together.

And they would go down fighting. She didn't care if these things could stomp her flatter than a pancake; she would fight them to the death. At least it would be a quick death.

Cole stopped changing as he led her through the dragons and toward the dais. She yearned to say so much to him, but the words remained trapped behind her lips.

She should have put up a fight when they came for her, but worried about Cole, she let them lead her out of the human realm and into this place. She was scared that if she resisted, they'd take it out on him.

Instead, she allowed them to take her away. Despite her willingness to go with them, they tore her shirt when they pushed her onto one of their horses. As they came around the last dragon, she tugged her sleeve up to her shoulder.

When her gaze settled on Malakai, he smiled smugly at her. She gritted her teeth as she resisted giving him the finger.

She had no idea what was happening here, but it couldn't be good, and Malakai had a role in it.

CHAPTER SIXTY-FOUR

"I TOLD you to stay where you were," the Lord said as his red eyes bored into Cole.

Cole didn't respond; he'd known he was risking the Lord's wrath when he disobeyed his command. But there was no way he was going to leave Lexi out there alone with the dragons.

"I am sorry, milord," Cole said.

The apology grated on Cole's nerves, and the words were a bitter acid on his tongue, but if he were to have any chance of saving Lexi's life, he had to play nice. He had to act like he considered the Lord his boss and respected him.

But if there were no dragons here, he'd slaughter this man in a heartbeat.

And they both knew it.

"I couldn't leave her out there alone," Cole said.

"You could, but you *chose* not to."

"She's my mate, milord; I could not leave her out there alone."

The malicious glee in the Lord's eyes set Cole's teeth on edge. *This* is exactly what he'd hoped to avoid revealing to this man, but he had no other choice.

And he suspected the Lord already knew. Lexi wouldn't be

here if the Lord didn't already believe she was something he could use against him.

"Is she now?" the Lord purred. "Let her go, Cole."

Cole's fingers tightened on her arm before he peeled them away. The Lord needed him to keep the dark fae in line and to hunt his brothers, so he might be able to disobey this man once; he wouldn't get a second chance.

And he wouldn't be the one who paid for his disobedience; Lexi would.

~

THE LORD CROOKED his finger and beckoned to her. "Come here, honey."

Lexi bristled over being called honey, but now wasn't the time to get all pissy about an endearment this man hadn't earned the right to give her. When she stepped closer, the Lord beckoned her onward until she stood only a few feet away from the steps.

When she stopped, he tilted his head to study her. Lexi forced herself not to shift and twitch beneath his scrutiny.

"Ahh," the Lord murmured after a minute.

Something was wrong with the Lord's eyes, and it wasn't just their solid, ruby red color. No, it was the madness churning behind those eyes that made them so off. There wasn't any morality or compassion in the man's gaze.

He didn't possess one *ounce* of kindness. He might have at one time, but that time was gone.

The dragons' claws scraped the ground as they shifted behind her. She chanced a glance back at Cole as the creatures closed around him again. The stony mask of his face didn't change. He had to be aware they were approaching, but he didn't show any sign of it.

"You're a beautiful woman," the Lord murmured, drawing her attention back to him. "I received word of your presence at the king's side throughout his father's funeral and coronation, but they underestimated your beauty. No wonder these men seek to claim you."

Her gaze shot to Malakai; her lip curled. She hadn't seen him since he attacked her. She'd hoped never to see him again but known it was inevitable.

She hadn't expected it to be like this. And she hadn't expected to learn he was trying to *claim* her.

"One of them says you're his mate, and the other wants you as his wife," the Lord continued.

Wife! Lexi's mouth went dry as bile rose in her throat. Malakai had come to this man to tell him he wanted her as his *wife!*

She'd rather be burnt to death by a dragon while *also* being chomped on by it.

"I also want her as my wife," Cole said.

"Is that so?" the Lord murmured while he ran his teepeed fingers back and forth under his chin. "I'm not sure how the dark fae will take to their king marrying a... what *are* you, honey?"

"I'm half human and half vampire," she managed to say around the lump in her throat.

The Lord released a humorless laugh. "Oh my. It must be your beauty they're fighting over then because it's certainly *not* your breeding."

Lexi bit her tongue. Telling this psycho off was probably not the best way to ensure a good end to this rather crappy day.

"Yes, I do not see that going over well with the dark fae, especially since they already have a half-breed as their king," the Lord continued. "We know how little they like outsiders, and their opinions on *humans*... well, let's just say, I have more tolerance for them, and I enjoy watching them burn."

If Hannibal Lecter had a baby with Annie Wilkes, it would be saner than this freak.

"It doesn't matter what the dark fae say or want," Cole said. "*I* am their king, and they will obey me. They sent three others into the trials against me, and *none* of them survived. They can send more dark fae into the trials, and I'll destroy every single one of them, just as I destroyed Aelfdane. That throne is *mine*."

Cole's voice remained guttural and distorted as he spoke, and his revelation about Aelfdane caused even the dragons to stop moving. She hadn't known this detail about the trials, but he'd only revealed this about Aelfdane to prove his strength and determination to the Lord.

She didn't know how the monster was going to take it.

"One must kill to rule, but one does not have to marry," the Lord replied. "And marrying a half-breed human is bound to irritate the already cantankerous dark fae."

Taking a deep breath, Lexi gathered her courage and asked, "Do I have a say in this?"

The Lord's eyes came back to her, and he smiled. It was the cruelest smile she'd ever seen. "You can say whatever you want, but it means nothing to me."

Lexi's fingers bit into her palms as the futility of her situation sank in. They were all rats to him, and he was the cat batting them around. Then the Lord's gaze went to her shoulder.

Lexi hadn't realized her shirt had fallen to reveal Cole's bite on her.

CHAPTER SIXTY-FIVE

IN THE MOONLIGHT spilling through the opening above, his bite on Lexi shone a brilliant silver against her creamy flesh. Too late, Cole realized the Lord had purposely waited until nightfall to bring them in here.

It was a good thing he'd admitted she was his mate because *this* was exactly what the Lord intended to learn about her when he brought them here.

And he'd done so because someone in the Gloaming had told him about Lexi being by his side. Malakai had a hand in these events, but one of *his* subjects came here to reveal a weakness to this man.

An image of Becca formed in his mind. It could have been anyone or more than one, but he couldn't shake the conviction it was *her*. He would find out who had betrayed him and make them pay.

The Lord turned to Malakai. "Do you still want a woman that another man has claimed?"

"I don't want him," Lexi stated.

The Lord waved a hand dismissively at her. "I don't care."

"He should have no right to her. She is the daughter of one of your most loyal soldiers, and *he* attacked her," Cole stated.

"Is this true? Did you attack the woman?" he asked Malakai.

"He didn't like seeing her with me and has convinced himself she wasn't perfectly willing," Malakai replied.

"That's not true," Lexi protested.

When Cole stepped toward Malakai, the Lord rose a little from his throne. "There will be no fighting in my hall!" he bellowed.

His words caused all the dragons to turn toward them. They moved closer until three of them were only inches away from him and Lexi. The three of them lowered their heads to glower at him.

"Cole," Lexi whispered and rested her hand on his arm.

He relaxed a little beneath her touch, but no matter what happened here, he would kill Malakai if the Lord decided to hand her over to him. It would mean his death, but so be it; she would at least be a little safer.

The dragons' attention shifted to her, and one edged a little closer to release a smoky breath that coiled over where her hand gripped his arm.

"Oh," she breathed.

"It's okay," Cole assured her. "You're going to be fine."

"Now," the Lord said as he settled on his throne again, "I don't care if he attacked her or not. He got a little overzealous, or she teased him; she is a woman after all. We all know how fickle they are."

When Lexi's hand tightened on his arm, Cole grasped it and gave it a gentle squeeze as Malakai laughed.

"That they are," Malakai agreed.

"Do you still want a woman that another man has claimed?" the Lord asked Malakai again.

"That bite will fade," Malakai replied. "And I will leave plenty of my own on her."

The Lord roared with laughter as he slapped his knee. He was crazier than the last time Cole saw him, and it was obvious the lunatic liked Malakai. Not only had he given the vamp a sun medallion to allow him to walk in the day, but he found the asshole amusing.

"You are correct!" the Lord agreed. Then, as suddenly as the laughter came, it vanished. "But, if I give her to *you*, then I will make an enemy of the king of the dark fae, and since I just killed the last one, I should probably keep this one alive for a little bit."

His attention shifted to Cole. "I should kill you. You're too powerful, and I don't like it." He leaned forward. "But as long as I allow you to have *her*, then I can control you. Before, I only had the threat of destroying the Gloaming to keep you in line, but now... now, I have something that means so much more to you... your *mate*."

He chuckled as he leaned back on his throne. "I couldn't have planned it any better if I tried. Any other dark fae king wouldn't have such a weakness, but you... oh, *you* have lycan blood in you, and the lycans will do anything for their mates.

"And oh, how I plan to use her. The second you step out of line, King Colburn of the dark fae, I will take her and give her to him"—he pointed a finger at Malakai—"and I will make you watch while he fucks her.

"From what she says, she will not be willing, so I'm assuming it will be brutal and something you will never forget. The *second* you mess up, you'll hear the screams of your mate as another takes what you think is yours but is *mine*. You may rule the Gloaming, but I control all the realms and everyone in them."

Cole's joints and bones popped as they twisted and shifted. With sheer strength of will, he shoved the wolf back into its cage.

"And no matter how powerful you are, you cannot stop my friends or me," the Lord said and waved his fingers.

Behind him, the dragons shifted again, and more of them crept closer.

"I want your brothers, Cole," the Lord said.

"You'll have them," Cole replied.

"Good, because if I don't have them soon, then I will have *her*." He thrust a finger at Lexi. *"I'll* fuck her before I give her to Malakai, but don't fret; I'll give her back afterward because she will *always* be my leverage against you. And as your mate, you'll take her back, even if she's sucked every dick in this realm."

∾

IT TOOK everything Lexi had not to vomit at the picture the Lord's words conjured. Her mind screamed denials at her even as her heart acknowledged the truth. This monstrosity would pass her around to every man he knew while making Cole watch.

What they would have to do to Cole to get him to watch would probably damn near kill him.

When the Lord finished with her, he would give her back to Cole, and Cole would take her back. And he would do it, not because she was his mate, but because he loved her. He would never blame her or hate her for what happened.

He *would* hate himself and never recover from it, but neither would she. They'd both be broken and battered by it and their helplessness, and all because this sick bastard was determined to destroy everything good in the world.

"If Varo and Orin aren't here by the end of the month, I'm coming for her," the Lord said. "So, you had better start hunting. And if you try to hide her from me, I'll level the Gloaming and more of the human realm in search of her. So, the two of you will have to decide between having *her* blood on your hands or *millions* of others' blood on them."

Lexi would never let that happen. She couldn't imagine much worse than being passed around to countless others by this monster, but the lives of millions staining her soul was one of them.

"What about me?" Malakai asked plaintively.

"You'll have to wait to see if you get a turn at her or find someone else. Do you believe she is your consort?" When Malakai didn't reply, the Lord turned to face him. "Do you?"

"I don't care if she is; she *will* be my bride."

"Not if I say no, and I am saying no… for now."

Malakai's gaze swung to her, and red flashed through his eyes. Lexi glared back at him.

"Colburn, take your mate and get out of my hall," the Lord said and waved dismissively at them.

Cole pulled Lexi's hand from his arm and kept hold of it. "Let's go," he said.

Before they could go anywhere, one of the dragons swung its wings forward. Their vast size blocked out the room as the lethal points at the bottom of those wings hit the floor on either side of Cole. He didn't acknowledge them.

Lexi glanced up at the creature as it rose over them, but she'd rather face its wrath than the Lord's. Then the dragon lowered its head to peer intently at her.

CHAPTER SIXTY-SIX

COLE STARED the creature down as he pulled Lexi into his arms. He locked her against his chest as the dragon's head swung back and forth while it studied them.

"How sweet," the Lord murmured. "And disgusting. Get out of my hall, but remember, I know where she is, and I'll find her if you don't bring me your brothers."

Cole glanced over at where Malakai remained sulking by the stairs. The Lord must have seen something on his face as he sat a little straighter on his throne.

"The two of you are to stay away from each other," the Lord said. "If something happens to one of you, I will not be pleased, and I do *not* like being displeased. Do you understand me, Colburn?"

"Yes."

But, to him, Malakai was a dead man walking.

He cradled Lexi's head against his chest and led her beneath one of the dragon's wings as they made their way toward the doors at the end of the hall. All the dragons were awake now, and their heads turned to watch them.

The last, and the biggest dragon he'd ever seen, rose onto its hind feet as they neared. It unfurled its wings, and its bellow shook the walls before it launched itself off the ground and soared toward the open ceiling.

The flap of its wings blew their hair back and plastered their clothes to them. Lexi trembled as she pressed closer to him.

Cole opened one of the doors and led her into the hallway beyond. They passed statues of golden dragons and the ill-fated arach who stood beside some of them.

He guided her out of the palace and down the front steps. As they strode down the walkway, he let out a loud whistle. A minute later, Torigon trotted into view. The magnificent animal's black coat shone in the moonlight as it trotted forward and fell in behind them.

As they left the palace gates behind, the monstrous dragon flew over the top of them. It glided so low that the fine lines etching its belly were visible.

His bones and joints cracked and popped as the lycan strained to break free in response to the dragon's clear threat to his mate.

~

COLE LED her to the portal that would take them out of Dragonia. They entered and emerged in the human realm, near the city.

When Cole used his powers to open a different portal, Lexi wasn't concerned about it weakening him. Instead, she considered it better that he released some of his power.

However, the opening of the portal didn't ease the thrum of his power beating against her. The thump of it sounded like a helicopter's rotors churning through the air.

His body swelled, changed, and contorted before returning to normal. She winced at the noises his joints and bones made. *Snap. Pop. Snap. Crack.*

She couldn't imagine the kind of pain this continuous changing caused him, but he showed no signs of it affecting him as his step didn't slow. His ciphers swelled with his muscles before constricting again.

He led her into the portal and through the darkness until they emerged at the edge of the lake. They were only fifty feet away from the manor; it was exactly as she left it, yet it all seemed so different now. Everything had changed in such a short amount of time.

Torigon followed them as they crossed to the manor before ambling away to graze. Cole's claws lengthened and retracted. *Crack. Snap. Crack. Pop. Snap. Snap. Snap.*

The song of the tree frogs and crickets wasn't nearly loud enough to drown out the continued contortion of Cole's body as he hurried her up the steps of the manor and opened the door.

He guided her inside and kicked the door shut with his heel. She didn't have time to speak before he pinned her to the wall and kissed her.

His fangs pressed against her lips, and his leg parted her thighs as he pushed it between them. Something cracked again, but the continuous noises ebbed as his tongue swept into her mouth.

When he seized her wrists and lifted them above her head to pin them against the wall, his claws grazed her skin but didn't draw blood. Despite the awfulness of everything they'd gone through today, his kiss made her forget about the Lord.

She had no doubt Cole meant to take her right there, and she longed for it to happen. She hadn't known how to help him regain control before, but she did now as her body arched into his.

He relaxed against her, and his claws retracted. Unable to stop herself, she bit his lower lip and swallowed his blood as he released a sexy growl.

She needed this as badly as him, but a clattering bang from the kitchen caught her attention. She tried to ignore it, but when something else banged, she tore her mouth away from his and turned her head toward the kitchen.

The realization someone was in her home doused her lust. Sahira was gone, and George would never let himself in; *no* one else should be in here. Cole's ragged breath warmed her ear as a cabinet door opened and closed.

"No one should be here," she whispered.

Cole stiffened before releasing her and stepping away. She had no idea who was in the kitchen, but as Cole stalked down the hall, she felt sorry for them.

She'd been his outlet for the pent-up violence, but that outlet was interrupted. Now, he would unleash it in another way. When his bones started contorting and cracking again, Lexi ran to catch up with him as he entered the kitchen.

She had no idea what she expected to find, but her jaw dropped when she spotted Orin on the other side of the island, stirring a pot on the stove. He was wearing one of Sahira's aprons that read *Bitch, I am the secret ingredient.*

If Cole didn't kill him, Sahira might. She loved her aprons.

From the corner of the room, Shade's tail twitched as the cat's golden eyes followed Orin. Sahira's familiar might claw Orin's eyes out if he got one drop on that apron.

When Orin looked up, he started to smile, but it froze when Cole stopped to glower at him. Lexi's eyes flew to the kitchen window; the curtains had been drawn shut. The lock on the back door was engaged, and the curtain over the window there was also closed.

That didn't stop her from scurrying over to the windows to make sure they were completely covered. When she finished, she noticed the bottle of birth control Sahira had left on the counter.

With her face burning, she grabbed the bottle and shoved it in her pocket. Orin had no way of knowing what was inside, but she still didn't like having it out in the open.

"I made sure nobody could see inside," Orin said.

"*What* are you doing here?" Lexi demanded.

Orin didn't take his eyes off Cole as he stirred whatever was in the large pot. Judging by the smell wafting from it, the arrogant ass was cooking *spaghetti sauce*. Incredulity warred with irritation as she scowled at him. If the remains on the cutting board near the pot were any indication, he'd used *their* stash of tomatoes to make it.

"I figured since the cat was out of the bag, no offense," he said to Shade, who twitched his tail in response, "I might as well make dinner for everyone."

"You shouldn't be here," Cole said.

Orin continued to stir, but he couldn't hide the small tremor in his hand. Cole was pissed in the tunnels, but this was a whole new level of angry as his bones continued to snap and pop.

Finally, he tore his eyes away from his brother to look at her. She saw the questions in his gaze, but she didn't have answers for him. Her loyalty lay with Cole, and she had no idea how much he wished to reveal to Orin.

"I shouldn't be many places, but here I am," Orin said.

Lexi rolled her eyes. The man was horrible at keeping his wise-ass comments to himself.

Cole slammed his hand onto the black marble countertop. "You put us all at risk by being here. You put *her*"— he pointed at Lexi — "at risk by being here. And she's already in far too much danger; I won't have her placed in anymore because you think you can do whatever you want."

Orin stirred as he studied Cole. "*Where* have the two of you been?"

"The Lord wanted to meet with me," Cole said. "And he brought her along for the ride."

Orin paled a little; he stopped stirring and stepped away from the stove. "What happened?"

Cole gave him a brief rundown on what occurred while Lexi chewed her bottom lip and paced from the back door to the kitchen window and back again. Stopping at the back door, she pulled aside a corner of the curtain and peered out.

The night remained hushed, but a malevolent air had settled

over the place. Things would never be the same. As long as the Lord lived, she would always be a pawn for him to use against Cole.

And she had a bad feeling that no matter what Cole did, no matter how well he played the game and obeyed the Lord, the insane man would never be satisfied. He would find a reason to punish Cole by handing her over to Malakai. Cole knew it too. That was why he was so volatile right now.

When Cole finished speaking, Orin was speechless for the first time since she met him. She turned away from the window to look at the brothers.

Orin remained in complete control while Cole was unraveling again. His joints cracked and popped, his face elongated and retracted as she returned to stand near the basin sink.

"I don't see anyone out there," she said.

"I made sure no one was around when I came out of the tunnel," Orin said. "I remained cloaked in shadows until I pulled the curtains over the windows."

"You shouldn't have risked it," Cole said.

"I didn't know the Lord had decided to have you over as his guests when I did," Orin replied.

When Cole leaned toward him, Orin gulped. Lexi had never seen him look anything less than perfectly composed, but it was clear Cole's instability unnerved him. No one spoke as the sauce on the stove bubbled.

Snap. Crack. Snap. Crack. Crack. Pop.

When sauce splattered the stainless-steel surface of the stove, Lexi reached to turn off the flame. Before her hand settled on the knob, Orin snatched it and drew it toward him.

"What is that?" he demanded.

Lexi had no idea what he was talking about until he lifted her hand to examine it. On the back of it, a swirl of silver ran across her flesh. She frowned at the marking, uncertain where it came from, but then she recalled the dragon's nose brushing against her.

"I'm not sure what it is," she said. "But one of the dragons touched me."

Orin's face was unreadable as he stared at her hand. Then, before she could stop him, he stuck her hand in the fire beneath the pot.

CHAPTER SIXTY-SEVEN

WHEN HER FLESH bubbled and sizzled, Lexi gasped and ripped her hand away. "What is *wrong* with you?"

The question was starting to slip from her lips when Cole hit Orin with an uppercut that shot his head back, lifted him off the floor, and sent him soaring ten feet backward. He hit the gray stone wall behind him with a loud thud.

Blood poured from his nose and mouth as he slid down the wall to the ground. Cole's shoulders hunched forward, his face and hands changed as he stalked toward his brother. His eyes burned silver, but blackness seeped across the whites of them.

And as he walked, something black emerged from him. It floated in the air around him as it seeped from his pores to darken the room. It took her a second to realize *shadows* were oozing out of him.

How is that possible?

Lexi gawked at him as she cradled her blistered hand against her chest. She'd seen a lot of things recently, but she'd *never* seen anything like the blackness emanating from him. The shadows rose around him like demons set free from Hell.

She'd sensed the increase of his power since he emerged from the trials, but now, she *saw* it. And it was a terrifying sight to behold. She had no idea how it was possible, but the shadows hissed as they weaved around him.

If this had happened while they were in Dragonia, they would be dead. There was no way the Lord would let him survive if he saw this.

Had he kept this hidden while there because she wasn't injured or because he'd known that unleashing it would get them killed? Or had he been pushed too far throughout the day and couldn't maintain control anymore?

She suspected the latter. Orin's actions were finally the breaking point.

Orin's feet kicked at the floor as he pushed himself further up the wall. He didn't get a chance to rise before Cole loomed over him. When one of the shadows snapped at his face, Orin recoiled.

"Holy shit, Cole!" he exclaimed when the shadow left a red welt across his cheek.

How is it possible for a shadow to hurt someone? She didn't have an answer for that, but these ones were out for blood and could inflict damage.

"You don't *ever fucking touch her!*" Cole roared.

He grasped Orin by the shirt and, as if Orin weighed no more than a discarded leaf, plucked him off the ground. When he slammed his brother into the wall, the manor shook from the impact.

"You *ever* touch her again, and I'll rip off your head and personally hand it to the Lord. Do you understand me?" Cole snarled.

The last four words were bit out in a mutated voice Lexi barely recognized. She'd never considered it possible for Cole to lose control so completely yet somehow manage to retain it.

"Do you understand me?" Cole gave Orin a sharp shake with each word he spoke.

"Yes!" Orin shouted.

His hands fisted, but he didn't swing at Cole. If he did, Lexi was sure a bloody, brutal battle would ensue. One they both knew Orin would lose.

"You better hope they find the harrow stone because I will *not* let her be raped and brutalized by the Lord and his minions. I will not let her become a pawn in our games and mistakes. Am I making myself clear?"

"Yes."

"We deserve whatever the Lord unleashes on us. She. Does. Not."

Cole shoved Orin away from him and turned toward her. Unprepared for the sudden motion, Lexi couldn't stop herself from retreating from him.

When he saw her reaction, he hesitated, but she quickly recovered and walked toward him as Orin slid to the ground. Cole met her halfway and tenderly clasped her wrist.

The second he touched her, some of his tension ebbed, and the shadows retracted a little. He guided her over to the sink, turned on the cold water, and gently held her hand beneath the cool flow.

The water trickling over the blister forming on her hand helped ease some of the sting. As he brushed the hair back from her forehead, the shadows fully retreated into him.

"Are you okay?" he asked.

"Ye-Yes," she stammered. "Are you?"

"Yes."

She might set him off again, but she had to say what they both already knew. "Someone from the Gloaming told the Lord about me."

"I know."

"Do you think it was Becca?"

"Yes."

"That means a member of your council is working against you."

"It's to be expected. Even my father had resistance when he

claimed the throne. The dark fae will test their boundaries, and I will be there to make sure those boundaries hold firm. No matter what it takes."

He sounded so confident in his ability to do so, but she couldn't stop the feeling of foreboding creeping down her spine. They already had so much going against them; they didn't need this too.

CHAPTER SIXTY-EIGHT

"THAT SHADOW THING; I've never seen it happen before," she said.

"Neither have I," he murmured.

"So, it's a new development?"

"Yes."

"Is it because you're king?"

"No, it's because I survived the trials. When I did, the shadows became as much a part of me as I am them. With or without the crown, that wouldn't change."

"I never saw it happen to Father," Orin said.

When Cole's head swiveled toward him, Lexi considered Orin either extremely brave or incredibly foolish to speak at all. The brothers stared at each other before Cole spoke.

"Neither did I, but that doesn't mean it never did. We also never saw Father in a rage."

"No, we didn't, but you came back different than him, and we both know it."

Lexi bit her bottom lip as she waited for someone to say something, but neither did. "Is that true?" she finally asked.

Cole turned his attention back to her. "I think so."

"But why?"

He shrugged as he tenderly ran his fingers over her hand. "I don't know."

"But you're going to be okay?"

"I'll be fine," he assured her. "If I'm different, it's because I'm more powerful and have newfound abilities."

"Like shadows that can inflict damage on another?"

"Yes."

"You have to keep that hidden."

"I know." He kissed her forehead. "Don't worry about me, love."

That was much easier said than done.

He focused on Orin again. "Do you care to explain why you hurt her?"

Orin slowly rose from his position on the floor. He approached the stove, turned off the flame, and lifted the towel sitting beside it. He studied Lexi as he wiped the blood away from his mouth and nose.

"Sometimes, the arach would get silver markings on them," he said.

"So?" Cole asked.

"So, your mate had a silver marking on the back of her hand. Don't you find that a little strange?"

Lexi studied her palm beneath the water before turning it over. The silver was gone. "The dragon must have had something on it that left a mark on me."

There was no other explanation. At one time, the arach were the most powerful immortals in existence, but she couldn't even create a portal, was physically weaker than most immortals, and had no discernible powers.

"You think she's an arach?" Cole inquired.

"I'm not sure what I think," Orin said.

"I'm not an arach," Lexi said. "It's said they could walk through a dragon's fire, and I can't withstand a tiny flame from the stove."

"I see that," Orin muttered.

A ticking against the window over the sink broke the ensuing silence. She and Cole stared at the curtain as the ticking paused for a few seconds before starting again.

"Did you send a letter to Niall?" Cole asked her.

"No, I never got the chance," she said. "They returned for me before I could."

Cole glanced over his shoulder at Orin. "Hide."

Orin slipped into the hallway and, drawing the shadows around him, disappeared. Cole kept one hand on her wrist beneath the water as he pulled aside the curtain. A crow peered in at them from where it sat on the sill.

Cole undid the lock and pushed the window open a little. The crow dropped a small piece of paper, cawed loudly, and took flight. Cole retrieved the paper, closed the window, and set the note on the counter beside the sink.

He released her wrist, dried his hands on one of the towels hanging from the kitchen cabinets beneath the sink, and tugged the curtain into place. Orin returned to the kitchen as Cole opened the note.

"Shit!" Cole hissed a second later.

"What is it?" Lexi asked.

"It's from Elvin. There's been an uprising in the Gloaming. The king's army is fighting to end it, but I have to return."

Is it ever going to end? But she already knew the answer to that.

No.

As long as the Lord sat on the throne, it would never end.

"They're testing their boundaries," she whispered.

"And I'm going to make sure they learn what a giant mistake that is, but you have to come with me. I cannot fight this battle if you're here where Malakai and the Lord can return for you."

"You can't take her to the Gloaming while it's in upheaval; there are countless enemies there," Orin said.

"Am I supposed to leave her here for *you* to protect?" Cole demanded. "In case you've forgotten, you're the most hunted man in all the realms."

"It's safer here than in the Gloaming."

"Not if she's in the palace; it will protect her."

"You're kidding." Orin snorted.

"I'm not," Cole said. "It already has."

Orin's eyes narrowed on her. Lexi didn't like the look in his eyes, and Cole must not have either, as he growled while stepping in front of her. The move drew Orin's attention to him.

"You have to return to the tunnels and stay there," he said.

"You don't know who you can trust in the Gloaming, and you don't have Brokk to watch your back," Orin said.

"Are you offering to come back to help me fight this rebellion?"

"I would, but do you want the Lord to hear about me fighting at your side? That would sign both our death certificates. However, returning to fight this battle alone is a risky thing, Cole. Enemies with friendly faces will surround you."

CHAPTER SIXTY-NINE

As MUCH AS Cole wanted to kill his brother for harming Lexi, Orin spoke the truth. If he could return to the Gloaming to help Cole against this insurrection, he would, but it would only result in the Lord hunting them both.

There was a lot of animosity between them, but they were brothers. They might one day kill each other, but they would also fight to the death *for* each other.

"I have to go," Cole said to Lexi. He clasped her uninjured hand tenderly in both of his. "Please, come with me."

"What if...." She paused to swallow her sorrow before speaking again. "What if something happens to you while I'm there? I won't be able to leave."

"I'll leave a portal open inside the palace. If something happens to me, you can return here. Hopefully, Sahira and Brokk will be back by then. Brokk will be able to get you somewhere safe and away from the Lord."

Because his death would not guarantee her safety from that madman.

"So will I," Orin said.

Cole gave him a nod of thanks before returning his attention to Lexi.

She bit her bottom lip before responding. "I've already asked George to stay on and help with the horses, so they'll be fine. And I'd prefer to be there... to know... to...."

Her voice broke, and she stopped speaking to look at the window.

He brushed the hair back from her shoulder and clasped her cheek to turn her face to him. "I'm going to be fine. The dark fae have no idea what they're messing with when it comes to me."

"That's for sure," Orin muttered, but when Cole shot him a look, he saw the curiosity in his brother's gaze.

"And there is Niall. I have him and other men there that I trust."

Lexi turned the water off and carefully dried her blistered hand. When Cole lifted her palm to examine the red welt, he glowered at his brother again.

Orin rolled his eyes. "She'll heal."

"Prick," Cole muttered.

"Then we should go," Lexi said.

"I'll be right back," Cole said.

He released Lexi and jogged down the hall to the library. He'd left his sword leaning against the wall there after returning from the tunnels with Lexi, Brokk, and Sahira. That all seemed like weeks ago, but a day hadn't passed.

Lifting the sword, he swung it onto his back and secured it there with the strap. He returned to discover Lexi filling her pockets with potions from one of the cabinets.

"What are those?" he asked.

"Sahira's skin-melting potions. They could come in handy."

He wouldn't turn down anything that would help keep her safer. When she finished, Cole claimed her good hand.

"Stay below, stay out of view, and stay out of trouble," he said to Orin. "I'll be back as soon as this is over."

"Don't rush on my account," Orin said with a dismissive wave of his hand. He dipped his spoon into the sauce before lifting it to take a small taste. "It needs some garlic, but you don't have any."

"Oh, well, I'm so sorry," Lexi retorted. "When this is over, I'll run down to the grocery store to get some for you. Oh, that's right, they don't exist anymore."

"That's okay," Orin said. "I'll make do without it."

Lexi stared incredulously at him before looking at Cole. "Can you hit him again?"

Despite his growing urgency to return to the Gloaming, Cole chuckled. "Anytime you want."

"Good."

Cole drew her against his side as he lifted his hand and placed his palm out against the air. Drawing on his power, he focused it before him as he worked to tear a veil into the fabric separating this world from the Gloaming.

Only the king could open a portal into the palace, and he pictured a door forming in his rooms in his mind. She would be safest there, and he would lead her straight into them.

When the portal materialized, Orin set down his spoon. "Good luck, brother."

"Same to you," Cole said. "And don't forget, Sahira can find you anywhere, so don't try to run."

Orin placed a hand over his heart as he feigned insult. "I would *never* dream of doing such a thing."

Cole watched his brother as he led Lexi into the portal and toward the battle waging on the other side.

CHAPTER SEVENTY

ORIN STRODE past the closed doors of the cells lining the corridor of this long-forgotten prison. Established centuries ago, the stronghold sat on an outer realm that was barely more than a floating rock spinning through the fabric of time.

Misery hung like a thick, cloying blanket over the place. The smell of despair, sweat, and tears choked the air. He despised this place and rarely came here, but there was something he had to do.

He wasn't concerned about the witch tracking him here. She could find him if she tried, but Sahira was otherwise occupied, and she couldn't track all his past locations. Besides, he'd be back before anyone realized he was missing and started looking for him.

Behind the doors, some of the prisoners wept, others shouted, some begged to be set free, and others remained eerily silent. They had either accepted their fate or snapped completely. He'd seen those broken ones, sitting within and staring at the wall while they wasted away.

They refused to eat, and most were skin and bones as time marched relentlessly on. He'd wondered if some of them would eventually die, but it hadn't happened so far.

He felt no guilt over their fate. They'd chosen their path when they decided to fight for the Lord, and they were paying the consequences of it.

The soft soles of his boots didn't make a sound against the stone floor as he walked. He couldn't see any of the prisoners behind their solid metal doors. He was aware they were there, but they didn't have the same luxury of knowing about his presence.

Halfway down the corridor, he stopped outside one of the cells. A single window sat high up in the door. The metal covering was firmly closed and could only be opened from the outside.

Stepping forward, he grasped the small knob and pulled it open. Directly on the other side of the door, a pair of red eyes glared out at him.

He had no idea how the vampire did it, but Orin had yet to open this window and not discover the man standing there. He was tempted to believe the vamp never moved away from the door, but that was impossible. The vampire had to sit, sleep, and shit; he couldn't do those things while standing there.

No, somehow, this asshole always knew when he was coming, and he was always waiting for him.

Hatred simmered in the vampire's eyes as they stared at each other. Then Orin smiled.

"Hello, Del," he greeted. "We need to talk about your daughter."

～

Turn the page for a sneak peek of book 3, *Shadows of Betrayal*, or download now and continue reading: brendakdavies.com/SBwb

Stay in touch on updates, sales, and new releases by joining to the mailing list: brendakdavies.com/ESBKDNews

**Visit the Erica Stevens/Brenda K. Davies Book Club on
Facebook for exclusive giveaways and all things book related.
Come join the fun**: brendakdavies.com/ESBKDBookClub

SNEAK PEEK

SHADOWS OF BETRAYAL, THE SHADOW REALMS BOOK 3

Cole released Lexi as soon as he stepped out of the portal and stalked over to one of the windows overlooking the Gloaming. His jaw clenched as flames from the torches they carried leapt high. The dark fae roused from their homes fled from the approaching army.

A couple of hundred dark fae crested the hill and marched toward *his* home. He couldn't make out who was at the front of the rebels, but he would make them pay for it when he found out who was behind this.

"Stay here," he said as he turned away from the window.

"I'm going to the front door with you," Lexi said.

Cole didn't take the time to argue as he strode toward the door; he flung it open and swiftly descended the stairs to the first floor. Lexi ran beside him as he raced for the weapons room.

When he arrived at the room, he pulled the door open and entered the cavernous space. Lexi followed him inside, and he closed the door behind them.

Countless weapons lined the walls, filled the trunks pushed against them, and stuffed the containers set into the floor. Only a few knew how to access those hidden containers.

He stopped and knelt in the middle of the white marble floor. After years of having his father drill it into his head how to access these weapons, instinct guided him to this spot.

When he was little, he used to have to count the steps straight from the door to the right place. Along the way, he hoped he didn't step too far to one side or the other because it would throw him off completely. Not anymore.

When he placed his palm against the floor, the marble heated, and a golden glow shone around the edges of his hand.

"Amazing," Lexi whispered as the floor slid back to reveal the thick, metal case beneath.

When the marble settled into place with a click, he leaned forward and pulled the case open to reveal the cache of weapons within. He only wanted the sword, though.

The black, oplyx stone in the center of the sword's hilt shone as he lifted and turned it over in his hands. The blade was lighter than it looked and even more lethal. He'd seen it cut through flesh like butter before. He pulled the sword halfway from its sheath and examined the honed blade.

"Is that yours?" Lexi asked.

"My father's."

"Is it fae metal?"

"No, but whoever started this rebellion won't survive its wrath."

Even though his people were rising against him, he wouldn't use fae metal against his kind. Those rebelling against him wouldn't survive, but he couldn't break one of the most sacred rules amongst the fae.

No matter what, the fae didn't wield fae metal against their own.

Of course, some didn't always respect that boundary. He was certain more than a few of them were marching across that field right now.

Cole dropped the sword he wore to the ground, slung his

father's sword over his shoulder, and secured it there by its strap. He would go into this battle wielding his father's weapon.

When he lifted his head, he discovered Lexi watching him with dread. Her sun-kissed skin was much paler than normal, and her full lower lip trembled before she stiffened it.

Bending, he clasped her cheeks in his palms. "I must go. Don't leave the palace."

"Please, be careful," she whispered.

"Always."

He kissed her forehead, her nose, and finally her lips before releasing her and walking away. As he crossed the floor, the panel he'd opened slid back into place with a click.

He didn't look back as he opened the door and strode out of the room.

~

LEXI STARED after Cole's back as he left. She didn't move until she heard the front door close. Then, she sprinted across the room and to the wall that caught her attention when they first entered.

There, she pulled down a small sword and the leather belt hanging with it. She slid the belt around her waist and sheathed the sword. Lexi had no intention of leaving the palace; she wouldn't become a distraction to Cole, and they'd kill her as soon as she stepped foot on that battlefield, but she wouldn't be weaponless either.

Next, she pulled down the throwing stars hanging on the wall near it. She reached for the stars and froze when she saw the intricate designs marking the thick metal. The sword she wore wasn't fae metal, but these were.

And fae didn't use fae metal against each other.

However, she wasn't fae. It wasn't against the rules for her to use them in a fight with a fae. Of course, it probably wasn't the best idea to use fae metal against the species she might rule one day, but it was a worse idea for them to rise against Cole.

And she would make them pay for that if it became necessary.

She pulled the stars and the brown satchel hanging behind them down. She tied the pouch to the other side of her waist and shoved the stars inside.

~

GATHERED BY THE GATE, the hundred or so soldiers of the King's army waited for him. Their horses pranced restlessly as beyond the gates, the torches drew nearer, and the terrified shouts of the fleeing fae folk resonated through the night.

At one time, the King's forces numbered much higher, but that was before the war. The war decimated those numbers.

He'd fought beside many of these men during the war, but their loyalty lay with his father then. He had no idea how many considered themselves loyal to *him*. He saved many of these men's lives during the war, but that didn't mean he could count on them now.

There was no way to know how long this rebellion had been in the works, whose loyalty was bought, or who organized it. Any of these men could be a relative of the organizer or organizers. Any one of them could have been paid to turn against him.

He was about to ride into battle to face his enemies with an untold number of them at his back. His skin prickled as he studied the men, but there was no way of telling which side they were on until they were in the fray.

"Bring me a horse!" Cole shouted to the stable boy running between the horses. The boy squeaked and ran into the stables.

He'd much prefer to ride Torigon into battle, but he'd left his steadfast mount at Lexi's. It was just one more thing working against him for this battle.

"Milord," Niall greeted as he rode up in front of Cole.

Out of everyone here, he trusted Niall the most. They were the same age. Niall's father was once a general in his father's army; they played on top of hay bales as children, ran through the fields, skipped rocks, shared dreams of being mighty warriors, and later trained together in the art of war.

They spent countless nights together carousing with women, drinking, and fighting. Niall saved him nearly as many times as Cole did him during the war. He was one of Cole's most trusted friends, yet Cole didn't know where his true allegiance lay.

He would find out.

The stable boy ran up to him with a bay stallion. The animal was not as large as Torigon, but he looked sturdy, his legs were in good shape, and he wouldn't shy away during the fight. All the horses in the stable were battle tried, and that was what mattered most.

Grabbing the saddle's pommel, Cole swung himself onto the soft, brown leather that hugged the horse's back and settled himself there. He seized the reins and nudged his horse in the side to ride before his men.

"Destroy all who rise against me but, if possible, leave the leaders of this rebellion to me. I will see to them!" he shouted.

A chorus of shouts went through the soldiers before Cole rode up to the palace gates. As he pushed them open, he kept waiting for an arrow or sword to pierce his back, but neither thing happened.

Raising his sword high, Cole led the charge out of the gates. His horse's hooves thundered across the ground as he led his men over the hills. He didn't have to look back to know those gates would close behind the last man; they wouldn't let anyone else enter.

The fleeing fae raced past him as the rebellion's army topped the crest of the next hill. Cole was nearly to the invading rebels when the first arrow whistled past his ear.

He was not surprised that it had come from behind and struck the ground twenty feet in front of him. Shouts sounded from behind him, and when he glanced back, some of the king's men had closed in on one of their own.

They knocked the fae from the saddle, and he disappeared beneath the pounding hooves of the horses. He would not be the last enemy to come at him from behind.

Cole turned back in the saddle and focused on the enemy coming down the hill toward him. When they were upon him, Cole swung out with his sword and sliced the head from the first fae as another arrow came from behind.

No one had passed him yet, so that meant the bolt had come from another one of his men. Before he could see who, the enemy flooded the area and surrounded him.

The clash of steel against steel, the shouts of men in battle, and the screams of the injured and dying rebounded through the air. The stench of blood filled his nostrils as did horse sweat, and the rich aroma of the earth churned up beneath the horse's hooves.

These sights and smells had haunted his nightmares since the end of the war, and he could feel those memories churning within him. He buried those memories even as he realized he would now have even more death haunting his sleep.

Blood splattered his face and clothes as he cut down one dark fae after another. He didn't know how many he killed outright, but he wouldn't leave any survivors when this was over.

His horse's hooves stomped over the bodies, but it never floundered. Cole deflected the blade of one fae but missed a second sword that sliced across his bicep. He gritted his teeth against the influx of pain as blood spilled down his arm.

Spinning in his saddle, he was about to destroy his attacker when Niall's blade severed his attacker's head. Niall's black eyes shone with fury when they met Cole's, and blood dripped from his black hair. Though he was pure dark fae, Niall was a little broader and heavier than most others.

When Cole nodded to him, Niall's grin revealed all of his even, white teeth. And then, he vanished as the enemy raced between them.

A ball of fire shot at his head. Cole ducked and threw up a hand to catch the flame in his palm. Spinning his hand, he flung the ball into the face of the dark fae charging at him.

The man screamed, and when his hands flew up to protect his face, Cole drove his sword into the fae. He sliced upward, cleaving the man in half from his chest, through his head. Once his sword was free, he chopped off the fae's split head and twisted in his saddle to face the horses coming at him.

He jerked his horse's reins to the side, and the horse instantly twisted away. The animal was fast and sure and managed to avoid being plowed into by a charging horse. Cole recognized his attacker as one of the king's soldiers.

The betrayal burned like acid in his throat. Cole shifted his hold on the sword and, swinging out with his free hand, he embedded his claws under the fae's chin and ripped the man from his horse.

The man kicked and made gurgling noises as his fingers tore into Cole's hand. Cole gripped the man's shoulder and tore the man's head off. Retracting his claws, he palmed the head and threw it at the next fae coming at him.

It bounced off the man's forehead and sent him tumbling out of the saddle. His horse continued toward them but veered away before running into them. When Cole aimed his horse at the fallen rider, the animal didn't hesitate before trampling the man.

Fire from the torches burst high as the enemy lost them, and it caught on the grass and homes. Controlled by another dark fae, those flames raced across the ground and encircled him and a dozen other riders.

Cole almost laughed out loud. He was sure that whomever was controlling the fire probably believed they would frighten or intimidate him, but these flames were pathetic after what he endured during the trials.

Kicking his feet free of the stirrups, Cole jumped from his horse's back and raced toward the flames.

On the other side of the fire, he spotted Durin with Nissa and Fiadh. Durin was a member of the council who Cole would gladly kill. Nissa and Fiadh were Aelfdane's brother and sister. Cole hadn't had any problem with killing Aelfdane, and he'd have less of one killing his siblings.

But now, he knew who was leading this rebellion against him, and he would make them pay for it.

As he stalked toward them, the three of them lifted their arms, and the flames surged higher. The fae who'd risen against him swarmed closer to the fire as the flames leapt higher.

Cole bellowed as he ran toward them.

~

Download *Shadows of Betrayal* and continue reading:
brendakdavies.com/SBwb

~

Stay in touch on updates, sales, and new releases by joining to the mailing list: brendakdavies.com/ESBKDNews

Visit the Erica Stevens/Brenda K. Davies Book Club on Facebook for exclusive giveaways and all things book related. Come join the fun: brendakdavies.com/ESBKDBookClub

FIND THE AUTHOR

Brenda K. Davies Mailing List:
brendakdavies.com/News

Facebook: brendakdavies.com/BKDfb

Brenda K. Davies Book Club:
brendakdavies.com/BKDBooks

Instagram: brendakdavies.com/BKDInsta
Twitter: brendakdavies.com/BKDTweet
Website: www.brendakdavies.com

ALSO FROM THE AUTHOR

**Books written under the pen name
Brenda K. Davies**

The Vampire Awakenings Series
Awakened (Book 1)

Destined (Book 2)

Untamed (Book 3)

Enraptured (Book 4)

Undone (Book 5)

Fractured (Book 6)

Ravaged (Book 7)

Consumed (Book 8)

Unforeseen (Book 9)

Forsaken (Book 10)

Relentless (Book 11)

Legacy (Book 12)

The Alliance Series
Eternally Bound (Book 1)

Bound by Vengeance (Book 2)

Bound by Darkness (Book 3)

Bound by Passion (Book 4)

Bound by Torment (Book 5)

Bound by Danger (Book 6)

Bound by Deception (Book 7)

Bound by Fate (Book 8)

Bound by Blood (Book 9)

Bound by Love (Book 10)

The Road to Hell Series

Good Intentions (Book 1)

Carved (Book 2)

The Road (Book 3)

Into Hell (Book 4)

Hell on Earth (Book 5)

Into the Abyss (Book 6)

Kiss of Death (Book 7)

Edge of the Darkness (Book 8)

The Shadow Realms

Shadows of Fire (Book 1)

Shadows of Discovery (Book 2)

Shadows of Betrayal (Book 3)

Shadows of Fury (Book 4)

Shadows of Destiny (Book 5)

Shadows of Light (Book 6)

Wicked Curses (Book 7)

Sinful Curses (Book 8)

Gilded Curses (Book 9)

Whispers of Ruin (Book 10)

Secrets of Ruin (Book 11)

Tempest of Shadows

A Tempest of Shadows (Book 1)

A Tempest of Thieves (Book 2)

A Tempest of Revelations (Book 3)

A Tempest of Intrigue (Book 4)

A Tempest of Chaos (Book 5)

Historical Romance

A Stolen Heart

Books written under the pen name
Erica Stevens

The Coven Series

Nightmares (Book 1)

The Maze (Book 2)

Dream Walker (Book 3)

The Captive Series

Captured (Book 1)

Renegade (Book 2)

Refugee (Book 3)

Salvation (Book 4)

Redemption (Book 5)

Vengeance (Book 6)

Unbound (Book 7)

Broken (Book 8 - Prequel)

The Kindred Series

Kindred (Book 1)

Ashes (Book 2)

Kindled (Book 3)

Inferno (Book 4)

Phoenix Rising (Book 5)

The Fire & Ice Series

Frost Burn (Book 1)

Arctic Fire (Book 2)

Scorched Ice (Book 3)

The Ravening Series

The Ravening (Book 1)

Taken Over (Book 2)

Reclamation (Book 3)

The Survivor Chronicles

The Upheaval (Book 1)

The Divide (Book 2)

The Forsaken (Book 3)

The Risen (Book 4)

ABOUT THE AUTHOR

Brenda K. Davies is the USA Today Bestselling author of the Vampire Awakening Series, Alliance Series, Road to Hell Series, Hell on Earth Series, The Shadow Realms Series, A Tempest of Shadows Series, and historical romantic fiction. She also writes under the pen name, Erica Stevens. When not out with friends and family, she can be found at home with her husband, son, and pets.

Printed in Dunstable, United Kingdom

68421823R00210